I0659189

ACTING ON IMPULSE

Contemporary Short Stories
by Georgette Heyer

WITH COMMENTARY BY
Jennifer Kloester
and
Rachel Hyland

Overlord Publishing
overlordpublishing.com

2 3 4 5 6 7 8 9 10

*With thanks to Ruth Williamson,
for unmatched attention to detail.*

~

For Georgette, forever and always.

CONTENTS

INTRODUCTION
BY JENNIFER KLOESTER

I began my Georgette Heyer research journey in May 1999 with my first visit to the wonderful British Library. Arriving at King's Cross Station (itself a name to conjure with!) and walking the short distance to the library, receiving a Reader's Pass and gaining access to the reading rooms in that amazing building was, to me, akin to winning a Golden Ticket and being admitted to Willy Wonka's Chocolate Factory. I was awe-struck by the King's Library housed in its magnificent multi-storey glass tower at the top of the stairs and by the beautiful Rare Books and Music reading room where, over the next ten years, I would spend so many happy hours pursuing all things Heyer. I'll never forget being allowed to take possession of Domenico Angelo's *School of Fencing*, published in 1787, and spending a glorious hour leafing through its pages. Heyer had used Angelo's guide in her own research and, though I did not know it then, this first foray into understanding her life and writing would mark the beginning of what has become a twenty-year adventure (which is still ongoing).

In 2001 I began my Doctorate on Georgette Heyer and her Regency novels. In 2002 I travelled to England to meet her son, Sir Richard Rougier, her biographer, Jane Aiken Hodge, and to return to the British Library to further my research. In the first year of my Doctoral studies I had discovered the existence of several untapped archives of Heyer's early letters and Sir Richard had generously granted me copyright permission to have access to these. It was here that I found the first clue that Georgette Heyer had written short stories in the early 1920s.

At the time, the only Heyer short stories I had seen were the eleven historical tales that made up the 1960 anthology, *Pistols for Two* – republished in 2016 under the title *Snowdrift*, and including three more historical shorts I was able to unearth – all of which had been published from 1935 onwards. However, here among the collection of her correspondence owned by the University of Tulsa was a letter in Heyer's own hand, written to her agent just a few months after her twentieth birthday, that said: "I've sent you another short story, and there is a third in the making." I was instantly intrigued. While I knew it was possible that these early short stories, sent so enthusiastically to her agent, might never have been published, I also knew that I had to find out.

The first challenge was working out where these early Heyer stories might have appeared. This was no easy task as the 1920s in England had been a Golden Age for short story writers with more fiction magazines published than at any other time. Scores of famous writers made their names writing for publications such as *The Strand Magazine*, *Nash's*, *The Happy Mag*, *Sovereign*,

The Quiver, Pall Mall, The Red Magazine and *Pearson's*, among many others. Writers like Agatha Christie, P.G. Wodehouse, Richmal Crompton, J.B. Priestley, Daphne du Maurier, A.A. Milne, Sapper, and Ngaio Marsh found homes for their short fiction on a regular basis. As Mike Ashley observed in his book *The Age of Storytellers*, the 1920s would also be "the last haven of the popular fiction magazine" as the rise of radio in the 1930s saw the demand for short stories begin to decline.

If Georgette Heyer *had* been published in one or more of these magazines, I reasoned, then it seemed likely that these would have been historical stories. Unfortunately, this gave me no real idea of which among dozens of likely magazines might have accepted her youthful tales. Fortunately, as I read through the archive of her letters I came across a clue. In 1936, Heyer had written two historical shorts and she wrote to her agent about them: "under no circumstances should they be offered to the cheap 'popular' magazines such as *The Red* & *The Happy*, etc." Here at last was a clue to at least a couple of magazines where I could start looking.

The biggest repository of UK magazines in the world is the British Library, and so I returned to that great institution and began my search for these forgotten Heyer works. One hundred and sixty microfilm reels later, I had found five short stories: three in *The Happy Mag* and two in *Red Magazine*. It was an exhilarating experience. There is nothing like that moment when, after pages and pages and *pages* have been examined, suddenly – there in front of you – is Georgette Heyer's name and above it the title of a story you have never heard of before. And then comes the thrill of reading for the first time the stories written when she was only twenty. I devoured "A Proposal to Cicely" (which was, I later discovered, republished in Mary Fahnestock-Thomas's *Georgette Heyer: A Critical Retrospective* in 2001), "The Little Lady", "The Bulldog and the Beast", "Acting on Impulse" and "Whose Fault Was It?". Five short stories, all set in contemporary times and each with something new to tell me about Heyer.

Of course, such finds only made me long for more, and by now I had learned from Heyer's letters that many of her novels had been serialised in the famous British magazine, *Woman's Journal*. This collection was housed at the Newspaper Library – that arm of the British Library situated at Colindale, about forty-five minutes from London on the Underground. Today, Colindale is no more, but between 2002 and 2011 I travelled there many times. Though it was something of a trek, I always looked forward to my visits there.

On my first visit I was somewhat taken aback by the starkness of the scene outside the station. On the opposite side of the narrow road and standing by itself like an old forgotten relative was a solid brick rectangular building. More prison than library, I thought at the time, unaware of how much affection I would have for it by the time my years of research there ended. Today, the British Library has moved its newspapers and magazines to Yorkshire. In time, I expect everything will be digitized and made available on the internet. Very convenient, of course, but I wouldn't have missed those long days at Colindale for anything.

The kindness of the staff, the great wooden trolleys stacked with twenty huge bound volumes of magazines, the anticipation of what might lie between the thick cardboard covers, the feel and smell of the pages as I turned them, always hopeful that the next page would reveal the eagerly-sought, cherished Georgette Heyer by-line. I always arrived early, before the reading room opened, and would then wait with other keen researchers in the downstairs cloakroom. A sparse space with just a few chairs and a table and nothing at all to indicate the "cave of wonders" that lay upstairs. It was always magical to me, being at the Newspaper Library.

I visited England nine times in pursuit of information about Georgette Heyer but my time there was always limited. Three full days, five full days, seven at the most was all the time I could allow for the magazine research on any one trip. The staff at Colindale were so kind and very understanding of my situation – an Australian far from home with a clear goal and limited time in which to achieve it, and they always allowed me more than my regulated allowance of four items at one time. They would bring up a huge trolley filled with great bound books – each one holding as many as twelve magazines for me to search.

It was in these that I found "Linckes' Great Case" and "The Old Maid," two very different stories written two years apart. "The Old Maid" appeared under the name of "Stella Martin" – the same name under which Heyer had published her third novel, *The Transformation of Philip Jettan*. At first I wasn't sure if the story was hers – after all, there could be another Stella Martin writing short stories for the magazines – but then I read the story. Definitely Heyer's. So many things in it resonated and today it remains one of my favourites of hers. In fact, I find it nearly impossible to separate Heyer from Helen, the story's main protagonist.

Those days at Colindale also revealed her historical short stories and serialised novels that had appeared in *Woman's Journal*. Heyer was first published in that magazine in 1935 and over the years she became one of their most popular "selling" names; husbands were known to snatch the magazine from their wives' hands if Georgette Heyer's name was on the cover. I loved *Woman's Journal* and not only because it had an index which made searching a lot quicker and easier, but also because it published so many well-known authors.

Over the years, I searched more than three thousand physical magazines, sometimes turning pages for eight hours at a time. My final reward for my (some would say obsessive) persistence came on a day when I was back at the main British Library. This is where *The Sovereign Magazine* was held and it was here that I found Georgette Heyer's earliest known historical short story: the tragedy entitled "Love". I'll always remember the moment when I turned the page and saw the title and with her name beneath it. It was all I could do not to jump for joy right there in the Rare Books and Music Reading Room. I had to suppress a desire to shriek with excitement and did a tiny little jig instead.

My final discovery came from a typewritten list of her many publication which I found in the Heyer Archive held by her son. Here were listed the various foreign serial rights and foreign publications of her novels. Here, too, was a list of her short stories. But most of these were the historical shorts her readers would come to know from her 1960 anthology, *Pistols for Two* – whereas not a single one of the contemporary short stories I had discovered at the British Library was included on the list. Only one short story title from the 1920s was listed and it was not a title I had found in any of the magazines I had spent so long searching. "'The Chinese Shawl' 1924 Tidenskronder" was how the entry read. At the top of the page was written "Danish Serial Rights." Another clue. I contacted the main library in Copenhagen and the remarkably efficient librarian very kindly effected a search for me and, in what seemed like no time at all, sent me the story. Of course, it was in Danish, which meant finding a translator. I eventually found two and so have two slightly more modern versions of this early Heyer short. It was only this year, and because of my collaborator Rachel Hyland's brilliance and persistence, that the original story finally came to light in a most unlikely publication.

Of these nine short stories, seven were contemporary shorts published in a single year (September 1922 – October 1923), one was a historical short (November 1923) and one was published in 1925 under Heyer's pseudonym. Each story tells us something about Georgette Heyer, about her development as a writer, her willingness to experiment, her ear for the language of the day, her attitudes to women and marriage, her attempts to write in different genres and her perception of love and relationships. These stories represent her juvenilia – they are not her best work, but nor are they anything of which to be ashamed. She was writing for money and for experience. She was working out her voice and trying her hand at different styles. These early stories, along with her early novels, helped build Heyer's writing "muscle"; they were an important part of her evolution as an author. They are also interesting, entertaining stories, reflective of their time and place. Even at twenty, Georgette Heyer was a good writer, and her earliest short stories reveal much of the superb stylist she would become.

Most of the stories included in this collection have not been seen since their first publication nearly one hundred years ago. Georgette Heyer's novels, however, continue to sell in large numbers around the world and she has become that rare thing – a perennial bestseller. Forty-five years after her death she is considered a classic author and, as her works endure and interest in Heyer continues to grow, her early short stories take on a new significance. In light of this, we wanted to make these stories available to readers everywhere and to offer an introduction and afterword to each story. The introductions place the stories in their historical and cultural context and give a sense of Heyer's life at the time. The afterwords offer readers a modern take on the stories' 1920s sensibilities and humorously highlight the many subtle and not-so-subtle differences between Heyer's time and ours. Of course, each story can be enjoyed in its own right without reading the commentaries, though we hope that they will add to the reader's enjoyment of these very early Heyer works.

"A PROPOSAL TO CICELY"

INTRODUCTION

As far as we know, "A Proposal to Cicely" was Georgette Heyer's first published short story. It appeared in print in the English journal *The Happy Mag* in September 1922. Brought out by George Newnes Ltd., who also published the famous *Strand Magazine*, *The Happy Mag* was a new publication, having begun in June of that year with a particular focus on humour. A monthly magazine, it would become most famous for the "William" stories written by Richmal Crompton. Although a claim in *the Age of Storytellers* that the magazine had "launched the career of Georgette Heyer" is untrue – she had already had considerable success with her first novel, *The Black Moth* (1921) and a second novel, *The Great Roxhythe*, was due out in the coming November – the publication of "A Proposal to Cicely" in *The Happy Mag* did mark the beginning of an intensive period of short story writing for her.

Unlike her first two novels, both of which had historical settings, "A Proposal to Cicely" was her first contemporary story. It is a romantic tale which tells of Cicely and her "first cousin once removed" Richard Spalding, who wants to marry her. So far, she has refused every one of "Dicky's" proposals and when the story opens Cicely is "absolutely sick" of everything and "ready to do something desperate." Richard takes this all in good part and there follows an illuminating conversation which reveals much about the characters.

Richard is one of those men of independent means so beloved of writers. He does not have to work but has money enough to live a life of leisure. Heyer describes him as "an athlete and an amateur boxer," but Cicely tells him "you don't *do* anything," though she does concede that he has stood for Parliament "and all that sort of thing." When Richard mentions in passing that he spent four years in the trenches, Cicely is "slightly mollified," though she tells him frankly, "I don't count that".

To the modern reader this abrupt dismissal of Richard's war service may read oddly; to Heyer's generation, however, it was an entirely appropriate response. She herself had been raised in an aspirational middle-class home and taught the importance of regulating one's feelings, keeping a "stiff upper-lip" in the face of adversity, and of the need for restraint and discretion when discussing serious matters. While it is acceptable for Cicely to throw a cushion across the room, or vehemently express her distaste for modern living and complain of being bored, it would be pushing the bounds of good taste for her to discuss in detail, or properly acknowledge, Richard's war service.

Though "A Proposal to Cicely" has less polish than her later stories and novels, she had already developed the knack of revealing character through dialogue: we quickly learn that Richard is intelligent, decent and well-bred and that Cicely is bright, impulsive and naïve. The dialogue is also an enjoyable throwback to an era when people said things like "honour bright!" "be a sport" "beastly" and "oh, rather!" When Cicely complains that she's sick of dances, she tells Richard that she's "been trotted round till I want to scream!"

Heyer herself attended dances and parties of the kind that bored Cicely, and her four later contemporary novels would also depict heroines who struggled with aspects of the post-War London social scene. As a young woman Heyer enjoyed dances, although she disdained studio parties and had no time for bohemians. Cicely is bored with town life, dances and society, and has decided to go "into seclusion." For an upper-middleclass girl enjoying all the delights of 1920's London, this meant an escape to the country. She and a friend take a cottage in a "quaint village" where they will escape from city life.

From here Heyer uses class difference as a driver for the rest of the story. Despite the destruction of so many mainstays of British life wrought by the Great War, England remained a strongly hierarchical society. Class still mattered and "A Proposal to Cicely" is the first of Heyer's stories to reveal some of the attitudes prevalent at the time. These, initially subtle, class differences are first made known during Cicely's exchange with a local farmer, Fred Talbot. In the secure knowledge that she is Talbot's "better," Cicely makes assumptions: "Come in to tea this afternoon, We're fearfully bored. An' then you can take us over the farm". She receives "a shock" when he tells her he's busy. Later in the story Heyer expresses the class differences more overtly: "Had he but known it, she was treating him as her inferior in that she still called him Mr. Talbot, and confined her conversation to farming." He is simply a "diversion" from life in a small village where there "was no tennis and no society."

But there were dogs. "A Proposal to Cicely" is the first time that Heyer brought dogs into a story and Cicely's "Pekinese" [sic], Chu-Chu San, may have been modelled on the Pekingese Heyer herself had owned in her teens. Richard's bull-terrier, Bill, is also a breed Heyer would own, though several years later. Though neither dog is as developed as Heyer's later canine characters, and serve rather as props, Bill does have a small dramatic role towards the end of the story. In this first short story, Heyer had not yet realised the full potential of the canine character, but it would not be many months before she did.

— *Jennifer Kloester*

A PROPOSAL TO CICELY

CICELY hurled a cushion across the room.

"*That's* how I feel!" she said, and glared at her first-cousin once removed, Richard Spalding.

"Good Lord!" he remarked, with a proper amount of sympathy in his lazy voice.

"And you sit there—idling about in my room—laughing at me! I quite hate you, Richard!"

"Oh, I say!" he expostulated, "I wasn't laughing—honour bright!"

Cicely looked scornful.

"I'm absolutely sick of it all. Dead sick of it." Cicely nodded so vigorously that her brown, bobbed curls seemed to jump. "I never want to go to another dance as long as I live."

"That's bad," said Spalding. "What's brought on this sense of repletion?"

"Everything. I've been trotted 'round till I want to scream! I feel like doing something desperate."

At that Spalding dragged himself upright and threw away his half-smoked cigarette.

"Oh, splendid, Cis! I hoped that if I waited long enough, you'd melt. When shall it be? Be a sport, now, and—"

Cicely covered her ears with her hands.

"No, no, no! I don't want to do anything as desperate as that!"

Richard sank back again.

"Thought it was too good to be true." He pulled a leather diary from his waistcoat pocket and proceeded, gloomily, to make an entry.

"What's that?" asked Cicely.

"Diary."

"But what are you writing?"

"'Friday. Proposed to Cicely. Refused.'"

In spite of herself, Cicely giggled.

"Dicky, you are idiotic! When will you give it up?"

"When we're married."

"We're not going to be!" Cicely's chin went up defiantly.

"You can't possibly tell. You never know what you may come to," said Spalding cheerfully.

"I'll never come to that! And now we've got on to that subject I may as well tell you, Richard, that that's another of the things I am fed up with. You ask me to marry you every day of the week, and I'm—"

"No, I don't!" Spalding was righteously indignant. "I've only asked you three times this week and three and a half last week. It's down in the book, if you want to verify it."

"Can't you be serious for one moment? That's one of the things I hate about you. You're too beastly flippant! You don't *do* anything. My husband'll have to be a worker!"

"He will be," murmured Richard.

Cicely disregarded him.

"I know you think you do a lot—standing for Parliament, and—and all that sort of thing—but you're just—flabby!"

Richard, an athlete and an amateur boxer, blew another cloud of smoke.

"Have you ever done a day's work—hard, manual work—in your life?" demanded Cicely.

"The complete park-orator? Four years in the trenches, that's all."

Cicely was slightly mollified.

"I don't count that," she said.

"No, I didn't think you would. What next?"

"You're too civilised. Too drawing-roomified. I'd want to feel that I could rely on my husband—not just that he'd be a great success at any party I took him to. All you think about is clothes and racing and whether your tie's on straight. It's not good enough for me."

"In five minutes' time I think I shall propose to you again," he said. "I'm sorry you're so sick of everything."

"I've found a remedy," said Cicely. "I am going into seclusion."

"What? Into a convent?"

"No, silly. I am going into the country. I've taken a cottage."

"Cottage? You? D'you mean to say Uncle Jim's mad enough to let you go off on your own?"

"Daddy knows that I am perfectly capable of looking after myself, thank you."

"Where *is* he?" demanded Richard, preparing to get up.

"He's out. Besides, it's nothing to do with you. As a matter of fact, I'm not going by myself."

Spalding looked slightly relieved.

"I'm going with a great friend of mine, Maisie Duncannon."

"What, that fat, stolid girl who's been hanging round here lately?"

"Y-es. That's one way of describing her. Are you satisfied?

"No, I'm not!"

Cicely reached out her hand to stroke her diminutive Pekinese. "Chu-Chu San is going, of course."

"That puts quite a different complexion on it," he said. "He'll look nice in the country. Stir the villagers up a bit."

"He's a lot pluckier than your rotten bull-terrier!" said Cicely fiercely.

Spalding brightened.

"I say, will you take Bill? Do, Cis! I'd feel a lot happier about you if you'd got a decent sort of guard."

"Chu-Chu *is* a good guard!"

"Oh, rather!" said Richard hastily. "But you must admit, he's a bit small, what? Take old Bill—please! I've been wanting to get him out of town for some time."

Cicely hesitated. She knew that the last statement was entirely without truth, but she reflected that Bill would bring with him a certain sense of security.

"He'd miss you," she said, uncertainly.

"Not a bit of it. Besides—" Richard checked himself. "Do take him, old girl!"

"It's awfully nice of you," Cicely thanked him. "If you think it 'ud do him good—"

"I do, most decidedly. By the way, where is this cottage?"

"Bly—I'm not going to tell you! No one's going to know 'cept Daddy, and he's promised not to tell a soul."

"Bly. I'll remember that."

"You'll never find it!"

Richard recognised the challenging note.

"Like to have a bet on it? An even bob?"

"I don't mind. *My* money's safe."

Richard smiled, and made a note in his pocket-book.

"Don't count your chickens before they're hatched," he said.

THE pony trotted down the village street in a leisurely, abstracted way, paying no heed to his mistress's voice. The excited barking of Chu-Chu San he took to be an encouragement to him to proceed. He ambled on.

"Whoa!" said Cicely, sharply. She tugged at the reins. "Whoa!" she repeated, more as a request. The pony still ambled on. "Oh, please, whoa!" begged Cicely. "Timothy *dear!*"

Timothy waggled one ear to show that he was attending to her. Chu-Chu-San yapped again and he waggled the other, accelerating his pace.

"Shut up, Chu-Chu! Whoa, you! *Stop!*"

Farther down the street a man stood, watching the pony advance. He was dressed in rough tweeds and riding-breeches, with stout leather gaiters, and he carried a short riding-crop. He observed Cicely's struggles without a smile. When the trap drew alongside he stepped forward and caught the rein. Timothy halted obediently and looked round.

"Oh, thank you!" sighed Cicely. "I don't know what I should have done if you hadn't stopped him. He's frightfully pig-headed. It takes ages to make him start, and when once he's got going he simply won't stop—oh, no, Bill, *don't* go and fight that dog, *please!*" She dropped the reins and hauled the departing bull-terrier back into the seat.

Her rescuer half-raised his cap.

"Glad to be of use. Dan Brown's pony, I think?"

"Yes," nodded Cicely. "But I'd no idea how tiresome he was, or I'd never have hired him." She smiled, and ran her eyes over him appraisingly.

He was fairly tall, and thick-set, with very broad shoulders, and a tanned face. Quite good-looking, she decided, and with a wonderfully square chin. Dogged and purposeful. And a grim mouth, too. Blue eyes that looked straight at you—almost steely. Cicely felt quite thrilled.

Under her frank scrutiny the man had flushed little, but his eyes held hers unwaveringly. Cicely was unabashed.

"Well, thanks very much," she said. "And if you wouldn't mind turning us round, I might get Timothy to walk back to the butcher's."

For the first time a hint of a smile crossed his face.

"I'll lead you to the butcher's if you like."

"Thanks awfully," she said.

For a few minutes they proceeded in silence, while Cicely studied the back of the man's head. Then he looked over his shoulder.

"I reckon you're the girl who's taken Miss Fletcher's cottage?" he said.

Cicely nodded. "Yes. Do you live near?"

"Mortby Farm."

"Do you really? Why, that's just at the back of our cottage! Do come in and see us some time! And, oh, I should like to go over your farm. George— that's the gardener, you know—says you've got the sweetest little pigs. Are you Mr. Talbot?"

"Fred Talbot. And you're Miss Duncannon, I daresay?"

"No, that's my friend. I'm Cicely Carruthers."

"Oh!" said Talbot, and relapsed into silence. He spoke no more until they came to the butcher's shop. Then he released the pony's rein, and again touched his cap.

"You'll be all right now. Mean what you said about my coming in to see you?"

"Oh, rather!" said Cicely. She descended gingerly from the trap. Talbot made no effort to help her, but watched her with an amused air. "Come in to tea this afternoon. We're fearfully bored. An' then you can take us over your farm."

She received a shock.

"Can't manage it this afternoon, I'm afraid. Can I drop in tomorrow if I have time?"

"Oh, certainly," said Cicely, not too pleased at this cavalier treatment. "Whenever you like. And thanks so much for helping me with Timothy. Good-bye!" She extended a slim, gauntleted hand. It was crushed in a grip that made her wince.

"Not at all," said Talbot. "Pleasure. Good-bye."

Half an hour later Cicely walked into the living-room of her cottage, and nodded briskly at Maisie Duncannon, who was flipping over the pages of a novel.

"You missed something by not coming with me, Maisie," she announced.

"Mr. Spalding hasn't turned up, has he?" inquired Maisie, a sudden gleam of interest in her eye.

Cicely blushed ever so faintly.

"'Course not. He won't either, thank goodness! I've been talking to an aborigine."

"Oh!" yawned Maisie, and returned to her book.

CICELY rather wondered whether Talbot would come at all, but he did, and stayed for over an hour. Maisie objected strongly to him, but then, Cicely reflected, Maisie was in the mood to object to anything. She was "bored stiff" with the country. So was Cicely, but she would not admit it.

For a fortnight it had been glorious. They had gloated over the quaint old village and told one another that they could live here content for months. At the end of the next week the simple life had begun to pall on them. There was no tennis and no society. The atmosphere began to be rather tense between the girls.

So Cicely welcomed the diversion in the shape of Fred Talbot. Maisie complained that he brought mud into the house. Cicely told her that she needn't speak of Talbot as though he were a dog. Maisie retorted that that was just what he was—a shaggy, uncouth sheepdog.

As Talbot came more and more frequently to Rose Cottage, Maisie, to show her disgust, retired either to her room or to the neighbouring woods.

So engrossed was Cicely in Talbot's farm that it never occurred to her that she was encouraging Talbot to fall in love with her. She was not at all flirtatious, and not one of her numerous adorers would have taken her frank, unaffected friendliness for anything other than it was meant to be.

But Talbot was not a society man; neither was he used to the ways of a Cicely Carruthers. The girls he knew belonged to the village of Blythe, or its environs, and were fifty years or so behind the times. This was his first experience of the modern girl. At first he was a little shocked at the free and easy way in which she wandered into his place, or invited him into hers; then he was no longer shocked, but thought he understood. He came still more frequently to Rose Cottage.

Another fortnight slipped by. Maisie had sunk into a sort of sullen apathy, but Cicely, tanned by the sun, and pulsing with energy, was on the road to becoming the complete farmer. She had come to associate Talbot merely with his farm. Had he but known it, she was treating him as her inferior in that she still called him Mr. Talbot, and confined her conversation to farming.

She had a rude awakening. She came into the cottage one afternoon, her hair dishevelled by the wind, and her shoes caked in mud, and collapsed into a chair.

"Oo! I *am* tired!" she remarked.

Maisie raised her eyes from the inevitable novel.

"I don't wonder at it if you will go mucking about a dirty farm," she said.

Cicely was roused to wrath.

"It is not a dirty farm! It's a beautiful farm! You don't know what you're talking about!"

"All right." Maisie shrugged her shoulders and went on reading. After a short pause Cicely continued:

"The last incubator lot are hatching themselves. Isn't it wonderful? And Mr. Talbot's coming here to-day, and afterwards he's going to take me to see the chicks coming out of the eggs. You've no idea how interesting it is, Maisie! It's simply—"

"Is that man coming here to tea?" demanded Maisie.

"Yes, he is. And I do think you might be civil. He's not at all a bad sort—underneath his extraordinary manners."

"Then I'm going over to see the Frasers," said Maisie, disregarding her. The Frasers were friends of hers, living some three miles away.

"All right, you can," answered Cicely. "I don't care."

She waited until Maisie had left the room, and then added: "And I hope Timothy runs away with you."

TALBOT tramped in at a few minutes past four. "Hullo!" said Cicely. "Sit down and I'll make the tea."

Talbot lowered himself into a chair. It did not occur to him that he might help his hostess. It did occur to Cicely, and she sighed. With all his faults, Richard—. She set the kettle down smartly, and came to the tea-table.

Talbot seemed rather thoughtful. Tea over, she lit a cigarette and saw that he was frowning.

"I don't like to see a girl smoking," he said heavily.

"Really?"

"I'd not allow my wife to smoke."

"Really?" said Cicely again. "But I am not your wife."

He looked full into her eyes in that bold, dogged way that had first intrigued her.

"Seems to me, my girl, we'd best come to an understanding," he said.

Indignation robbed Cicely of words. Fred Talbot to address her as "my girl"! With an effort, she controlled herself.

"I don't know what you mean," she said icily. "Will you have a ciga-rette?"

"No." He brushed it aside. "Reckon you know all right. I want you to marry me."

"What?" Cicely gasped. "To—" Again, she controlled herself. "Thanks very much," she said lightly, "I'm afraid not. I'm sorry you should think—think—"

"Reckon I think what I'm meant to. I don't pretend to understand you town-girls, but I know what I want, and I get what I want."

Cicely drew herself up.

"Mr. Talbot, you forget yourself. Please don't say any more! I had no idea you were—you had—you wanted to marry me, or I shouldn't have—well, anyhow, don't let's talk about it. It's a pity to spoil a very pleasant friend-ship, isn't it?"

He smiled rather grimly.

"Suppose you cut out the fine talk, my girl, and come to grips? I don't know why you should pretend you'd no idea I wanted to marry you. You've been in and out of my place for weeks. I'm not a fool, my girl, and I know what to make of that."

"Don't call me that!" exploded Cicely. "I'm not your girl, and I won't have such an—such an impertinence! I came to your farm because I was interested! We were just friends, as you very well know! I've never given you the right to talk to me like this!"

"THINK so?" He rose and stood over her. "You were just playing, were you?—leading me on?"

Cicely pushed back her chair and sprang up.

"How dare you?" she cried. "How dare you say such a thing to me? Please—go! I am exceedingly sorry you should have made such a dreadful mistake—but to blame me? Why, I've never been anything but friends with you!"

He came nearer.

"Reckon a girl's not friends with a man unless there is something more," he drawled.

Cicely backed to the wall.

"Mr. Talbot, will you please go? If I were not alone here, you would not dare to speak to me in this way. I tell you, once and for all, I am not going to marry you. If you really care for me, you'll go now."

"I'm not going. You've had your fun with me, and now you'll pay for it." He strode forward as he spoke, and gripped her by the shoulders.

Panic seized Cicely, at the mercy of this dreadful person.

"Bill!" she shrieked. "Bill, Bill, Bill!"

From the garden came the sound of yelping barks. Bill showed no signs of coming to the rescue. Only he barked and barked in wild excitement.

Talbot crushed Cicely against him. She could not even struggle under his iron hold. She was kissed roughly on her panting mouth, and then—

Someone pushed open the cottage door.

"You owe me a bob," said a lazy, pleasant voice. "Get down, Bill!"

"Richard!" sobbed Cicely. "Oh, Richard!"

Still holding her with one arm, Talbot wheeled about. Cicely never quite knew what happened next. All that she remembered was that she was suddenly whisked from the farmer's hold and deposited on the sofa. And Richard's voice, dangerously sweet, was inviting Talbot to come outside. Then the two men seemed to disappear, shutting Bill into the cottage.

Cicely crouched on the sofa, shivering still, and Bill snuffed and whined at the door with suppressed excitement.

Then, after what seemed to Cicely countless ages, the door opened and Richard strolled in, calm and imperturbed. He passed the palm of his left hand across his knuckles and looked at his flushed cousin.

"Has—has he—gone?" asked Cicely, in a very small voice.

"Oh, yes!" said Richard.

"Did—did—you—hurt him much?"

"I hope so," said Richard, and there was a short, uncomfortable pause.

"How—how did you—find me?" she inquired, with would-be carelessness.

"Process of deduction. What was that poisonous blighter doing in your cottage?"

"Ha — having — tea," said Cicely, nervously.

"Where's that fat fool—Maisie?"

"Gone to—to see some friends."

"What does she mean by leaving you with a man like that?"

"She—she doesn't like him."

"Shows her good taste. Don't you know better than to ask a brute like that to tea with you alone?"

Cicely blinked away a tear.

"I—I didn't kn—know he—he'd—I always d—*do* ask my friends to tea!"

"Your father's house is rather different, isn't it?"

A muffled sob came from the sofa. Cicely was staring down at her hands, biting her lips. Richard went to her and sat with his arm about her shoulders. "Poor little kid! I won't rag you any more. Don't cry, Cis."

Cicely shed a few tears into his coat pocket, and sat up. She mopped her eyes with a diminutive handkerchief.

"I—I am glad you came," she sighed. "I n—never thought you would." There was another pause.

"Are—are you staying at the inn?"

"I am."

"Are—are you going to stay for long?"

"Looks as though I'd better," said Richard drily.

"Oh!" Cicely digested this. Then she spoke again. "P'raps you'll be able to manage Timothy," she said, hopefully. There was no answer.

CICELY looked at him sideways. She sat for a moment, twisting a cushion-tassel. Richard said nothing at all, but watched her with that curious look in his eyes.

A tiny smile came, shyly. And Cicely came to him and dived her hand into his waistcoat pocket.

"What do you want, Cis?"

"Diary," said Cicely briefly.

It was handed to her. She hesitated for a moment, not looking at him. Then she opened the book, and sucked the pencil. She scribbled diligently, and shut the book with a snap. Richard was watching her half-smiling, half-anxious. Cicely held out the book.

"There you are! I've finished with it."

Richard took it. He slipped his arm round her once more. Cicely subsided meekly, and buried her face in his coat.

Richard dropped a kiss on to the fluffy head.

"Am I allowed to read what's written here?" he asked.

"If you—like," said a muffled voice.

He opened the book. The last entry was written in a round, sprawling hand. It was quite short.

"Tuesday. Proposed to Cicely. Accepted."

THE END

READING "A PROPOSAL TO CICELY"

This one packs quite a punch, and even were it not only Georgette Heyer's first published short story, but also her first published contemporary tale, there would still be a lot to examine in here. First, there is the suave, devoted Richard, whose chronicle of his many proposals to the firebrand Cicely is quite touching and sweet. But then you can't help but think him a bit stalkery, too, unable to take no for an answer and all, and that is less sweet—but also more, somehow? (This is because romantical tales such as this have warped us all, of course, and our expectations of a fictional hero's behaviour towards our heroine do not at all match what we would accept in real life.)

Then we have Cicely, entitled and naïve, certainly, but a woman we cheer for, nonetheless—at first, anyway. When our story commences, she is terribly weary of her privileged life of wealth and beauty, and decides on a tree change as the cure. Not for her, the social whirl and a suitable marriage! For her, the countryside, and a light flirtation with what we'd call nowadays a "bit of rough." In fostering the plebeian Talbot's friendship and/or attachment to her, she is equal parts living dangerously and being determinedly egalitarian – when her friend and companion, the sensible if snobbish Maisie, objects to Talbot, Cicely doubles down on her efforts to befriend him, making herself free of his farm to simultaneously prove a point, give herself an illicit thrill, and, above all, alleviate her *ennui*.

Which leads us, of course, to the almighty subject of class difference. This is, of course, a hallmark of Heyer, not just in her historical works but also in her contemporaries, especially in her arguably most challenging outing, 1930's *Barren Corn*, in which a well-educated member of London's rarefied gentry falls into *mésalliance* with the post-War equivalent of, in Victorian literary terms, a simple country maid, to the misery of all. (Including, it must sadly be admitted, many of the book's readers.) Here, it manifests in Cicely's utter disregard for Talbot as a man, or even as a person. To her he is a mere prop to her vanity, a sop to her boredom, and she is utterly astonished that he would presume to think of her as a potential mate, with their stations in life so very different, he a farmer and she a gentleman's daughter. She takes it for granted that he will know his "place," and that she could never be in any real danger from him, her "inferior." Indeed, it is evident she has never felt in real danger from any man, for which we can only envy her.

Talbot, for his part, is assured of his own superiority over her, having misread Cicely's signals entirely and also somehow believing that even if she had been signalling a romantic interest with her visits and her invitations, she'd consent to have him tell her what he'd "allow" her to do. In the space of a very few paragraphs, Talbot goes from mistaken to menacing, pitiful to predatory, and the shock of this sudden transformation rings so very true that a surge of adrenaline races through you, as your stomach plummets and fear grips.

It is very, very well done.

The very real threat of sexual violence is thrust upon the reader in quite the most dramatic fashion here – even *The Black Moth*, the publication of which predated this story by a year, and which features as one of its leads a serial abductor and rapist, is not so blatant about the looming dread its heroine faces – and in reaction to it, our independent Cicely comes over all winsome and compliant to the suddenly masterful Richard, whose timely arrival at this hidden away backwater of a cottage could not have been luckier for him, or her, or even Talbot, most probably. Cicely, shuddering in the aftermath of her would-be suitor's anger and assault, rashly clings to her childhood companion (and cousin – here we have the first of Heyer's consanguine couples, eventually culminating in *The Grand Sophy's* first cousin pairing) as a safety net, as a protector, and meekly accepts his oft-delivered marriage proposal, at last.

It's understandable, but also kind of lowering, to see Cicely brought so helpless by this encounter. It is maddening to see Richard believe himself validated in his opinion that she is not to be trusted to take care of herself.

Though there *are* hints that perhaps the old defiant Cicely is still in there somewhere. I actually like to think that she breaks off the engagement a couple of weeks later, and goes off to see the world with the much-maligned Maisie. (I'll never forgive Richard for being so unnecessarily mean about her, the jerk.) Indeed, this is the one and only Heyer romance that has ever left me hoping that the Happy for Now does not become a Happily Ever After, post-book. Richard – despite his four years serving in World War I, which is very subtly mentioned herein – is clearly a dilettante, and our Cecily needs more from her partner.

She especially needs someone who won't badmouth her friends.

Is that really so much to ask?

The name Richard, by the way? Georgette Heyer *really* liked that name. Not only did she bestow it on several of her characters – Richard Carstares of *The Black Moth*, Richard Carmichael of *Helen,* Major Richard Fawcett of *Pastel,* Richard "Diccon" Dangerfield of *Beauvallet,* Sir Richard Wyndham of *The Corinthian* and Richard Chartley of *The Nonesuch*, plus Vidal's groom Richards in *Devil's Cub* – she also gave it to her son. *[Note: For a time, he too was known as "Dicky." It was not until he went to Cambridge that a close female friend suggested he become "Richard," after which he was Dicky no more. - JK.]*

Dogs would also come to be a regular feature in Heyer's works, but happily none of her future creations ended up with such a misapplied name as Chu Chu San, which one can only assume came from the title of a "Japanese Fox Trot" written by one Joseph Samuels in 1919, and which would be fine, except that Pekinese [sic] are from China, and you just know that Cicely –

and, by extension, Heyer – did not even think about that for a moment. Then again, "Chu" is a Chinese name, and "san" is Japanese, and Joseph Samuels was neither, so it is all of a 1920s cultural appropriation-y piece, really, isn't it?

Not that things are all that much better a century or so later, but at least now we know it's wrong. Heyer – and, from the evidence, the majority of her contemporaries – did not. It's so hard to stop ourselves from judging the past by the standards of the present, and our aspirations for the future, isn't it?

But we must. Or we could never read, well, pretty much anything ever again.

– Rachel Hyland

"THE LITTLE LADY"

INTRODUCTION

Georgette Heyer's second short story, "The Little Lady", was published in *The Red Magazine* in December 1922. *The Red*, as it was affectionately known, was, as Mike Ashley observes, originally intended as "an adult all-fiction magazine," but frequently included stories by boys' adventure writers. Founded in 1908 and part of "the first wave of all-fiction magazines," it had a circulation of 90,000 for its twice-monthly publication. *The Red Magazine* was sometimes described as the "progeny of *The Strand* magazine" and early editions included stories by Jack London, O. Henry and Rafael Sabatini. It offered readers a wide range of well-written short stories including mystery, adventure, dramatic, and humorous, with about a third of the magazine's contents being romantic tales.

"The Little Lady" undoubtedly falls into this latter category.

An unusual Heyer story, "The Little Lady" definitely belongs to this group of Heyer's juvenilia. A whimsical tale of lost love and chance encounters, the story was written in her teens. Its hero, Peter, has quarrelled with his fiancée and left London in a rage. Another of Heyer's independent young men of means, he finds his way to a country inn, and walking in the woods one day he meets a strange young woman: Bride is elusive, ethereal, elfin, and dressed as though she "had stepped from the pages of Jane Austen."

From Bride's first appearance, Heyer creates an almost mystical atmosphere of uncertainty and doubt. Is Bride real? A ghost? Mad? Heyer compels the reader to wonder. She also raises doubts about the time in which the story is set. Though its opening is clearly 1920s England and Peter drives his car to the country, Bride seems to come from a different time and place. She is otherworldly and strange. More than fifty years later, Heyer would write *Cousin Kate*, another unusual story and one in which a young man goes "mad." Torquil's madness is far more intense and dangerous than any behaviour we see in Bride, but it is interesting that Heyer touched on the subject so early in her career.

There is no knowing exactly when she wrote "The Little Lady", though it was likely after 1918, at the end of the Great War. Heyer turned sixteen in August of that year and may have written it around that time. This is lightweight, sentimental fiction, with a mystical, magical element, that is unlike anything else she ever wrote. These elements suggest a more youthful pen than her later shorts. Here, too, is Heyer's first– and most overt – reference to Jane Austen. Throughout her life, Austen would remain her favourite author, but the use of Austen's name in this story has none of the subtlety or humour of later references.

"The Little Lady" also has an adolescent's sentimentality; none of her later stories would come to be so saccharine. Instead, Heyer would find her voice with more fully developed characters, sharper dialogue and her own particular brand of humour.

– *Jennifer Kloester*

THE LITTLE LADY

I.

HE was tramping through the wood, hands thrust deep into his trousers-pockets, brow lowering, and lips in a sullen curve. He was very, very angry. Hurt, too, and like a sulky schoolboy. He had quarrelled with Ruth, and she had flung his ring back at him, telling him to go away and never to come back again. Well, he wasn't going back.

A rotted piece of tree-trunk lay across the cutting; he kicked it petulantly out of his way.

It wasn't his fault, anyway. She had started the row—at least, he thought so. He really couldn't remember quite how it had begun or what it was about. He only knew that they had both been furious and that everything was at an end. Ruth was absolutely unreasonable, too. Probably it was just as well that the engagement was broken off.

A rabbit scuttled across the path and was lost in the bracken. Peter scowled after it; he was in no mood for rabbits. A thrush singing in some nearby tree made him look savagely round. How dare the bird be happy when he was in black despair? He strode on, shoulders hunched forward.

Yes, the row had upset him. He had gone back to his flat and had hurled some clothes into a portmanteau. He rather thought he had snarled at his servant, but he wasn't sure. Then he had flung out of the place to his waiting car and driven blindly off Heaven knew where! He hadn't cared where he was going to. He had just driven out of London, through the suburbs, out into the country and on, on till dusk came. Then he had come upon this place, with its bubbling stream and its quiet beechwoods. He had liked the old inn, and, in any case, one place was as good as another to him now.

He had intended to move on next day, but somehow, for no particular reason, he had stayed. He had been here almost a week and still he felt no more at ease in his own soul. He had come to a clearing in the wood where the golden sun filtered through the trees in great patches. He flung himself down upon a mossy bank and sat hugging his knees, staring gloomily before him. The sunlight played about his bare head, caressing his cheeks, but it awoke no gladness in him. He blinked at it, and shifted farther into the shade.

A crackling of twigs sounded on his left, and the flick of leaves brushing against an alien presence. He turned his head apathetically.

Through the undergrowth a little lady came, pushing her way. She paused for a moment on the edge of the clearing, standing on tiptoe, like some startled faun, timidly regarding him.

Peter looked at her with some interest. Her hair was cut short and clustered in feathery curls about her head. She was dressed in white muslin, high-waisted and blue-sashed, with tiny puff sleeves and sandal shoes. Rather eccentric, Peter thought, but quite pleasing to the eye. She looked very young, too, hardly more than a child. but it was difficult to tell with that short hair.

For a moment they stared at one another, he curiously, she with a half-shy, half-mischievous look on her little, pointed face. Then she took one or two dancing steps forward, light as thistledown upon the grass, and curtseyed to him, laughing. The sound of her voice was like fairy bells, ethereal and far away. Peter saw that although her eyes were smiling they were very sad.

He struggled up awkwardly.

"I hope I'm not trespassing," he said. "I thought the woods were not private?"

She danced back a few paces.

"Oh, no! Not private now."

She laughed again, pointing her tiny foot.

"They were once, I suppose?" he asked for want of something better to say.

"Yes—oh, yes! A long, long while ago."

She came back to him, seeming hardly to touch the ground, so light was she. She hesitated a moment and sat down on the bank. She stretched out her hand in a shy, inviting gesture. Peter obeyed the summons and sank down beside her. The little lady possessed an odd magnetism; he found himself drawn to her almost irresistibly.

"D'you live here?" he inquired, smiling at her.

Her eyes flew up to his and he saw his smile reflected in their wistful, blue depths.

"No, not now. They all went away," she said sadly. "I only come here sometimes. Once I lived here."

She made a gesture with her hand, embracing the wood. His smile grew.

"What, in the wood?"

The rippling laugh bubbled up again.

"Oh, no! Over there." She pointed, and his eyes followed the direction of her finger.

"There? Carbury Place lies that way, doesn't it?"

She clapped her hands.

"That is it!"

"Then you are a Dering?"

She shook her head.

"No. I am Bride. Only I never was one," she added, sighing.

"Bride. What an unusual name! I beg your pardon. That was rather rude of me! Does it mean Bridget?"

"No. Oh no! Just Bride."

He did not wish to appear inquisitive, so he did not question her any further. They sat in silence for a while till she looked up and spoke again.

"Everything has changed," she said, "but the beechwoods are always the same."

"Do you come here often?" he asked.

"Not now. I used to—oh, very often! But now hardly at all. Only when I am wanted."

The friendly, shy smile peeped out. He came to the conclusion that she was younger than he had thought.

"When you're wanted?" he repeated. "How can you tell when that is?"

"I can't tell. I just know. I felt to-day that someone needed me, so I came, and then, of course, I found you. You want me, don't you?"

"I?" he said, taken aback. He looked down at her sharply, but there was no suspicion of coquetry in her face. She spoke, too, as if she were stating a natural fact. "I want you?"

"Yes. You do, don't you?"

He laughed.

"You quaint child! Why should I want you?"

"Because you're so unhappy," she answered simply.

He started.

"How do you know that?"

She smiled wisely, tenderly.

"I always know. Tell me."

"Tell—" In spite of himself he was amused. "My dear little girl, why should I?"

"Because I came to help you," she said.

"Very nice of you, I'm sure!" he replied. "But I'm not in the habit of pouring forth my woes to chance acquaintances."

He laughed shortly and bitterly. A shadow seemed to cross her face.

"Ah, you don't want me after all!" she said wistfully. She rose. "Good-bye!"

Suddenly he felt an overwhelming desire to keep her beside him.

"Oh, don't go!" he cried. "Forgive me! I didn't mean to be so boorish! Fact of the matter is—I'm going through a—rather bad time. My own fault, I suppose."

She was on tiptoe, hesitating.

"Please!" he said. "Don't go!"

The elfin smile danced across her eyes. She sat down again.

"No, I won't go. Not yet. Tell me what is the matter."

"I should bore you—horribly," he said diffidently. "Besides, it's such an extraordinary thing to tell a stranger—"

"Ah, but I am not like other people!"

"No, you're not," he said, considering her. "It's a curious thing, but I feel as if I'd known you all my life."

She nodded, full of understanding. He started to snap a twig into little pieces, not looking at her.

"It's—a quarrel," he said with difficulty. "I quarrelled with—the lady—who was—to have been my wife."

"Ah!"

It was a sobbing sigh. He glanced up, flushing, and saw that her eyes were full of tears.

"I say, you mustn't cry!" he exclaimed. "After all—it's my funeral."

She shook her head, smiling through her tears.

"I was crying for myself," she explained. "Why did you quarrel?"

"Blessed if I know!" he said ruefully. "I think we were both fed up—out of sorts. 'Twasn't my fault," he added sulkily. "I didn't start the thing."

"No! Go on."

"There's not much more. She—chucked my ring at me—and I came away. Down here. I've been here a week. Silly sort of tale, isn't it?

"Oh, the pity of it!" she sighed. "Do you love her still?"

He reddened, fidgeting with the twig.

"Yes. Can't help it."

She stretched out her hand, supplicating.

"You'll go back, won't you?"

He did not answer. Her fairy-voice held a quivering note of tragedy.

"If you only knew! The heartache, the remorse. Just a quarrel—a lover's quarrel—and everything at an end?"

"I'm not going to go back and grovel," he muttered, still sulky. "I've got some pride left."

"Only pride. To break both your hearts."

He turned.

"You speak—as though you understood," he said wonderingly.

She nodded.

"So well—oh, so well! I quarrelled, too, you see. I didn't think it was my fault; he didn't think it was his. And we were both proud. I never saw him again." Her long lashes were glistening, but she shook away the tear-drops. "Oh, that was long, long ago!" She held out her hands to a dragon-fly that darted past. "Too long to remember now."

"I say, I'm awfully sorry!" Peter stammered. "Was he—did he—"

She was stroking the moss with fingers that trembled.

"He was killed," she whispered.

"I'm most awfully sorry!" he repeated. "In the war?"

"Yes. In the war. But it's so long ago."

He thought she was perhaps a little mad.

"I'd no right to tell you my wretched trouble. It has upset you."

"Oh, no, no! Why, I shouldn't have come if you had been happy."

"Wouldn't you? Don't you talk to happy people?"

"They don't need me, you see," she explained. "I only come here to help those who want me. Because my own heart broke and it hurts me—oh, so terribly!—to see things go wrong between other lovers."

"You dear little lady! D'you know what you reminded me of when you first appeared?"

She looked inquiring.

"No? A dancing flower, perhaps. I was called that once."

"It suits you. No; I thought you had stepped from the pages of Jane Austen. But, of course, your hair is short."

Her hands flew to her head; her eyes crinkled charmingly at the corners.

"They cut it off. When I was ill, you know. After—after I knew that he was killed."

"It's topping. It never grew again?"

"No. Something happened, and I was different."

Her eyes became grave again, even a little shrinking. He put out his hand to lay it on hers, but she eluded him, and sprang away.

"Oh, no, you must not touch me!"

She danced back, sparkling with laughter.

"Mustn't I? Why not?"

"You couldn't, and you wouldn't understand. I am only a ghost, you see. You might be frightened of me. People are, and that hurts so. They think I am mad. But I'm not. Oh, I'm not! I'm just—dead!"

"Poor little will-o'-the-wisp!" he said gently. "Come and sit down. Don't be frightened. I promise I won't touch you."

She drew nearer, her head tilted to one side.

"I mustn't stay. I ought to go now."

"Oh!" Disappointment sounded in his voice. "Don't go yet!"

"Ah, but I must! I only came to comfort you. And I have done that, haven't I?"

He rubbed his forehead.

"Yes. Funny. 1 didn't think anything could comfort me. Are you a wizard, little lady?"

Her laugh tinkled out.

"Oh, no, I am just Bride! You'll go back, won't you?"

His face clouded over.

"I don't see how I—"

"Please, please! Does it matter whose fault it was, after all?

"She may not want me to go back."

"Oh, yes, yes! You will go—you must go!"

"She said she never wanted to set eyes on me again."

"She didn't mean it. Never, never!"

She shook her little head till the curls danced.

"How do you know?"

"It was just a quarrel," she said softly. "She will be so sorry—as you are."

An unwilling smile came to his lips.

"Oh, so you know that, too, do you?"

"Of course," she answered gravely.

"I expect you think me a pig-headed fool."

"No. Only mistaken. Please say you will go back. There's so much unhappiness—so much."

He got up, throwing away the broken twigs.

"I will go back. It's frightfully nice of you to bother about me. You've helped no end. I was a fool. I knew it, really; only I had to have you point it out to me. Thanks most awfully!" He held out his hand, but she skipped away, laughing. His face fell.

"I say — aren't you going to shake hands?"

"No. Oh, no!" Her fingers fluttered to her lips, twice. "There—and there!"

He followed her.

"I shall see you again, shan't I? I'd like to tell you if it's all right, and thank you."

"No, I shan't come again. You're happy now, and you don't need me. Good-bye."

He expostulated.

"You don't really think me such an ungrateful brute? Of course I want you."

She smiled, shaking her head. Then she curtseyed and ran into the undergrowth. The leaves fell back into place, screening her from his sight. Once again, from a long way off, came the sound of fairy laughter. Then all was quiet.

The wood seemed desolate suddenly. Peter stood for a minute, listening. Then he sighed and went back along the cutting through which he had come.

II.

PETER was shown into the drawing-room. He went over to the window and fidgeted. Presently the door opened, and Ruth came in. She paused on the threshold, rather pale. Peter stepped forward.

"Ruth, it was all my fault! I'm *awfully* sorry! Can't—can't we be friends again?"

She gave a little cry, and ran to him.

"Oh, no, it was my fault! I don't know what possessed me. Oh, Peter,

Peter!"

She buried her face on his shoulder, half laughing, half crying, and for a long while remained so, clinging to him.

Later, seated side by side on the sofa, Peter told her of the little lady in the wood. She listened, her hands in his, and at the end of the story her eyes were wet.

"Poor little lady! She just disappeared? She didn't come back?"

"No. She dived into the bushes, laughing. She had the most extraordinary laugh, Ruth. Like tiny silver bells, only that sounds rather rot. Frightfully fascinating, and a bit—what shall I call it?—elfin. She had an elfish little face, too."

"I wonder who she was? She didn't tell you her name?"

"No. At least, yes. She said her name was Bride, and that she used to live at Carbury Place. By the way, darling, that's a topping old house! You've no idea what a lovely part of the world it is down there. I'm going to take you one day. It's not far, though I spent hours getting there." He laughed. "I haven't the vaguest notion as to how I managed to get so hopelessly lost!"

She reached up her hand to stroke his face.

"I have," she said. "Poor old Peter! Oh, my dear, I thought you'd never come back!"

"Sweetheart!" He caught her to him.

A LADY and gentleman walked into the parlour of the Three Fishers' Inn. The land-lady, Mrs. Tippit, came forward. She recognised Peter, and dropped a bob-curtsey, smiling.

"It's pleased I am to see you, sir!"

Peter shook hands.

"I've brought my *fiancée* down to lunch, Mrs. Tippit."

Mrs. Tippit dropped another curtsey.

"Eh, dear!"

She beamed upon Ruth, who blushed a little, and dimpled.

Peter struggled out of his light overcoat.

"Mrs. Tippit, I wonder if you could help us? We want to find a certain lady whom I met in the woods when I was staying here. 'Fraid I can't tell you much about her, 'cept that she was young, with short curls, and dressed in a rather eccentric way." He tossed his motoring-gloves on to the table. "She said she used to live at Carbury Place. Oh, and her name was Bride! Does that convey anything to you?"

The landlady placed a chair for Ruth, and shook her head with a short sigh.

"Ah, sir! So you met Miss Bride? Everyone knows her, poor little lady. You understand, sir, that she's—" Mrs. Tippit touched her forehead significantly. "Not—not quite *mad*, sir, if you know what I mean, but sort of soft, as we say in these parts."

Peter sat down on the edge of the table.

"Yes. I guessed that, of course. She did me a jolly good turn, and I want to find her. Where does she live, and what is her name?"

"Flower, sir. She's Colonel Flower's daughter. Him that used to own the Place, before the war." Mrs. Tippit sighed again. "County, sir. Not like the present owners. They made their money in soap, or jam, I forget which. Colonel Flower had to sell the Place during the war. It were a ter'ble blow, sir, I give you my word. Carbury Place had been in the family for generations, you see. They live at Red Roofs now. About a mile to the west of the Place."

"Poor things! I wonder they can bear to remain here, and see their old home in other hands," said Ruth. "I know I couldn't."

Ever ready to gossip, Mrs. Tippit sat down opposite Ruth, and smoothed out her apron.

"It was all on account of Miss Bride, ma'am. You see, after Captain Jermyn was killed—"

"Captain Jermyn?"

"That would be her lover. You know, Ruth," interposed Peter softly.

"You're right, sir. Captain Jermyn was engaged to Miss Bride. The handsomest, jolliest gentleman you could wish for! He always had a smile for one, an' was that kind-hearted—well! Everybody said about here that you couldn't find a nicer couple than our Miss Bride and Captain Jermyn. And then they went and quarrelled, sir! No one thought much of it at the time. We all saw the captain go away in his car, scowling fit to die. But, as I said to my husband, lovers' quarrels end in kisses." Mrs. Tippet shook her head sadly. "This one didn't. He never came back. I think he was too proud, and as for Miss Bride— She was as gentle as you please until you happened on that pride of hers. Touch her there, and—my word! Well, all I know is that Captain Jermyn never came here again and Miss Bride never spoke his name! Just held her pretty head high, and pretended not to care. Then the war came, and nat'rally Captain Jermyn, being a Regular, was one of the first to go out. A change came over Miss Bride then." Mrs. Tippit touched her eyes with a corner of her apron. "Poor, sweet little thing! I remember her coming here and saying to me in her pretty voice, "I've written to Anthony, Jessie." Bless her! She'd be sure to tell me one of the first, me having maided her when she was a child. She'd written to beg his pardon, ma'am. An' the very next day there was a notice in all the big newspapers to say that he was reported missing."

"Oh," Ruth slipped her hand in Peter's. "How dreadful!"

"You may well say so, ma'am. From that day onward Miss Bride changed. It came gradual, but very soon we all knew that her brain was—was queer. Not exactly mad, just queer, like a child, sir. When the news came at last that Captain Jermyn had been killed, it seemed hardly to touch Miss Bride.

All she said was, 'It's so long ago! So long ago! Too long to remember now!' over and over again, till I could have cried to hear her. Then the smash came, and Colonel Flower had to sell the Place. They didn't dare leave the neighbourhood, because Miss Bride was always wandering through the beechwoods, where she and the captain used to sit. They did try to take her away, but she fretted herself sick, and they had to come back. They took Red Roofs—that was when Miss Bride was so ill, and they cut off her hair. They've been there ever since."

She stopped, looking inquiringly at Ruth, who had drawn closer to Peter.

"Peter, *we* might have—" She shuddered.

"Sh!" commanded Peter, squeezing her hand. "Mrs. Tippit, which is the quickest way to get to Red Roofs?"

"Your quickest way to find Miss Bride, sir, is to go through the woods. She's more likely to be there than anywhere. If she isn't, you've only to keep on towards the west, and you'll come to Red Roofs. 'Twon't take you long. By the time you're back, I'll have lunch ready for you. A nice chicken, sir, with a raspberry pie to follow. It's in the oven now."

"Topping!" said Peter. "I'll leave it all to you, Mrs. Tippit."

"An' you couldn't do better," said the beaming landlady.

III.

THEY went through the beech-wood, hand-in-hand, along the same cutting that Peter had trodden a fortnight before, in a mood so black that he had not smiled when a bob-tailed rabbit scuttled comically across the path. He and Ruth went slowly now, and their conversation was very private.

Seated on the stump of a tree, against a background of soft green foliage, they found Bride twining daisies into a long chain. She looked up at the sound of footsteps, and the daisies tumbled to the ground as she sprang to her feet. She would have run away into the bushes, had not Peter stepped forward with hands outstretched.

"Little Bride! Have you forgotten me? Don't go away!"

She paused on tiptoe, looking from him to Ruth. Her hands were clasped behind her; she stood half turned away, in the attitude that Peter remembered so well, poised for flight.

"Have you forgotten the poor wretch whom you comforted, Bride? I've come to thank you."

The elfish little smile peeped out. Bride came forward, dancing.

"Yes, I remember. Of course, I remember. Did you—oh, did you go back to her?"

"Thanks to you, little lady. Here 'she' is—come with me to tell you that it's all right again."

Bride nodded and smiled to Ruth.

"I am so glad! I could not bear to see you so unhappy. It hurt me so. Do you understand, I wonder?"

She had drawn closer to Ruth, and sank down on her knees now, waving to Ruth to sit down on the tree-stump.

"I do understand." Ruth stretched out her hand. "And I'm—so very sorry!"

"For me?" The little lady looked up at her wonderingly. "It's so long ago! Too long to remember! And you—you are happy now?"

"Very, very happy," Ruth answered. "But if it had not been for you, we should both have been miserable still."

The little lady came to her feet. She pressed her hands to her eyes, hiding them, but they saw her lips quiver.

"That hurts, too. You are happy, and you don't want me." Her hands came away, and she was smiling again. "Never mind, I'm not real, you know. I died—oh, long, long ago! Thank you for coming."

She kissed her fingers to them, and danced back, laughing a little.

"Ah, don't go! Not yet." Ruth got up quickly. "Please stay. Just a little longer."

"No. Oh, no! You don't want me now. Goodbye.

Peter held out his hands again.

"Little lady, won't you let me touch you?"

She came forward, tentatively.

"Touch me? Why must you? You see, I'm dead."

But she held out her hand.

Peter took it gently, and bent to kiss the slender fingers. And as he did so he heard a quick step behind him, an exclamation, and a cry from Ruth. He turned, and saw a tall, black-haired man standing watching him. He had come down the cutting, and stood now a few paces away, his hat in his hand, a frown in his anxious eyes.

The little lady moved first. A sobbing sigh escaped her, and she went falteringly towards the newcomer.

"You've—come back—at last! Anthony, forgive me!"

As one in a dream Peter saw the strange man go to meet Bride, and heard him speak.

"I've come to ask your forgiveness, Bride."

Then the little lady seemed to crumple up, but the man's arms were round her, and she fell against his breast. The black head was bent over hers for a long minute, and then raised swiftly.

"Whoever you may be—please—she has fainted! Would you—"

Ruth ran to him. Between them they laid Bride down upon the soft moss, while Peter ran to where he knew a brook wound its way through the wood.

"You're—you're—Captain Jermyn?" Ruth asked.

He was kneeling beside Bride, chafing her cold hands.

"Yes, yes. She's so cold. Do you think—will—"

"She has only fainted," soothed Ruth, a hand on the little lady's wrist. "My *fiancé* has gone for water. It is all right."

"Your *fiancé*? I was afraid when I saw—Ah, the colour is coming back into her cheeks. Bride, Bride! Look up! I ought not to have startled her so." His eyes never left that pointed, elfin face.

"Hush! She'll come round. Give her time."

"I went up to the Place and heard that Colonel Flower had sold it, and that—my Bride—my beautiful Bride—was mad!"

"It happened when she heard that you were killed. Oh, why have you stayed away all this time?"

He stroked the feathery curls back from the little lady's brow.

"I was taken prisoner. Nearly killed." He touched a long scar on his temple. "It knocked me silly. Couldn't remember anything. I was sent into Switzerland after a time with a batch of prisoners. Didn't know who I was or anything about myself. At the end of the war I was shipped over to England and Dr. Strange—you've heard of him? He's a marvel—put me right. It took ages, but he did it, and I'm here."

Peter came running in with his brandy-flask. Ruth took it from him, but it was Jermyn who bathed the little lady's forehead.

She gave a fluttering sigh, and her long lashes lifted. Straight into her lover's eyes she looked, and, smiling as one awakened from a long sleep, stretched out her hands.

"I've been—dreaming! Anthony dear!"

Ruth and Peter drew away quietly to the cutting. Just once they looked back, and the little lady was in Jermyn's arms, her lips to his. One of her tiny white hands caressed his dark head, the other clung to the collar of his tweed coat. Silently Ruth and Peter went down the cutting. Not until they came out on to the road did Peter open his lips.

"We're told that the age of miracles is past," he remarked.

Ruth caught her breath on a sob.

"Oh, my dear! The poor little thing—and he! It's—it's a good world!"

"Not so bad," agreed Peter, and kissed her.

THE END

READING "THE LITTLE LADY"

It is quite incredible to me, that if this story had ended with its first "chapter," two thousand-some words in, it would stand as Georgette Heyer's only paranormal work.

You come through that first encounter between the lovelorn Peter and ethereal Bride quite ready to be convinced that she is the ghost she claims to be – the atmosphere of the wood, from the outset, is deliberately eerie and otherworldly, as is the sprite-like Bride herself, and had the story concluded with her disappearance into the leaves, her work on this earthly plane complete when she convinces Peter to return to his fiancée Ruth and apologise for the fight that ended their engagement, then "The Little Lady" would have remained the vaguely supernatural fairy tale that it initially appeared.

But Heyer does not end it there, instead giving us Peter reunited with his Ruth, the two of them determined to return to that enchanted wood to thank Bride for her intercession in their relationship – and, no doubt, to check on her wellbeing. It is interesting that neither Peter nor Ruth believes for an instant that she might be other than mortal, as far as we can tell, despite her lachrymose words and the bell-like distant laughter and her anachronistic mode of dress—which is never explained, by the way. Instead, they are filled with pity over her plight, the desolate young woman left mad with grief after the Great War has taken away her one chance at lasting happiness.

Of course, it is estimated that upwards of 750 000 British soldiers died in that war, with a further quarter million dying as a result, which was something like 12% of the nation's total population at the time. There were many young women similarly stricken with such losses – Heyer, too, lost those close to her; everyone did – so when the story takes a turn from the paranormal to the psychological, and we are told, with some relish, by the local hostelry's landlady the tragic tale of Bride's lost love, Captain Jermyn, we begin to understand that sweet, soulful Bride is not dead but dissociative, and the story becomes one of coping with trauma and a study in human behaviour, making it clear that real world demons – and ghosts – are even scarier than their fictional, sepulchral counterparts.

The continued story also acts, perhaps, as a way to exorcise some of those ghosts and demons – especially given the wish-fulfillment nature of the conclusion.

The too-fortuitous return of the earnest Captain Jermyn, who knows how many years later (he was one of the early casualties; the war began in 1914 and ended in 1918; the story was published in 1922 – it could well be that he was MIA, presumed dead, for eight years at the time of this tale), right when Bride has allowed the gentle Peter to take her hand and thus prove her corporeality, is something of a convenience, and can't help but seem rather too pat. We'd rather believe Bride was long-dead than that her long-lost love should return, with an amnesia backstory to explain his continued absence, exactly at that moment. But in a world ravaged by war, and with *so many* loves lost to so many young ladies just like Bride, the happy ending must have been a tender and even healing vision of what might have been, and it is very understandable that it should have come from the pen of one then still so young. (Bearing in mind, Heyer was just twenty years of age when this story was published, regardless of how much earlier she may have penned it.)

It is not a story that is particularly Heyer-esque. Not at all. Well, except that the reported histrionics of Peter and Ruth perhaps hold some parallels in the tempestuous beta couple Isabella Milborne and George Wrotham in *Friday's Child* (1944), and Heyer's knack of building a character in just a few broad strokes is entirely present here, especially in her establishment of Mrs. Tippit, the expository force of the story.

Indeed, throughout her works, Heyer always had a way with succinctly conveying the characters of assorted landlord and landladies, and Mrs. Tippit is no exception, even if the fact that she keeps curtseying to Peter and Ruth seems confusingly anachronistic now. But this is a contemporary story to the time in which Heyer lived, we must assume she knew what the obeisance habits of the working classes were – there is no indication that our happy couple have jobs of any kind; they seem to be of the moneyed, idle drawing-room set – and hey, the domestics in *Downton Abbey* (which covers the years of 1912 – 1926) curtsey and bow all the time, so we must assume that it was still, somehow, a widespread thing, even in that increasingly democratic age.

However, the remainder of the story remains remarkably free of any indicators that Georgette Heyer was in any way its author. Her favoured turns of phrase are absent, as is any sign of witty repartee – it is, in fact, a withal humourless narrative, unusual, though not unique, in the Heyer canon. It reads like a writing exercise, like a work penned by a hopeful youth soon after the war had ended, and then repurposed as a way to make some quick cash from publication, after her name became established so unexpectedly with the 1921 success of *The Black Moth*. It's possible that she set out to write a ghost story, or a parody of one – perhaps, originally, it even ended with Peter determined to reconcile with Ruth, and Bride disappearing into the ether, her mission complete.

I, for one, wish it had. But I understand why it didn't.

– Rachel Hyland

"LINCKES' GREAT CASE"

INTRODUCTION

Though short-lived, published bi-weekly only from December 1922 to May 1925, *The Detective Magazine* is notable as being Britain's first magazine to focus solely on crime fiction. Edited by George Dilnot, himself a regular contributor and "crime aficianado," the magazine was unusual in publishing both fiction and non-fiction. It often included articles by former police officers, Superintendents and even Chief Inspectors, all writing about their most memorable cases. Edgar Wallace contributed a four-part serial, "The Flat", and Stanley Rubenstein wrote "Sheer Luck Again" featuring "Sheerluck Combs", an obvious parody on the famous Sherlock Holmes stories that had been so successfully published in *The Strand Magazine*. Georgette Heyer's first-known detective story, "Linckes' Great Case", appeared in March 1923.

Ironically, there is a mystery about this mystery story. Significantly longer than any of Heyer's other contemporary short stories, her first foray into detective fiction is an aberration. Not only because it was her sole attempt at writing a short story in the detective genre, but also because "Linckes' Great Case" is not very well-written. Instead of Heyer's usual deftly-drawn characters, Roger Linckes and his colleagues are two-dimensional and not very interesting. The plot is basic and unfortunately transparent and the timeline is ludicrous. The story unfolds over several months and the poor "hero" looks increasingly inept as the "appalling mystery" of who is selling government secrets to the Russians continues to prove insoluble.

Of course, Linckes gets there in the end but only long after the reader has figured out the answer to this rather dull tale. Though typical of hundreds of similar magazine stories of the 1920s, "Linckes' Great Case" is not typical of Heyer. Where is the sparkling dialogue? The humour? The interesting plot? Where are the characters who – even in Heyer's most lightweight stories – live for the reader? Only in the few romantic moments between Linckes and Autonia – "Tony" – does the story come alive. It is as though Heyer as creator is missing from her own story, which begs the question, was this detective story solely hers?

Heyer's father, George Heyer, was also a writer and was said to have written detective fiction under a pseudonym. Father and daughter often read and edited each other's work and made suggestions for improvements or change. Later in her life Heyer collaborated with her husband, Ronald Rougier, in writing her detective novels. Of those twelve novels, only *Death in the Stocks* and *Penhallow* were written without Ronald's input, and *Death in the Stocks* is considered by many people to be her best detective story. Though her husband was only responsible for the "how" of those novels, Heyer was happy to collaborate with him when writing her mysteries. Is it therefore possible that George Heyer was behind his daughter's sole foray into short detective fiction? Did he offer advice, or even write some or most of the story himself? It is a tempting solution to the mystery of how Georgette Heyer, already such an inventive and entertaining author, came to write anything as ordinary as "Linckes' Great Case."

— Jennifer Kloester

LINCKES' GREAT CASE

*A mysterious leakage of Cabinet documents and the trust of a very charming
young person gave Linckes the chance of his life.*

I.

THE chief paused and glanced sharply across the table to where Roger
Linckes sat facing him, listening to his discourse.

"It is a big job," Masters said abruptly. "So much is at stake. It's not like
safe stage robbery, where Lady So-and-So's pearls are stolen. It's—well, the
whole country—perhaps all Europe—is implicated. Maybe I'm wrong to set
you on to it. You're very young; you've had very little experience."

The younger man flushed slightly under his tan.

"I know, sir."

Masters looked him over thoughtfully, from his grave young eyes to his
brogued shoes. He smiled a little.

"Anyhow, right or wrong, I'm going to let you see what you can do. I
must admit I haven't much hope. Where Tiffrus and Pollern have failed, a
comparative tyro isn't likely to succeed. But you did exceedingly well over
that Panton affair, and it's just possible, you might hit on a solution to this
mystery." He drummed on the table, frowning. "I've known it happen before.
I suppose the big detectives get stale, or something approaching it. Let's hope
you'll bring fresh ideas into the business. How much do you know about it?"

Linckes crossed his legs, clasping his hands about one knee. "Precious
little, sir. You've seen to that, haven't you? Nothing known to the papers, I
mean. All I know is that there's a leak in the Cabinet. Knowledge of our
doings is being sold to Russia and to Germany. You say it has been going on
for some time. The Soviets got wind of our new submarines. Hardly anyone
in England knew about 'em, and yet Russia discovered the secret! Someone
must have duplicated the plans and sold them—probably he's done it many
times before—and that someone must be one of those in the small circle of
people who knew all the details of the new subs. In fact, he must have been
a pretty big man. It only remains for us to find out which one."

"Very easy," Masters grunted. "It might have been a secretary."

"It might," conceded Linckes.

"You don't think so?"

"I don't know. It doesn't seem likely. Who was in that circle?"

"The Government knew all about the submarines," Masters answered.
"But the actual plans at the time of the betrayal had been seen only by Caryu,
the Secretary for War, Winthrop, the Under-Secretary, and Johnson for the
Admiralty, and the inventor, of course, Sir Duncan Tassel. That rather dishes

your theory, doesn't it? Naturally, Tassel is above suspicion; so is Caryu; so are the other two."

"Are you sure that no one else knew of the plans?"

"No, I'm not sure. I'm convinced that someone else did know—must have known. Winthrop swears no one could have known, but he can't supply a counter-theory. He's more or less running the investigation, you know."

"What does he say?"

"He's terribly worried, of course. We thought at first that his secretary was the man, but we can't find the slightest grounds for suspicion against him, and Winthrop's had him in his employ for years. It's the greatest mystery I've struck yet. We've been working to dis-cover the betrayer for months, and we're no nearer a solution now than we were when we began. And still it goes on. Take the affair of the negotiations with Carmania. They leaked into Russia, we know. Or take the case of the submarines. Those plans weren't stolen, they were just copied. The only person, seemingly, who could have done it was Winthrop. He alone knows the secret of Caryu's safe. The plans were with Caryu for three days. All the rest of the time they were with Tassel, and they never left him for a moment. The thing must have been done during those three days that they were in Caryu's safe, because before that date they were incomplete, and dates show that they can't have been copied after they were returned to Fothermere. Now, having whittled the date down to three days, how much nearer the solution are we? Of course, everything points to Winthrop."

"Or Caryu," said Linckes quietly.

"My good youth, are you seriously accusing Mr. Caryu? Even supposing that he is the man we're after—which he isn't—would he have copied the plans while they were in his house? He's not a fool, you know."

"Where was he during those three days?"

"At home. Winthrop went round to his house, and together they examined the plans. That was on the first day, and Winthrop left the house soon after nine in the evening. Shortly after he had gone Caryu put the plans into his safe. He had them with him next day at the War Office, and put them into the safe when he came home. Not even his secretary knew of their existence. They were returned to Tassel on the following afternoon."

Linckes' forehead wrinkled in perplexity. "When did Johnson see them?"

"Before. He worked with Tassel, you see."

"Um! And where did Sir Charles Winthrop go when he left Caryu's house that night?"

"He went straight down to his place in the country—Millbank. Took Max Lawson with him. He was there for the rest of the week, with a small house-party. That wipes him off the list."

"What sort of a man is he?" Linckes asked. "All I know is that he's fairly young, very clever, and good-looking, rich, and an orphan."

"He's an awfully decent chap. Everybody likes him. Son of old Mortimer Winthrop. the railwayman. Mortimer separated from his wife when Charles was a kid. You know Charles' history. She went abroad with the other child, I believe, and Mortimer kept Charles. Did awfully well in the Secret Service during the war, and rose like a rocket. He'll be a big man before long, if this awful business is cleared up. Of course, he feels pretty badly about it. Means he'll perhaps have to resign his post."

"Yes, I suppose so. What about Tassel?"

"Tassel? My dear Linckes, if you're going to shadow him I shall begin to regret I ever put you on to the case. Why, you might just as well suspect Caryu!"

"Ah!" said Linckes, and saw the chief's lips twitch.

The telephone-bell rang sharply before Masters had time to speak again. He unhooked the receiver.

"Hallo! What? Sir Charles? Yes, put him through to me at once, will you?" He nodded at Linckes. "I thought Winthrop would ring up. I told him about you. Our White Hope. Yes? Hallo! Is that Sir Charles? Good-morning! Yes, he's here now. Yes, I've told him all I know. No, I don't think so. Well, he hasn't had much chance to yet. What? Yes, certainly! Now? All right, Sir Charles, I'll send him along. What? Oh, I see! Yes, all right. Good-bye!"

He put the receiver back.

"Sir Charles wants you to go along to his house now, Linckes—16, Arlington Street. Get along there as quickly as you can, will you? I want you to put every ounce of your brain into this. It's a big chance for you, you know."

Linckes rose, and drew a deep breath.

II.

HALF an hour later he stood in the library of No. 16, Arlington Street, taking in his surroundings with appreciative eyes. He was examining a fine old chest by the window when Winthrop came in.

Linckes turned. He beheld a tall, slim man of perhaps thirty-five years old, with an open, handsome face, in which sparkled a pair of dark eyes, singularly expressive, and fringed by long black lashes. Winthrop held Linckes' card in his hand, and he came forward, smiling. The smile dispersed the slight sternness about his mouth, and left it boyish and charming. Very simply he told Linckes all that he knew, while the young detective listened intently, occasionally putting a question.

"And that's all," Winthrop ended ruefully. "'Tisn't much to go on, is it?

"No; very little. You don't suspect anyone yourself?"

"I don't. I admit it looked like the work of an outsider, but I just don't see how it can be. Masters first suspected Ruthven, my secretary; but that's impossible. I can account for all his movements, and I know that he didn't go near Caryu's place during the three days that the plans were there, for the simple reason that he was with me at Millbank."

"There might be an accomplice."

Winthrop screwed up his nose, perplexed.

"Well, of course there might be. But, considering that Ruthven himself doesn't know the key to the safe, I don't see how that helps. Besides, Caryu has a most elaborate alarm thing in his safe-room. Only he and I know the workings to it. Either of us could enter the room without disturbing it, provided we did not try to get in at the window, or any funny trick like that, but no one else could. Whoever did it must have watched the place for months; might even have been in the household. Probably was, because there were no signs of burglary. We had no idea anything had been tampered with until we had ample proof that Russia had learnt the secret of those new subs. I tell you it's absolutely incomprehensible!"

Linckes pulled out his cigarette-case, frowning. He started to tap a cigarette on it absent-mindedly.

"The servants have been accounted for I suppose?"

Winthrop's white teeth gleamed in an infectious laugh.

"Oh lor', yes! They're all being watched and interrogated, and Heaven knows what besides. We don't think they have anything to do with it. It's too big a thing."

"I may act as I think fit?" Linckes asked.

"Absolutely! Interview all the servants, or anyone else you like. I say, don't smoke your own cigarette. Have one of mine."

Linckes suddenly became aware of the cigarette in his hand.

"I beg your pardon!" he exclaimed. "I ought to have asked you if you minded smoking. Well, thanks very much!" He took a cigarette from the box Winthrop held out to him, and inspected it. "'Fraid I don't usually indulge in this brand. I smoke gaspers as a general rule."

He lit the cigarette, smiling.

"Do you? I only smoke these. Sometimes, but very rarely, a cigar."

"Of course, I really prefer a pipe to anything," Linckes remarked.

Winthrop shook his head. "Can't rise to that. I think they're ghastly things. Look here! Have I told you enough? I mean, ask me any question you like."

"I think I've got enough to keep me occupied for a few days, thanks. I'll be getting along now if you don't mind." He rose and held out his hand.

Winthrop jumped up.

"Right-ho! And try your damnedest, won't you? We're trying to keep a brave front. But—well, it's serious. Just as serious as it can be. And until the mystery is solved Caryu and the rest of us are in a pretty sultry position. And —and it happens to mean rather a lot, to me especially, to have the thing cleared up."

"You may be quite sure that I shall do my best," Linckes told him. He gripped Winthrop's hand, and as he did so the door opened.

"Charlie, it really is too bad of you!" chided an amused voice. "I suppose you've quite forgotten that you asked me to lunch with you at the Berkeley? I beg your pardon I'd no idea you were engaged. Daddy, he's deep in business."

"Well, you shouldn't burst in on him in that unceremonious way," answered Caryu. He came leisurely into the room and cast a quick glance at Linckes. "Sorry to intrude like this, Charles. Autonia's fault!"

"How was I to know that he was engaged?" demanded Miss Caryu aggrievedly. She sauntered forward, bowing to Linckes.

"I'm not engaged, I'm sorry to say," retorted Winthrop. "I hadn't forgotten, Tony, honestly. I was detained, but I was just coming. Caryu, may I introduce Mr. Linckes?"

Linckes found himself the object of a keen scrutiny.

"Very pleased to meet you!" said Caryu, and shook hands. "You're not Tom Linckes' son, by any chance?"

"Yes, I am, sir. Do you know him?"

"Very well. We were at college together. Hope you'll be able to help us in this business."

Tony, who had just seated herself on the table, looked up. "Oh, are you the new detective, Mr. Linckes?" she asked interestedly.

"Autonia!"

"Well, all right, Daddy. You can't help my knowing. How do you do?"

She extended a small gloved hand to Linckes, who took it, and stammered something that seemed to him inane.

"I hope you'll solve the mystery," Tony said. "You don't look frightfully Sherlock Holmes-y, you know!"

She smiled mischievously. It was then that Linckes' heart changed hands.

Then he took his leave of them and went out, all thoughts obscured for the moment by the picture of Miss Autonia Caryu sitting on a table with her slim ankles crossed, and a friendly smile on her beautiful red lips.

III.

NEARLY three months slipped by, and found Linckes disgruntled. Caryu had been very kind to him. So, too, had Caryu's daughter.

He was a little puzzled by Winthrop. He had been drawn to him from the very first, but he was at a loss to understand his moods. One day Sir

Charles would be flippant and gay, the next irritable and restless; he was sometimes most inconsequent and absent-minded. Yet with all this nervous temperament he was undoubtedly clever, always charming, and an eminently responsible person. Once Linckes spoke tentatively to Tony about him, and the girl had laughed.

"Oh, Charlie's an extraordinary man!" she had said. "A perfect darling, but quite mad! They think an awful lot of him at the War House, you know. Under that flippant manner of his there's heaps and heaps of brain. Everybody loves him, but he's a dreadful trial!"

"A trial?" had asked Linckes. "Why?"

"Well, he's so — so moody. And he will forget things. Sometimes he'll say a thing to me and contradict it within an hour. When I tease him about it, he just laughs and says, 'Oh, did I? That was just hot air, then.' It's a pose, I think. He used not to do it so much."

Linckes' eyes narrowed.

"Funny! Doesn't seem quite to fit in with his reputation, somehow."

"That's why I say it's a pose," Tony had answered triumphantly. "'Cos really he's a most capable person. Daddy says he's got a huge grip on affairs. And—and now this beastly traitor business has cropped up, and if you can't solve the mystery it means Charlie and Daddy'll be under a sort of cloud, and it's—it's such a *shame!* I mean, everyone who knows Charlie knows that he's such a—such a splendid man! Why, look at the things he did during the war! Daddy says he was simply wonderful! Mr. Linckes, *please* do try and solve the mystery! I'd—I'd like to put the man who did the thing in *boiling* oil! I *would!*"

"Of course I'm going to try my hardest to get to the bottom of it all," Linckes said. He tried to speak carelessly. "I—I suppose you're awfully fond of Sir Charles?"

At that Tony had opened her eyes wide.

"Well, naturally. He's like a dear elder brother, and I've known him ever since I was a kid."

Linckes' depressed spirits suddenly soared high. A little colour stole up to the roots of his brown hair.

"You bet I'll never rest till I've found the man who's doing the dirty on us all!" he said impulsively. "Would you—er—would you be pleased if *I* discovered who it is, Miss Caryu?"

Tony had become suddenly interested in her shoe-buckles.

"I—I hope you'll do the deed, certainly," she answered.

Linckes took his courage in both hands. "I mean to. And—and if I do succeed I'm going to ask you a question, Tony."

"Oh—oh, are you?" had said Tony in a small voice,

NOT many days after his conversation with Tony, Linckes presented himself at Winthrop's house, with nothing at all to report. He found Sir Charles writing at his desk. He barely looked up at Linckes' entry, and the detective knew that one of his black moods was upon him.

"Oh, hallo!" said Sir Charles. "Sit down! Any news?"

"Not much. The butler is now wiped off the list of possibles."

"Well, I never thought he was a possible." Winthrop pushed his chair back impetuously. "I'm dead sick of the whole business! The wretched culprit, whoever he is, is just one too many for us."

"I'm dashed if he is!" Winthrop's ill-humour seemed to react on Linckes. "Hang it all, he must give himself away *some* time!"

"Why? He hasn't done it so far."

"Pretty soon he'll be trying to bring off another little coup," said Linckes savagely, "and then I'll get him!"

"Hope you will, that's all I can say. Help yourself to a cigarette."

Winthrop pushed the box across to Linckes, taking out a cigarette himself. He lit it, and began to smoke in silence. Linckes glanced at him idly, and suddenly a furrow appeared between his brows. It struck him that Winthrop was smoking in a curious way, rather as though he were puffing at a pipe. Usually he inhaled with almost every breath, sending the smoke out through his delicately chiselled nostrils.

"If I didn't know you loathed pipes, I should say you were in the habit of smoking one," remarked Linckes.

The dark eyes looked an inquiry. "You're treating that unfortunate cigarette as though it were one," Linckes explained.

Winthrop laughed, throwing the cigarette into the fire.

"Am I? Well, I'm worried. I suppose it's a nervous trick. I feel inclined to do something desperate. If only there were a clue!"

Linckes sighed.

"It's all so hazy," he complained. "You can't even know for certain that the plans of the submarines *were* sold. You can't prove it."

"Well, if the fact of Germany building submarines almost in accordance with those plans isn't proof enough, I'd like to know what is!" Winthrop retorted irritably.

"Oh, I believe they were sold all right, but it can't be proved. 'Twasn't as though the plans were stolen. There wasn't even a sign of anyone having tampered with the safe. The room—"

"For goodness' sake don't let's go all over it again!" Winthrop begged. "We've torn it to bits. Oh, yes, I'm getting peevish, aren't I?" He smiled reluctantly. "You'd be peevish in my place."

"You're certainly a bit morose," admitted Linckes. "What a mercurial sort of chap you are! A fortnight ago you were perfectly cheerful, and then you were suddenly plunged into despair!"

"Can't help it. Made that way." Winthrop picked up his pen, and started to address an envelope. "Oh, now the beastly pen won't write! Damn! I hate quills!"

"Then why use them?"

"Heaven knows! I used to like them awfully. Yes, John?"

The butler had entered the room.

"Mr. Knowles to see you, sir."

Winthrop's brow cleared as if by magic.

"Knowles? Show him in, will you? I say Linckes, do you mind if I interview this man? I won't be many minutes."

Linckes rose at once.

"Rather not! I'll clear out for a bit, shall I? Can you give me a little time when you've finished? There are one or two questions I want to ask you."

"Of course! Show Mr. Linckes into the drawing-room, please, John."

Linckes went to the door just as Winthrop's visitor entered. As he went out Linckes cast him a passing glance, and noted that he was an elderly man with grizzled black hair and a short beard and moustache. He bowed slightly, received a pleasant smile in return, which vaguely reminded him of someone, and went out.

He had not to wait long. Presently, from the drawing-room window, he saw Knowles descend the steps of the house and hail a passing taxi. As the vehicle drew up beside the kerb, he turned and saw Linckes. He nodded slightly, smiling, and after speaking to the taxi-driver got briskly into the cab. He let down the window, and as the taxi moved forward looked up at Linckes with a strangely mocking expression in his eyes.

Then the butler came to tell Linckes that Sir Charles was at liberty.

Winthrop was standing with his back to the fire when Linckes came in, smoking, and he greeted the detective with his old, sunny smile.

"I say, I'm awfully sorry to have turfed you out like that!" he exclaimed. "My time's not my own, you know. What do you want to ask especially? Didn't you say there were one or two questions?"

Something about him was puzzling Linckes. The frown had quite disappeared from Winthrop's face; the nervous, irritable movements had left him. He was smiling in his own peculiarly charming fashion, and as he looked at Linckes he sent two long columns of smoke down through his nose.

"Every track turns out to be the wrong one," Linckes answered bitterly. "I begin to think we shall never get to the bottom of it all."

Winthrop went to his desk and picked up the despised quill. He held it poised, smiling at Linckes.

"Oh, come! Don't lose hope, Linckes! Something must leak out soon."

Linckes stared at him.

"Well, I like that! Only half an hour ago you were groaning that nothing would ever be discovered!"

"Yes, but that *was* half an hour ago," Winthrop, explained. "I've taken a turn for the better since then."

"You certainly have. You've cheered up wonderfully. Did your visitor bring you good news, or what?"

"Knowles? Nothing to speak of. Now, who on earth has been mucking about with my pen? Beastly thing won't write."

Linckes leaned forward a little in his chair, eyes narrowed suddenly. "You said how well it *did* write a moment ago," he said deliberately.

Winthrop turned the pen round in his hand, scrutinising the bent nib-end that bore unmistakable evidence of having been jabbed down into some hard substance. Winthrop looked up quickly, and for an instant their eyes met.

"I don't remember saying any such thing," he replied.

A tiny smile hovered about the corners of his mouth, as if of triumph.

"But you did!" insisted Linckes. "What an appalling bad memory you've got!"

"My dear Linckes, it's your memory that's at fault. I believe I cursed the pen."

He glanced up again, one eyebrow raised quizzingly.

"Did you?" Linckes laughed. "I must be going to pieces. Yes, I think you did. Still, you *did* say that you always liked a quill, didn't you?"

"Of course I did! It's true, too. Well, I'll see what I can do for you in the matter of Burton, Caryu's secretary, that you were asking about. Anything else?"

"No, not at present, thanks. I must be getting along."

Winthrop laughed, and held out his hand.

"I'll see you tomorrow, I suppose?"

"Oh, I'm sure to come along to report," Linckes answered, and went out, his temples throbbing with excitement.

IV.

A MONTH later Linckes was shown into Caryu's study. Caryu looked at him hopefully, for there was a glitter in Linckes' eyes, and a very purposeful look.

"You've got a fresh suspicion?" he said, with the glimmer of a smile.

Linckes sat down opposite him.

"Yes, sir, I have. And I've come to ask your help."

"Have you, indeed? I'm sure I have to imitate the famous Watson, haven't I? I shall meekly do your bidding, being myself quite in the dark."

Linckes laughed.

"That is about the size of it, sir," he confessed. "But I really believe I've got on to the right track at last."

"Any clue?"

"No, sir. Pretty strong suspicion, though."

A shadow crossed Caryu's face.

"Only a suspicion, Linckes? I seem to have listened to so many."

"This time it amounts to a conviction, sir. And, because I'm practically certain in my own mind, I'm going to have the cheek to ask you to do something that'll seem quite insane to you."

Caryu moved a paperweight uncertainly.

"I'm not at all sure that I shall comply, then. What is it?"

Linckes clasped and unclasped his fingers rather nervously.

"Sir, you've got the plans of the new plane here, haven't you?"

The elder man smiled a little.

"You ought to know, Roger. You and your colleagues are supposed to be keeping an eye on them. But if you imagine they can be taken out of this new safe, you're wrong. No one knows the secret of the combination except myself."

"I know, sir. I don't expect the thief to attempt it. I want you to tell Sir Charles, when you see him tomorrow, that you have made one or two suggestions on the plans, and are sending them by your secretary to his house for him to see."

Caryu reddened.

"What are you driving at?" he asked levelly. "What do you mean?"

"Just that, sir. I think Mr. Fortescue carries documents to Sir Charles' house fairly often? Minor documents, I mean."

"Certainly. But I do not understand—"

"I know, sir. I want you to give Mr. Fortescue a package containing blank sheets. Keep the plans in your safe."

Caryu drew himself up. "Linckes, you must please explain yourself. I don't know what crack-brained notion you have got into your head, but if you are insinuating that Sir Charles is the criminal, I may as well tell you that it is an impertinent and foolish suggestion."

"I'm not insinuating anything, sir. I can't even tell you who I suspect. But I do beg of you to just do as I ask without mentioning my name. It can't do any harm, and I believe it'll enable me to find the man who's betraying us all."

Caryu's face softened a little.

"You think that whoever is doing it will try to intercept Fortescue on his way to Winthrop's house? It is rather improbable, isn't it? He has only a few yards to go."

"That's just what I'm counting on, sir. It's too short a distance for him to take a taxi. He doesn't, I know, for I've often been with Winthrop when he has come over with a letter for you, or, as I said, some minor document."

Caryu was silent for a moment. He looked Linckes over, frowning.

"And when Fortescue comes to Winthrop and gives him a package of blank sheets," he said sarcastically, "what am I to say to Winthrop? You don't seem to understand that if that happens my action in sending blank sheets amounts to a very serious insult."

"No, sir. If Fortescue does arrive, unmolested, and with the blank sheets, you can explain why it was done. You don't suspect Sir Charles. I haven't said that I do. It's quite simple."

Caryu smiled faintly. "Very well. I will tell Winthrop that among other things I am sending him the plan of the new 'plane. Are you satisfied?"

"Yes, sir. Thank you!"

Linckes rose and prepared to depart.

"What happens if Fortescue is sandbagged?" inquired Caryu. "What will he think of your little plot?"

"Not much chance of that, sir," Linckes grinned. "From Park Lane to Arlington Street isn't a far cry, and it's never exactly deserted. But don't tell Fortescue anything, will you? Not even that you are supposed to be sending plans. Send him off at the usual time."

"'The usual time' covers a wide margin," remarked Caryu. "I shall send him at about six in the evening. That is the most usual time."

"Then tell Winthrop, sir, casually. And thanks awfully!"

He shook Caryu's outstretched hand, and went to the door.

"Mind you, I think you've got a bee in your bonnet," Caryu warned him. "If you haven't—well, it'll be a fairly large feather in the bonnet instead."

V.

"GOT another fit of the blues, Winthrop?"

Sir Charles looked up, smiling.

"Getting rather frequent, aren't they? Sorry I'm such a surly brute. It's very nice of you to consent to stay and dine with me."

Linckes leaned back in his chair, crossing his legs.

"It's jolly nice of you to ask me," he retaliated. "I don't wonder you're feeling depressed."

Winthrop gave a short sigh.

"'Tisn't very surprising, is it? We don't seem to get any forrader, do we? Since your ingenious Burton theory there haven't been any fresh suspicions, have there?"

Linckes turned sharply. Caryu's secretary had just come into the room. Linckes looked him over quickly, conscious of a sinking sensation of disappointment somewhere in the region of his stomach.

"Good-evening, Sir Charles! Mr. Caryu sent me with one or two things for you to sign."

Winthrop had risen.

"Yes, that's right. Oh, don't go, Linckes! It's nothing private."

Dully Linckes watched Fortescue lay his dispatch-case on the table and insert a key into the lock. After a moment's twisting and turning he drew it out again and looked up at Winthrop, rather white about the mouth.

"Funny!" he said uneasily. "It won't open!"

Linckes' heart leapt. He lounged back at his ease, outwardly careless, but his eyes never left Winthrop's face.

"Won't open? Perhaps you've got hold of the wrong key?"

"No; it's a special lock and key."

Fortescue's eyes were rather wide.

"Then something must have gone wrong with the lock," said Winthrop impatiently. "You must force it."

"Ah!" Relief sounded in the secretary's voice. "That's it, of course. I got hung up on one 'island' in the middle of Piccadilly, and when half the people surged forward into the road there was a bit of a scrum, and I dropped the case. I suppose that did it."

"You dropped it?" Winthrop asked. "Rather careless, surely!"

Fortescue flushed.

"Yes, Sir Charles. But it fell at my feet, and I'd picked it up in a flash."

"I see."

Breathlessly Linckes watched the secretary burst open the lock.

"Mr. Caryu told me to ask you to run through his memorandum concerning the Crosstown Barracks, sir. Here it is!"

He was turning over some long envelopes. One of these he handed to Winthrop, who took it and pulled out several folded sheets. There was a moment's silence, broken only by the crackle of paper as Winthrop spread open the papers. Then Linckes saw Sir Charles look up sharply at Fortescue, the lines about his mouth suddenly grown stern.

"Ah, yes!" he said quietly. "Anything else?"

"Yes, sir. Mr. Caryu placed several documents in the case. I don't know what they were, but he told me to give—"

"Give them to me, please. Thank you!" Winthrop cast a hurried glance at each of the sealed documents handed to him. Then he laid the whole sheaf down upon his desk, and shot the secretary a long, keen look. Lastly he turned to Linckes.

"This is a case for you, I think," he said.

"Oh!" Linckes sat up. "What is the matter?" He looked inquiringly from Winthrop's impassive countenance to the secretary's surprised, vaguely nervous expression. "Anything wrong?"

"A very great deal. Come and look at these documents. You too, Fortescue."

Linckes went to the table and spread open the various sheets. Looking over his shoulder, the secretary gave a startled gasp. But Linckes' heart was beating madly. Every sheet was blank, not only the supposed plans.

"Good heavens!" he said.

"Exactly!" Winthrop turned to Fortescue. "Mr. Fortescue, I saw Mr. Caryu this morning. He informed me that he was sending certain important papers. Did you know this?"

"No, Sir Charles. Oh, heavens! Surely—"

He broke off, staring blankly at Winthrop.

Winthrop sat down at his desk.

"Your case was stolen, Mr. Fortescue. Presumably when you dropped it in Piccadilly."

"But—but, Sir Charles, it was only on the ground for an instant. Besides, who *could* know that the case contained anything important?"

"I'm afraid I cannot tell you that," Winthrop said coolly. "Will you please try and remember the exact circumstances of your dropping it?"

"I—I crossed to the 'island', Sir Charles, and waited for the stream of traffic to pass. There — there were a good many people on the 'island', and, as I said, there was a lot of pushing and barging. There was a stout woman who rather lost her head and tried to make a dash for the other side of the road, and had to get back again to the 'island' in a hurry. She must have pushed the man standing next to me. Anyway, he fell against me, and I lost my balance, and—and I dropped the case."

"And this man," said Winthrop. "Was he by any chance carrying a dis-patch-case?"

The secretary moistened his lips.

"I—I'm afraid I didn't notice, sir. I dare say he was. It was at an hour when most men are coming away from business, and— Oh, heavens!" He ended on a stricken note. "What a *fool* I am! What a damned fool! If only I'd known that there were important papers in the case! Sir Charles, it—they— they weren't the new plans?"

"That is precisely what they were," Winthrop answered.

He unhooked the receiver from the telephone and called a number. While he was waiting to be connected he glanced at Linckes, smiling rather wearily.

"Well, here's your chance, Linckes. And he's got away with it, the scoun-drel! Hallo! Is that Mr. Caryu's house? Put me through to him, please. Winthrop speaking. Thanks!"

Again there was a pause. Then he began to speak into the telephone. Quite calmly he told Caryu all that had happened. At the end he hung up the receiver and nodded to Fortescue.

"Mr. Caryu wants you to go back, Fortescue."

Some of the pallor left Fortescue's face.

"Mr.—Mr. Caryu doesn't suspect me, sir?"

"No. You'd better get along as fast as possible. Tell Mr. Caryu that I shall come round at once."

"One moment!" interposed Linckes. "Can you remember what the man who fell against you looked like?"

"Just—just ordinary," answered the unhappy secretary. "He was middle-aged, I think, but I won't swear to it."

"I see. Thank you! Winthrop, I won't stay to dinner, if you'll excuse me. I'll get right on to this at once."

Winthrop nodded.

VI.

IT was close on eleven o'clock that same evening, and Arlington Street was very quiet. One or two people passed down the road, and presently someone left Winthrop's house and went away in a large limousine. Several people had visited Sir Charles that evening, and he himself had returned from Caryu's house shortly after eight.

For some time after the last visitor had departed there was silence in the street, and then the chunk-chunk of a London taxi made itself heard, and in a few moments a car drew up outside No. 10. A man in an overcoat and opera hat got out, paid the driver, and mounted the steps to the front door. He pressed the bell, and stood waiting to be admitted. He was a medium-sized man, inclined to stoutness, and with a short, grizzled beard. The butler opened the door.

"Is Sir Charles in?" asked the newcomer. His voice was rather hoarse and guttural.

"Yes, sir. But I don't think he's seeing anyone else today."

"Would you ask him if he will give me a moment?"

The man handed John a card. The butler read it.

"Oh, Mr. Knowles, sir! I beg your pardon! Will you come in while I see if Sir Charles is still up?"

Knowles entered the house, and the door closed again.

From the shadowy depths of the area two men rose stealthily, and crept up the steps to the street.

"Got him!" Linckes whispered. "Your revolver ready, Tomlins?"

His companion nodded.

"Yes, it is. Wish I knew what you're about."

"You soon will know," said Linckes grimly. "Your men are prepared?"

"Inspector Gregory's at the back of the house, Mr. Linckes, and Inspector Marks is just down the road. He'll come up to the house with Sergeant O'Hara as soon we get in."

"All right. Don't forget that all you've got to do is to follow me and to do as I say instantly."

"No, sir. Carry on!"

Linckes ran lightly up the steps of the house and rang the bell. After a short pause the door was opened.

"John, is Sir Charles up?"

"Yes, sir. Oh, is it you, sir? Come in!"

Linckes walked into the hall, followed by the other detective. John looked at Tomlins surprisedly.

"Sir Charles is engaged just at the moment, sir. But if you'll wait—"

"Oh, is he? We'll just wait here, then. Don't bother to stay, John."

He turned to Tomlins.

"The library is at the bottom of this passage. It'll be locked, and we shall wait in absolute silence outside. There are two men in the room, and when they come out you are to cover Sir Charles Winthrop. Leave the other to me. See?"

"Can't say I do, sir. But I'll do as you say, of course."

"Then follow me. Not a sound, remember!"

In perfect silence the two men took up their stations on either side of the library door, revolvers held ready. The murmur of conversation could be heard within, and although neither Linckes nor Tomlins could distinguish any word spoken, they could hear that the talk was worried.

Then, after what seemed an interminable time, the key scraped in the lock, and Winthrop opened the door. Behind him stood the man Linckes had seen entering the house a few minutes ago.

For a moment there was dead silence as Winthrop stared haughtily from one levelled revolver to the other. Even now Linckes could not but admire the indomitable courage and sang-froid that Sir Charles displayed.

"Really, Mr. Linckes!" he said, faintly amused. "May I ask what you think you are doing?"

"Hands up, please!" Linckes said sternly. "If you attempt to escape I shall shoot!"

Winthrop shrugged slightly, and raised his hands. Still he preserved that air of haughty bewilderment. But the man beside him had grown very pale, and was biting his under-lip. The hands that he held up were trembling.

Linckes advanced into the room, covering his man.

"I may be doing you a grievous injury, Sir Charles, but I do not think so." With his free hand he drew a silver whistle from his pocket and blew three shrill blasts upon it. "Mr. Winthrop, will you be so good as to remove your wig and your beard? Your make-up is excellent!"

Disregarding Tomlins' levelled revolver, Sir Charles lowered his hands. He sank down into his chair, and regarded Linckes with a twinkle in his eye.

His fine lips smiled generously.

"Do tell me how you found out," he said pleasantly. "Take the wig off, Alec. The game's up!"

With starting eyes Tomlins watched the pseudo Mr. Knowles tear off his wig and beard. Night black hair with a faint crinkle in it was revealed, and when the man had rubbed his face with his handkerchief, removing most of the cunning make-up, the detective's jaw dropped.

"Sir—Sir Charles!" he gasped. A little, low laugh came from Winthrop.

"Wonderful, isn't it? Quite difficult to tell us apart." He paused, listening to the sudden pandemonium without. "Well, you've roused the whole household, Linckes, and I suppose your assistants are even now invading my house. You must allow me to congratulate you. I never thought you'd discover me. And I've had a fair run for my money, haven't I? I don't regret it a bit. Poor Alec's looking rather glum. But then he always was rather peevish. That was what made you suspect me in the first place, wasn't it? Jolly clever of you to think of that blank sheet scheme. I ought to have guessed, of course. Fact of the matter is, you took me in. I didn't think you suspected me."

VII.

TONY dabbed at her eyes, and gave a tiny sob.

"It's so awful, Roger! I c-can't bear to think of Charlie doing such a thing. I—I just can't realise it. It—it seems impossible!"

Linckes patted her shoulder uncomfortably.

"And—and somehow I can't feel angry with him. He was always such a dear!"

"I know. He was just one of those people who couldn't run straight. 'Twasn't altogether his fault. And one must admire his courage."

Tony was silent for a moment, still mopping her eyes.

A pair of soft arms stole round his neck.

"No; and I can't help admiring you!" whispered Tony.

THE END

READING "LINCKES' GREAT CASE"

It's not that it's boring, exactly. It's... fine. But as a devotee of Heyer's crime fiction, especially her Inspector Hannasyde novels, it is somewhat disappointing to read this rather pedestrian tale of stolen documents and the pursuit of the very obvious thief that takes so, so, *way* too long to unfold.

When it comes to Georgette Heyer, no matter what the genre, we expect more than "fine."

Of course, everyone has to start somewhere, even authors who saw such overnight success as Heyer, and because her first novel was such a tour de force, and is still in print nigh on a century later, it is easy to forget that she was so very young when she wrote it, and that even when this later story was published, in March of 1923, she was not yet even twenty-one years of age.

The theory propounded in the introduction to this piece, that perhaps George Heyer had a significant hand in this somewhat plodding outing, is certainly one explanation for its somewhat lacklustre nature (with apologies to George Heyer, who was an author and poet and general polymath, and whom Georgette adored), but I would offer up an alternate theory: it's all the younger Heyer's own work, but is just not very good, because not all early work is. And perhaps it is very different to her "style" simply because she had not yet figured out what that was.

Take, for example, her historical fiction novel *The Great Roxhythe*, published in 1922, and her 1923 contemporary novel *Instead of the Thorn*, both wildly different – and, it must be said, less successful – than *The Black Moth*. That *The Transformation of Philip Jettan,* now known, in slightly modified form, as *Powder and Patch*, was also published in 1923 showcases Heyer's range of experimentation during this period of her writing career, and *Linckes' Great Case* could very simply be yet another one of her attempts to find her voice, and her passion, and extend herself beyond the Georgian romps that evidently came so naturally to her.

Certainly, the developing romance of Linckes and Tony, the privileged daughter of a government minister, is pure Georgette, although it is interesting that their class difference does not seem to make much of a difference here – it might be a subtle distinction, but the sprightly Autonia (erk, what a name!) appears to be a scion of the County set while Linckes is, though well-spoken, clearly a working man hailing from the stolid middle class—even if their fathers *did* go to school together. Although, honestly, quite what Tony finds to so admire about Linckes is perhaps a bigger mystery than who stole those dratted documents could ever be.

The culprits are in many ways the most compelling characters of this narrative, for all that they are terribly incompetent and only get away with it for so long because Linckes is even more so. Sir Charles Winthrop is a smooth devil, and there are shades of the supercilious Duke of Andover/Avon model about him – it is understandable that Linckes falls into something of an infatuation with him, and we know that Heyer was very into male friendship narratives at this time, given *The Great Roxhythe's* central pairing of the Marquis and his devoted secretary, Christopher. Far better developed than Linckes/Tony is Linckes/Sir Charles, especially since the morose Alec constantly keeps Linckes guessing, making it seem that Winthrop is blowing hot and cold, and making him all the more fascinating to a young and easily-impressed ingenu like poor Roger Linckes as a result.

I've read more than my share of pulp detective fiction of this era, and *Linckes' Great Case* is not wholly unlike much of what was being published at the time – in fact, it's something of a cut above even the other stories published *even* in the very same issue of *Detective Magazine* in which it appeared. ("The Karlovna Jewel Mystery" by T. B. Donovan is especially dire.) The characters are two-dimensional, certainly. But they do have their charms, and occasional witticisms, and they're not entirely inconsistent with Heyer's later works. If only the mystery at the centre of this tale had been solved over the course of days and weeks rather than weeks and months, it might stand as an impressive first attempt in the field.

But it's not *Heyer*, not yet anyway, and that is what leads to the speculation that she didn't write it entirely by herself – we don't want to believe that someone so remarkable could have turned in something so relatively ordinary.

But I think she probably did.

And I think that's… fine.

– *Rachel Hyland*

"THE BULLDOG AND THE BEAST"

INTRODUCTION

Heyer returned to *The Happy Mag* for her fourth excursion into short fiction. "The Bulldog and the Beast" was published there in March 1923, the same month that "Linckes' Great Case" was published in *The Detective Magazine*, although the two stories are completely different from each other. Unlike "Linckes", "The Bulldog and the Beast" is a romantic tale, and there is a noticeable difference between the two stories in style, tone, and execution. "The Bulldog and the Beast" is more tightly plotted than "Linckes" and the story is far more engaging. It is also a decided step up from either "A Proposal to Cicely" or "The Little Lady" for here it seems, Georgette Heyer had found her short story "voice."

From the first sentence we are amused and a little intrigued. Beginning with: "Upon the stairs which led to his flat, Hugh Ruthven met the bull-dog," the story quickly evolves into a clever three-hander with Hugh, Mr. Sykes (the engaging and intelligent canine), and Katharine Testram, the bulldog's adoring owner, all becoming inextricably linked. Mr. Sykes is instantly lovable and the way he directs the action is comical and clever. Sykes is the lynch-pin of the story and Heyer's pithy romance is lifted above the average by his presence. Though there is instant animosity between the man-hating Miss Testram and the cynical Mr. Ruthven, both protagonists love Mr. Sykes and in Heyer's world this is a sign of both good character and intelligence.

Heyer had dogs through much of her life. From her mother's beloved Dachshund to her own Pekingese (the very same who was perhaps the model for Chu-Chu San in "A Proposal to Cicely") and her grandmother's terriers, she knew and loved dogs from early childhood. As an adult, Heyer had a Sealyham terrier named Roddy; after Roddy came her adored bull terrier Jonathan Velhurst Viking (known as Jonny), and her magnificent wolfhound, Misty Dawn. Jonny would be her last four-legged friend, but Heyer would always have fictional dogs – delightful imaginary dogs who would come to life in her books. Mr. Sykes epitomises Heyer's emotional connection to dogs and he would prove to be the fictional forerunner of the memorable canines that would eventually populate her Regency novels: Ulysses in *Arabella,* Tina in *The Grand Sophy* and Lufra in *Frederica.*

Like those felicitous creations, Mr. Sykes is delightful and Heyer brings him endearingly to life. Sykes snorts and waddles and snuffles and squirms his way through the story as he tries his best to bring his belligerent owner and the man she detests together. Heyer is finally hitting her short story straps here and allowing her natural wit and humour a much freer rein. Her voice is crisp, her characters more fully realised, and the story flows from the first sentence.

As always, class attitudes are inherent in Heyer's depiction of upper middle-class people in 1920s England. Katharine is only poor because her once-wealthy father has invested his money badly. Her father has died and she must earn her living as a paid companion to a difficult great-aunt. Hugh Ruthven is one of Heyer's independent men of means and, though he lives in a flat, he has a man-servant, a cook, and a parlour maid. Hugh also has a racing-car, is often at home during the day, and has no apparent need to work. This is the aspirational world so popular with readers after the Great War. Heyer needed only to sketch these details in lightly but she did so with a deftness that fleshes out her characters and evokes her readers' empathy.

"The Bulldog and the Beast" is the first of three short stories which would signal the tone of the clever comedic novels yet to come.

– Jennifer Kloester

THE BULLDOG AND THE BEAST

UPON the stairs which led to his flat, Hugh Ruthven met the bulldog. They eyed one another silently for a moment, until the bulldog signified his approval of this new acquaintance by a loud snort.

"I entirely agree with you," said Ruthven.

The bulldog seemed pleased with this remark: he snuffled engagingly by and waddled upstairs in Ruthven's wake. With his latch-key held ready, Ruthven again addressed the bulldog.

"Like to come in?" he inquired.

The bulldog said that he would. He said it quite plainly, with his ears and tail.

In the cosy hall, over a sweet biscuit, they made friends. The bulldog then wandered about the hall on a tour of inspection. He was interrupted by a girl's voice, calling from without.

"Sykes! Sykes! Where are you, Mr. Sykes? Here, boy!"

The bulldog waddled to the door, and looked over his shoulder at his host.

"My dear Mr. Sykes," Ruthven addressed him, "if you belong to a member of what we blindly and mistakenly call 'the gentle sex', you have my sympathy."

The bulldog seemed to deprecate this remark. The voice called again and he snorted loudly.

Ruthven rose languidly.

"You are mistaken," he said. "When you have had more experience of women you will know that there is nothing harder, more cruel, and more treacherous. Do you still wish to rejoin your mistress?"

Mr. Sykes wagged the whole of his hindquarters.

"You do. Far be it from me, then, to seek to detain you. Farewell." Ruthven opened the door and watched Mr. Sykes waddle out. A dark girl stood at the head of the stairs. She greeted her strayed property joyfully, but in the middle of her welcome, she perceived Ruthven, and a hard light came into her eyes.

"I must apologise for harbouring your dog," Ruthven said smoothly, yet with that bitter note in his voice.

"Not at all," said the girl stiffly. She called to Mr. Sykes, and went into the opposite flat. The door shut with a decided click.

Katharine Testram eyed Mr. Sykes sadly.

"Sykes, how *could* you?" she demanded.

Mr. Sykes squirmed apologetically.

"A man!" said Katharine. "Don't you know that men are hateful, cruel, fickle creatures?"

Mr. Sykes cocked his ears a little.

"They are!" averred Katharine stoutly. "Don't you forget how a man treated me—and how a man treated poor Lucille."

Mr. Sykes licked her hand.

"You can't judge all men by two rotters," said his ears.

"They're all the same," said Katharine, positively. "'Cept you."

From which cryptic remark it will be gathered that a man had treated Katharine very badly. As was indeed the case.

A year ago her father had died, leaving her his blessing. And that was all he had to leave, save some debts. It had been a severe shock to Katharine, for she had always expected to be well-off, and had never troubled her head about money-matters. But Mr. Testram had been led astray in his invest-ments, with the result that Katharine was left with just fifty pounds a year, and a bulldog. She was engaged to be married—and her fiancé broke it off.

Now she was acting as companion to her great-aunt, a crotchety, exact-ing old lady who never failed to impress two facts upon her niece: one, that she had allowed her to keep Mr. Sykes as a great concession; two, that Katharine should not expect to be mentioned in her will.

Only the dread thought of having to part with Mr. Sykes induced Katharine to remain with Mrs. Hilton. She would have preferred to seek a living in almost any other way, but she realised that were she to strike out on her own, Mr. Sykes would have to be sacrificed. And Mr. Sykes was all that remained to her.

MR. SYKES, having once tested the hospitality of Hugh Ruthven, that sore and jilted woman-hater, and found it good, made a point of visiting him reg-ularly. Hardly a day passed but Ruthven would hear an inquisitive snort out-side his door and when he went to open it, in would come Sykes with his rolling gait, and his expectantly cocked ears.

They became fast friends, to the annoyance of Sykes' mistress. Once she marched across the strip of passage separating the two flats, and coldly demanded her property from Ruthven's man-servant. She was asked to come inside, and very reluctantly she did so.

Ruthven came to her, Sykes at his heels, and the sight of her dog placidly following him, infuriated Katharine. Her dark eyes flashed, and her lips grew hard.

"I must really ask you not to entice my dog to visit you!" she said sharply.

Ruthven raised his eyebrows slightly. He bent to pat Mr. Sykes.

"You are labouring under a delusion, Miss—?"

"My name doesn't matter. Come, Sykes!"

"Not in the slightest," drawled Ruthven. "As I was saying, you are mis-taken. I have never—er—enticed your dog. He seems to like my company."

"Then may I ask that you will not admit him again?"

Ruthven smiled a little mockingly.

"Certainly you may."

Katharine's colour rose. "I don't know how you managed to bribe him," she said bitingly, "but I beg you will discontinue your efforts. I do not allow him to stray away to other people's flats. I very much object to it."

Ruthven looked her over, still faintly smiling.

"One would almost imagine that you had some grudge against me," he remarked languidly.

Katharine drew herself up.

"I know nothing about you except that you persist in encouraging my dog to come into your flat, but I dislike the whole of your sex." She could have bitten her tongue out as soon as the foolish words had left her mouth.

Ruthven's eyes widened.

"How very interesting," he replied. "I, myself, abominate the female of the species. Now we understand one another. I am glad you called today, as I have been wishing to see you. I should like to buy your dog."

Katharine swept to the door.

"He is not for sale," she said stiffly. "Sykes!"

Ruthven bowed her out. He shut the door and addressed himself sardonically.

"There you have the worst type of woman," he informed himself. "A spitfire. I wonder who the man was?"

"Don't you go over there again!" Katharine adjured Mr. Sykes. "He's a perfectly hateful creature. How dared he smile at me like that?"

Mr. Sykes snuffled aggrievedly.

"He may be handsome," said Katharine severely, "but he's a Beast!"

Mr. Sykes waddled away. There were times when he found his mistress a trifle wearisome.

MISS TESTRAM and Mr. Ruthven lost no time in finding out each other's names. Whenever they chanced to meet, either in the lift or upon the stairs, they cut one another dead. Only Mr. Sykes continued to gravitate between them. There was that in Mr. Ruthven that appealed to him. And Ruthven continued to admit Mr. Sykes into his flat.

Also he maintained a deaf ear to Miss Testram's voice without, calling her property, so that she was compelled, mostly, to cross his threshold. Why he did this he had no idea. It was of course ridiculous that he should want to see the lady, for on these occasions they were exceedingly hostile towards each other, not to say rude.

One day when Katharine called at Ruthven's flat for the straying Mr. Sykes, Ruthven greeted her with a malicious smile.

"I regret to say that Sykes is not with me," he said.

"Not with you? Then where—I don't believe you!"

Ruthven bowed.

"Give him to me at once, please!"

"He isn't here."

"Then where is he?" she demanded suspiciously. "Have you stolen him?"

"You can hardly expect to answer that question," he replied. "Have you lost him?"

"You know very well that I have!" she snapped, and hurried out.

Two hours later, Ruthven strolled out of his flat and inquired casually of the hall-porter whether Miss Testram's dog had been found. On being told that Miss Testram's dog had not been found, he went out and slid into his racing car.

He spied Mr. Sykes at length, plodding homewards, quite near the block, with an end of rope trailing behind him.

Ruthven slowed down and invited the somewhat grimy Sykes to enter the car. Relievedly the bulldog clambered in and licked Ruthven's hand by way of thanks.

Arrived once more at the block of flats, Ruthven surveyed his protégé gravely.

"Mr. Sykes. honesty compels me to remark that you are not over-clean."

Mr. Sykes heaved a large sigh.

"Also—to put it plainly—that you smell."

Mr. Sykes wagged his tail guiltily.

"I suggest that we repair to my flat. I can hardly return you to the Spitfire in that condition. A bath is what you need."

Mr. Sykes, hearing the hated word, followed him dejectedly into the lift.

"MR. RUTHVEN'S compliments, miss, and he has found Mr. Sykes, and will return him as soon as he is dry."

"Found him? Oh, thank heaven! Where is he? Send him to me at once, please!"

"You see, miss, the dog was a bit dirty, and Mr. Ruthven has been washing him," explained the man.

Katharine hesitated. Then she came out of the flat and shut the door. "I'll come and fetch him," she said.

She found Mr. Sykes wrangling amicably with his host and an old towel.

"Thank you for taking so much trouble over Sykes," she said frigidly. "I am sorry I accused you of stealing him."

"Not at all," answered Ruthven, just as coldly. "Won't you sit down?"

"I should prefer to take him home at once, thank you."

"Certainly," shrugged Ruthven.

A month later, Ruthven slit open a letter addressed to him in an unknown but palpably feminine hand-writing, and read as follows:—

"Dear Mr. Ruthven,

"Circumstances over which I have no control compel me to part with Mr. Sykes. If you still wish to purchase him, perhaps you will communicate with me. I enclose his pedigree. I am asking twenty guineas for him.

"Yours truly,

"Katharine Testram."

Ruthven read the document through twice. He did not glance at the pedigree, but rose and went to his desk. In his neat, masterly hand, he answered the letter in this wise:—

"Dear Miss Testram,

"I enclose a cheque for twenty guineas. If you will send Mr. Sykes over to my flat at your convenience, I can promise that he will receive every attention, and an appreciative owner. I trust you will visit him whenever you wish.

"Yours truly,

"Hugh Ruthven."

"Now, confound it, why have I asked the girl to visit him?" exclaimed Ruthven. He twisted the letter in his hand, undecidedly. "Oh, well! Let it stand!"

With trembling lips Katharine gave Mr. Sykes a last hug.

"He—he'll—be good to you, darling. He—he's got a hard, cruel m-mouth, but he likes you. An'—an' it was—it was a n-nice letter! Only I sh-shan't ever c-come to see you—cos—it'ud—m-make you so miserable. Be—besides he— abominates—women!" She kissed the top of Mr. Sykes' head, and hurriedly departed, while the sympathetic parlour-maid took Sykes and a receipt to Mr. Ruthven's flat.

For Katharine's great-aunt was dead at last, to the great relief of her family. An attack of bronchitis had carried her off, and Katharine was left, practically penniless. She had tried hard to find a post as companion to some lady who would not object to her keeping Mr. Sykes, but that lady did not seem to be in existence. Either she herself possessed a dog, or a cat, or had a rooted objection to them. Try as she might, Katharine could find but one solution to the problem. Mr. Sykes must go to the hated Ruthven.

RUTHVEN stretched his legs to the fire, and frowned down at Mr. Sykes, lying uneasily at his feet.

"I've been finding out one or two things about your late mistress, Sykes," he said.

Mr. Sykes lifted his head. A hopeful gleam came into his worried eyes, and he snuffled eagerly. The word "mistress" had caught his attention. Ruthven patted him.

"Sorry, old man. That was not my meaning. She's in a bad way, you know. She's very hard up."

Mr. Sykes gave vent to a short, gruff bark. He waddled to the door.

"All right," said Ruthven. "But it's only for your sake, remember!" He pulled out his pocket-book and drew from it a slip of paper. "Radclyffe Gardens," he read. "Beastly hole. Come along."

Mr. Sykes followed him joyously out. Twenty minutes later the manageress of the boarding-house eyed Ruthven curiously.

"Miss Testram has gone," she announced.

"Gone! Where?"

The manageress folded her hands.

"Our charges were too high for Miss Testram," she exclaimed. "I believe she has gone into rooms."

"Will you please give me the address?" said Ruthven coldly.

"Oh, certainly!" She disappeared into her office, drawing her skirts away from Mr. Sykes. Presently she emerged. "Bryan Road," she announced, with a small sniff. "No. 245."

"Thank you," bowed Ruthven. "Come along, Sykes." Once in his car again, he frowned at Sykes. "Bryan Road?" he said. "Do you call that a proper place for a girl like the Spitfire?"

Mr. Sykes sneezed.

"I should think not," said Ruthven. "And you must understand that it is solely on your account that I am seeking her out."

He imagined a quizzical gleam in the bulldog's eye. He promptly stared Mr. Sykes out of countenance.

Miss Testram had rented a bed-sitting-room over a furniture shop. Ruthven and Sykes climbed slowly up the dingy staircase, and knocked at Katharine's door. Mr. Sykes snuffled violently, for his nose had caught a whiff of his mistress's scent.

Katharine opened the door, and the instant he set eyes on her, Ruthven decided that she looked wan and underfed.

"What—oh, *Sykes!*" Katharine fell on her knees, and received Mr. Sykes' heavy body in her arms. For a little while he occupied all her thoughts, and the air was filled with mingled snuffles, tears, and laughter. Then Katharine stood up, brushing her hand across her eyes.

"I—beg your pardon. I—what—"

"I brought Mr. Sykes to see you," said Ruthven. "He misses you rather badly."

"He's getting thin," she reproached him.

"I know. May I ask what you are doing?"

"I—I take in—typing," she said, as jauntily as she could.

Ruthven looked hard at her.

"Yes? Well, is there any reason why you should not keep Sykes with you, now that you are in all day?"

A sudden flush dyed Katharine's cheeks.

"Oh! Oh, could—" She collected herself. "I—I'm afraid I can't—offer to—to buy him back—just at present," she said with difficulty. "It's—very kind of you."

"No, it is not," contradicted Ruthven. "I can't have a moping dog on my hands. If you'll take him, you'll be doing me a favour. There is no immediate hurry for payment. I hope you will—er—pay me at your convenience."

Katharine's eyes filled.

"Do—do you—really mean—it?" she asked.

"Of course I mean it!" he answered roughly. "But I must ask you to let me—er—visit him occasionally."

"I don't—feel I ought—"

"I shall not take him back with me, so if you don't keep him, he'll stray."

"I—I haven't much choice, have I?" she said with a tired sort of smile. "Thank you very, very much. I—I hope you'll come to see him—whenever you like." She held out her hand.

Ruthven took it, and found himself saying:

"Er—I wonder—could you lunch with me tomorrow?"

Katharine was surprised.

"Lunch with you? It's very kind of you, but—"

"And Sykes, of course. I'll call for you."

"But—"

"Please don't argue!" said Ruthven, curtly, and departed.

A MONTH later, after several lunches, two teas, and some motor-drives with Katharine, Ruthven received a letter from her.

> "Dear Mr. Ruthven,
>
> "It's no good. I can't keep Sykes. He frets terribly for you, and I can't bear to see him growing so thin. Will you please take him back? He likes you better than me.
>
> "Yours sincerely,
>
> "Katharine Testram."

Ruthven spent half an hour staring into the fire. Then he carefully folded the letter and put it into his pocket-book, together with another in the same hand-writing. Next he wrote an answer to Katharine.

> "Dear Miss Testram,

"I will call on you on Thursday morning, if you have no objection, to discuss the matter of Mr. Sykes.
"Yours sincerely,
"Hugh Ruthven."

Before Ruthven left his flat on Thursday, he gave a few parting instructions to his servant, concerning lunch, and the preparation of a certain room. The servant was, as he put it, completely flabbergasted at the extraordinary announcement Mr. Ruthven had made, two days before. He had talked it over with his wife, Ruthven's cook, and they agreed that it was incomprehensible.

When Katharine opened her door to Ruthven that morning, it was quite obvious that she had been crying. Ruthven perceived it at a glance. However, he did not remark on it.

"Put your things on," he commanded, "and bring Sykes."

"But—"

"I am not going to argue about it, Katharine. Put your hat on."

Katharine blushed, for her had never addressed her by her Christian name until now.

"I don't understand—"

"I can't and won't talk to you here," interrupted Ruthven. "I'll explain in the car. Go and do as I tell you."

Katharine went with surprising meekness. Not until they were driving along the street did she venture another question. Sykes, panting blissfully, was wedged in between them, trying to lick both their faces alternately.

"Where—where are you taking me?" Katharine said.

"I've thought it all out carefully," said Ruthven, "and I've come to the conclusion that we'd better get married. So I bought a ring and a special licence, and I ordered a wedding brunch at home, and—"

"But it's impossible!" cried Katharine, as soon as she had recovered from her first surprise. "You don't love me—I hardly know you! I don't like men! You don't like wom—"

"I can't help that. We owe it to Sykes."

Katharine started to laugh hysterically.

"Oh, please take me back! You're—you're quite mad! I can't possibly marry you! It's too rid—ridiculous! I—" Ruthven turned down a side-street.

"Katharine, do you, or do you not love me?"

"No, of c–course I d–don't!"

"Well, I do love you," Ruthven told her. "I don't know what it is about you, but I can't live without you. And I'm not going to. So don't start arguing again."

Katharine fumbled for her handkerchief, sniffed, and started to cry, quite quietly. Mr. Sykes sought frantically to comfort her. Mr. Ruthven slowed down and took Katharine's hand in his.

"Don't cry, Katharine! Poor little girl, you've had the devil of a time, but don't cry! I'm going to change all that, and you shan't ever be unhappy again, Katharine. If you don't stop, I shall have to kiss you, and there's someone looking!"

Katharine gulped, and clung to Ruthven's sustaining hand. Ruthven kissed her fingers.

"Will you marry me, Katharine? Sykes clearly wishes it."

Katharine nodded, mopping her eyes.

"Yes, please, Hugh," she sighed. "The—the man isn't looking now."

Mr. Sykes sniffed, and his grin spread from ear to ear.

MR. SYKES gave the bride away. He was the first to embrace her after the ceremony in the dingy registry office, and he snorted so loudly that there could be no mistaking his delight.

Later, when the newly married pair sat before the fire in Ruthven's flat, occupying one chair between them, Sykes lay down at their feet with a contented wriggle.

"I believe he planned it from the first," remarked Ruthven into Katharine's hair. "You know, your hair smells of violets, darling."

"Does it?" She laughed a little. "D'you think Sykes really thought it all out?"

"I do. Look at him now! Absolutely triumphant. Sykes, you old rascal, you undertook a superhuman task, for we both hated one another."

Sykes blinked at him for a moment.

"We did," averred Katharine. "For—oh, for ages!"

Mr. Sykes snorted scornfully, and disposed himself afresh, with his back to them.

Mr. and Mrs. Ruthven looked at one another.

"I don't think he believes us," said Katharine.

"No, I don't think he does. He's got too much sense," answered Ruthven.

Mr. Sykes heard the sound of a long kiss, and he wagged his tail drowsily. Then he rolled over on to his side and closed his eyes. He felt that his labours were at an end.

THE END

READING "THE BULLDOG AND THE BEAST"

One of the great tropes of romantic fiction is the Enemies to Lovers archetype, in which our plucky pair hate each other with some passion at first sight, but eventually snipe their way into love. This is not a trope that is unknown among Heyer's works, but it is uncommon, and when she does employ the formula it is usually her heroines who despise her heroes, while the heroes are alternately indifferent (Worth in *Regency Buck*), intrigued (Sylvester in, of course, *Sylvester*) or utterly smitten (Simon in *Simon the Coldheart*).

But here, in this very early outing, we have a meet-cute that leads to a very stiff correspondence between two broken people, both of whom are soured on the opposite sex after bad breakups and who have decided to live forever alone, in that very melodramatic way of the recently heartbroken. Slowly, through the kind offices of Mr. Sykes the bulldog, our misogynistic Hugh Ruthven and our misandrist Katharine Testram come to appreciate the good in one another, and when Katharine's increasing penury draws out Ruthven's protective instincts, he calls it love.

And then Katharine agrees to marry him, after only "several lunches, two teas and some motor-drives," and despite having just told him categorically that she is not in love with him, because actually she is, and probably was from the first. Nothing else can fully explain her immediate animosity when Sykes importuned him so grievously as the story commenced.

I have a lot of questions about what is going on with Sykes. How is he permitted to roam the apartment building in which they live? How does he "get out" so often? He's obviously an inside dog – who is opening the door of Katharine's locked apartment while she is out and letting him escape? Or is he some kind of mystical dog, as the last paragraph alludes, whose purpose on earth is to matchmake cynics and/or provide providers for apparently unemployable women?

Could it be that "The Little Lady" was not, after all, Heyer's only flirtation with the supernatural?

And, hey. Ruthven is, as far as we can tell, also unemployed. At least, if he does anything to earn his crust, we never hear of it. Yet he has a car, and twenty guineas (equivalent buying power today of around £1,200; that is one expensive second-hand bulldog!) to spare on a whim, and can get married… also on a whim. Ah, these idly rich gentlemen of the 1920s! I shouldn't wonder if Ruthven was a member of the Drones Club. Richard Spalding of "A Proposal to Cicely" surely was – the P. G. Wodehouse influence over these stories is pretty self-evident.

It is quite strange, meanwhile, that Heyer refers to Hugh Ruthven as

"Ruthven" throughout this tale, which feels quite incongruous when he is not a lord of some kind. In her historical novels, most of which dwell in the aristocracy, you'll get a "Cardross" or a "Damerel" and won't necessarily learn the gentleman's first name for a good deal of the book. (Giles and Jasper, respectively.) True, in those more formal times, we also have "Mr. Beaumaris" and "Mr. Carleton," who are only rarely Robert and Oliver to us, but in *Instead of the Thorn*, for example, Heyer's first contemporary novel, published in 1923, our – I guess? – hero is known to us almost from the outset as "Stephen." One might think this is a deliberate choice made by Heyer here, to demonstrate the distance Hugh feels towards humanity in general, and Miss Testram in particular, but even at the story's happy conclusion, she persists in last-naming him, so it just seems to be the mode of address she decided he deserved. It's like he's straight out of the prefect's study in a Boy's Own boarding school story, but when Katharine (who is, crucially, Katharine pretty much from the off) – calls him Hugh, he does not in any way object.

Curious.

Although, Katharine did name her dog the very formal Mr. Sykes, and her last name is the unfathomable and irregular Testram – the kind of word that your brain wants to read differently, and you are forced to really look at, not to misinterpret it entirely – so clearly nomenclature is a problem for this story all over the place.

Especially as, in its originally published form, the word bulldog was consistently rendered "bull-dog" (we fixed it), and I can find no reference anywhere to that being the standard. Ever. Even the title, as printed in *The Happy Mag*, does not use this eccentric hyphenation.

Just another instance of Georgette Heyer leading the vanguard with her linguistic uniqueness, I guess.

This is a really, really cute story for all that, though.

– *Rachel Hyland*

"ACTING ON IMPULSE"

INTRODUCTION

In June 1923 Heyer had her fifth short story published, this time in *The Red Magazine*, which had published her second short, "The Little Lady", the previous year. The new story was very different from that sentimental tale, and it has some additional early signs of what would become Heyer's trademark humour. "Acting on Impulse" is, following on from "Bulldog and the Beast", another light-hearted story, this one featuring an impulsive, youthful hero in Kenneth and a kind but practical heroine in Ursula.

Though it is a romance, most of the action centres, not on Kenneth and Ursula, but on Kenneth and his father, the choleric "old General Mount." The General is instantly recognisable as one of those crusty, irascible, yet soft-hearted men so popular in the fiction of the time. Kenneth's only parent lives a comfortable, well-heeled life, with a clear code of conduct and a valet. Whisky and cigars are his weakness and Kenneth puts them to good use in accomplishing his latest mad plan. Kenneth is another of Heyer's wealthy young men with only themselves to please. He is charming and lively with a great deal of bonhomie. He also has a strong, determined streak and will not be diverted once he has settled on a scheme.

Heyer's heroine, however, is the first properly independent female in her fiction. Ursula is "an orphan, and she supported herself by painting posters and illustrating magazines." She is intelligent and outspoken and knows how to manage Kenneth and, in the end, his father. This sort of character would appear five years later in Heyer's most autobiographical novel, *Helen*. In that novel Angela Lorne is a friend of Helen's, and an artist who does "poster-work" and illustrations for short-story magazines. She lives in a Chelsea flat with a large studio and is described as, "capable and fairly hard, and entirely independent."

In "Acting on Impulse" Ursula is not "hard" but she is strong-minded and sure of herself. When the General discovers that she is "a modern girl who worked for her own living" he is apoplectic. For a man of his generation a "self-supporting girl" is the same as a bohemian and that, as he tells his son, must see an end to the affair. But Kenneth is determined.

He is the "creature of impulse" and it is his "ingenuous boyishness" that drives the unlikely but entertaining plot. The action is fast-paced, the dialogue is pure 1920's literary England, with such smile-inducing phrases as "topping," "top-hole" and "awfully bucked," and the plot has enough twists and turns to keep the reader amused. Heyer's hand is sure throughout the story and with some wit and more good humour than she would achieve in *Helen*, she brings the tale to its obvious conclusion.

Though only her second short for *The Red Magazine*, "Acting on Impulse" would be Heyer's last for that publication.

– Jennifer Kloester

ACTING ON IMPULSE

I.

EVERYONE who knew him or had ever known him agreed that Kenneth Mount was mad. His nurse had said it most emphatically when, at the age of five, Kenneth had left his bed while she was having dinner and climbed on to the roof through the trapdoor, clad only in his pyjamas. The only explanation he had been able to give for his extraordinary conduct was that he had wanted to see the man in the moon. When she indignantly demanded whether he could not have done that from his bedroom window, he replied that he hadn't thought of it.

His father said that he was mad; his mother, when she was alive, said that he was "just like his father," which meant practically the same thing. It was a source of wonderment to all his friends and relations that he had escaped expulsion from school, but escape it he did; nor was he sent down from college, although there he had had some anxious moments on that score. Why he was spared no one knew. It may have been that his ingenuous boyishness appealed too strongly to the authorities, or that they realised that there was not an ounce of vice in his composition.

The fact of the matter was that he was purely a creature of impulse. Once he proposed to an elderly spinster because she told him that she was no longer attractive. Strange to say, she did not take offence, but thanked him for his offer and refused it.

He was twenty-six when he became engaged to Ursula Fenton. He had known her for some six months or so, and they were great pals. She was an orphan, and she supported herself by painting posters and illustrating magazines. She took a great interest in the irresponsible Kenneth, and he went often to her studio in Chelsea, just as a friend. There was so little of the lover in his behaviour that Ursula was considerably surprised when, at ten o'clock one morning, he presented himself at her door, hatless and breathless, and delivered himself of this sentence:

"I say, Ursula, will you marry me?"

Another girl might have been offended by this sudden proposal, but Ursula knew her Kenneth. She drew him into the studio and shut the door. She was a very business-like little lady.

"Sit down and pull yourself together, Kenneth! What on earth do you mean?"

Kenneth ran his fingers through his dishevelled hair, which made it stand upon end in short, crisp curls.

"Marry me—be engaged to me! You know!"

"When did you have this brain-wave?" demanded Ursula.

"This morning. I was having breakfast alone—pater's got a cold—and it suddenly struck me how topping you'd look sitting opposite me—pouring out the coffee an' all that. It's the way your hair curls against your cheek, and the way your nose goes squiggly when you laugh. Ursula, it must have been coming on for months. Do marry me!"

They became engaged, and it was all Ursula could do to prevent Kenneth from dashing off there and then to buy a special licence. She dragged him down from the clouds and reminded him that he must first tell his father. Also she would not marry him for at least six months, because she wasn't at all sure that he wouldn't regret the engagement.

Kenneth rushed home to break the news to his father.

Now, old General Mount was a choleric man. He worshipped his son, but there were times when he could be as obstinate as a mule. He wanted tactful handling, but today Kenneth was in no tactful mood. He burst into the general's bedroom and sat down on the side of the bed. The general sneezed violently and swore. A man labouring under a severe cold in the head is hardly in his most amenable frame of mind.

"Look here, sir," said Kenneth excitedly, "I've got a great piece of news! I'm engaged! Engaged! Engaged to be married!"

Another, more violent, sneeze shook the general.

"Engaged be damned!" he choked.

"No—no, not at all! You don't understand, sir! She's the most extraordinary girl you've ever seen in your life! Absolutely wonderful! When she laughs, her nose is all squiggly. Oh, she's top-hole! And she's got the sort of eyes—"

The general raised himself on one elbow.

"Who is this girl?" he snarled.

Kenneth stared at him in surprise.

"Why, didn't I tell you?"

"No, you did not, sir!"

"It's Ursula Fenton. You know."

"I tell you I do not know! Never seen the girl in my life!"

"Haven't you? I say, this won't do!" Kenneth sprang up. "I must buzz off and fetch her along. You'll—"

"Stop!" The general sat up, shivering. "What the devil d'you mean by it, sir? I won't have her here! I won't see any girl in bed! Damn it, I say I will not!"

Kenneth came slowly back to the bedside.

"Can't you get up?" he asked disappointedly.

"No, I can't! You don't seem to understand that I'm very unwell! How dare you come bursting into my room like this?"

Kenneth pushed him gently back on to his pillow and tucked him up.

"I'm awfully sorry, sir. Clean forgot you'd a cold. I'll have to bring Ursula along later."

The general eyed him malevolently.

"I don't want to see her! You're mad—mad!"

That set Kenneth off once more. For ten minutes the general was incapable of stemming the tide of his eloquence. When Kenneth at last paused, he shot forth a number of questions. He discovered that Ursula was a modern girl who worked for her own living. The general was old-fashioned; one of his pet aversions was the self-supporting girl. When he further discovered that Ursula was an artist his rage knew no bounds.

Kenneth must clearly understand that this miserable affair must end at once. If he married this bohemian he would be cut off with a shilling, he should never enter his father's house again, he— At this point, the general's old servant who had entered the room, led Kenneth forth, sternly and silently.

Kenneth knew that his father's bark was a good deal worse than his bite. He fully expected the general to cool down in a few days' time. But for once the general was adamant. The mere mention of Ursula's name drove him into a fury. Kenneth waited a month, and still there were no signs of relenting. So Kenneth went to consult Ursula. It was not the first consultation by any means.

"It's no good," Kenneth said. "He simply won't give in. Won't even see you. We shall have to get married and trust to luck. He'd never disinherit me."

"I'm not going to do that." A frown creased Ursula's pretty brow. "It isn't fair. After all, you're all he's got."

"Well, he shouldn't be so pig-headed," said Kenneth. "If only he'd consented to see you he *couldn't* object."

Ursula smiled a little.

"Silly old Ken! You know, you've mucked this pretty thoroughly. You ought to have told him gently, and not when he was in bed with a cold."

"I s'pose it was rather stupid," agreed Kenneth dejectedly. "The worst of it is, I don't want to upset him. I mean to say, we're frightfully good pals and I don't want to have a row."

"'Course not. Are you quite sure I couldn't go to see him?"

"Good lord, no!" Kenneth was horrified. "He'd have apoplexy! No, there's nothing for it, Ursula. We've got to get married on the Q T and break the news by degrees. I'll get a licence, and—"

"You won't! If your father doesn't give his consent, I won't marry you."

No argument had any effect upon her. Kenneth tried many. He would have gone on arguing until midnight had she not ejected him.

Kenneth drove back to South Kensington, wrapped in gloom. He was trying to think of a way of persuading his parent. Such a way eluded him, and he spent the evening brooding over a pipe and staring blankly at the general.

Next morning he awoke suddenly. He lay for a few minutes, frowning at the bed-post. Then, suddenly, his brow cleared, and he bounced out of bed.

"I've got it!" he shouted. "Got it, got it, got it!"

II.

THE general was a little uneasy about his son. Kenneth had seemed very preoccupied for the last few weeks. Ursula's name had not once passed his lips, but somehow the general did not take this as a good omen. And Kenneth was very often absent from home. Day after day he drove off in his racing-car and did not return until late at night. He offered no explanation for his strange demeanour, and the general was too proud to ask for one. He felt that his son was not pleased with him. Not that Kenneth was anything but polite to him. In fact, he behaved to his father as if nothing had happened. But there was just a faint undercurrent. The general did not like it.

About three weeks after the interview with his *fiancée*, Kenneth walked into his father's club, attired for motoring. It was just after lunch, and he banked on finding his father in a mellow mood. There was a purposeful gleam in his eye as he went into the smoking room, but when he bent over his father, who was enjoying a siesta, his voice was as gentle as cooing doves.

"Pater, I want you."

The general opened his eyes. He grunted. "Hallo! What do you want?"

"You," said Kenneth firmly. "Come on, sir."

The general was drawn protesting from his chair.

"What is it?" he demanded. "What's the matter? What do you mean by coming and disturbing me like this?"

Kenneth led him out of the room, rather like a nurse with a refractory child.

"I'll explain as we go," he said. "Where's your coat?"

"I don't want my coat! If the house is on fire tell me so at once and have done with it!"

"No, no," said Kenneth soothingly. "Nothing like that. Ah, here it is! Come along now."

The general was put into his coat. Kenneth buttoned it up and handed him his hat.

"That's right. Now we're ready."

"B-but—where are we going?" stuttered his father.

Kenneth conducted him to the door.

"Oh, just for a short run in the car! I want you to come out with me. Glorious day, you know."

The general showed a marked tendency to hang back.

"I don't want to go for a run! It's too cold! Damn it, what's the matter with you?"

"Do come sir!" begged Kenneth winningly. "It's ages since you and I went out together."

The general hesitated. But the engaging tone was too much for him. It *was* a long while since he had been anywhere with his son.

"Very well," he grumbled. "But I don't like motoring in the winter."

Kenneth paid no heed to this last feeble protest. He put his father into the car and tucked him up in a large rug. Then he got in himself and started the car.

For some time they went in silence, but when they drew out of London into the suburbs the general put a question.

"Where are we going?"

"Oh, just to a rather jolly little place I know of," answered Kenneth. "Very pretty run."

There was a pause.

"Didn't I see a suitcase on the back of the car?" asked the general.

"Some togs I wanted," explained Kenneth.

Then he launched forth into a flow of conversation which did not abate for quite an hour. By that time the general was becoming uneasy.

"Surely it's time we turned back," he said. "Where are we?"

"Hampshire," said Kenneth. "It's not much further."

"I should hope not! We shall be disgracefully late as it is. What's the point of coming so far?"

Kenneth laughed.

"It's all right, sir. Just wait a bit, and you'll see."

The general became suspicious.

"Look here, Kenneth, if you're doing something mad, understand me, I will not have it! Turn round and go back! I order it!"

Kenneth shook his head.

"Sorry, sir. Can't be done."

He turned a deaf ear to all his father's commands and imprecations until at last the general relapsed into sulky silence. Presently Kenneth switched on his lights, for it was growing dark. The general shivered and drew the rug closer about him.

"Nearly there," said Kenneth cheerfully.

The general's reply was unfit for publication.

Half-an-hour later Kenneth pulled up outside what looked like a high fence. He jumped out and fumbled with a key.

"Where the devil are we?" shouted his father.

He saw that the fence had a large gate adorned with barbed wire and broken glass. Kenneth opened it and got back into the car. In silence he drove through the gateway and again got out. The stupefied general saw him relock the gate and pocket the key.

"And now we are in," said Kenneth triumphantly.

"What the hell are you about?" barked his father. "Have you taken leave of your senses?"

"No. When we get into the house I'll explain. Sit tight, it's a bit bumpy." Kenneth drove slowly over a surface that resembled a ploughed field. Through the gathering darkness they could see a cottage, some yards distant. Before it Kenneth stopped again. "Jump out, sir. You'll find the door on the latch. I'm just going to shove the car into the shed. You'll find matches and candles inside. I won't be a minute!"

The general seized him by the coat collar and tried to shake him. As he was a small man, and Peter stood six foot two in his stockinged feet, this attempt failed.

"Explain yourself this instant!" raved the general.

Kenneth disengaged himself.

"Now look here, pater, keep cool! I'm not going to explain out here. Go into the house and light a candle!"

"Where *are* we?" cried his father.

"In Hampshire—on the moor. Now do get out, sir!"

The general fought for words. Kenneth pushed him gently out of the car. Then he drove on and parked it in a ramshackle shed. When he came back to the cottage he found his father had lighted a candle and was engaged in ramping up and down the uneven floor of the kitchen like one possessed.

Kenneth shut the door and threw his gloves on to the table. He picked up the matches and knelt down before the fireplace. It was ready laid and the wood was dry. Kenneth tended it for some moments, and then stood up. Next he lighted an oil lamp and set it on the table.

"Now we're comfortable," he remarked.

"Comfortable?" roared the general. "*Comfortable?* You young scoundrel, what do you mean by it?"

"Well, I'm just going to tell you," said Kenneth. He coaxed his father into a chair. "I'm afraid you won't be awfully bucked at the scheme, but I can't help it. You see, you wouldn't listen to the idea of my marriage to Ursula, so I had to think of a way of *making* you see reason. I wanted to marry Ursula without your consent, but she wouldn't have it at any price. Said it wasn't fair, and so on and so forth. So I thought it all out carefully, and suddenly I had an absolute brain-wave. Sort of impulse, if you know what I mean. Woke up one morning and the thing came to me. I decided that the best thing I could do would be to kidnap you. Jolly sound scheme, don't you think? Anyway, I didn't waste any time, but jumped out of bed and set about it. I found this little shanty the very first day—saw it was empty, and bought it. Chap who owns it was glad to get rid of it as it's practically breaking down, 'sides being such miles from anywhere, and not water-tight. I didn't think that mattered much, so I closed the deal and set about making preparations. Got a fence shoved up and brought a few miles of barbed wire down from London. Jimmy Fairfax helped me to fix it up inside the fence, and I can tell you it's a pretty neat thing. Took the deuce of a time to do, though, but I don't grudge that. Well, then I imported a lot of food-stuff in tins, and some furniture and what not, and here we are. That suitcase you saw has got your clothes in it. Shaving tackle, and all the rest of it. I don't think I've forgotten anything."

The general had listened in silence, not because he did not wish to interrupt, but because he could find no words suitable to the occasion. Now he made a choking sound in his throat, and waved his hands.

"You—you" —again he choked— "impudent young scoundrel! Confound your abominable cheek. You—you think you can keep me here?" He sprang up and stalked to the door. "You'll drive me back to town at once. At once, I say!"

Kenneth sighed.

"Do come back, pater. It's no good going out into the cold. You'll only walk into the entanglements. Do be reasonable!"

"Reasonable! Reasonable! How—how *dare* you, sir? Is it reasonable to bring me down here? Is it?"

"Honestly, sir, I think it was an A 1 notion. But if you don't like it—"

"Like it! Damme, who would like it? You young devil. When I get back home I'll turn you out of the house. Impertinent puppy! I'll—"

Kenneth made him come back to the fire.

"No, pater, don't get annoyed. If you don't like it, all you've got to do is to give your consent to my marrying Ursula. Then I'll run you up to town at once."

The general glared up at him under his bushy brows. "Trying to force my hand, are you?" he snapped.

Kenneth smiled a little, a smile of pure mischief.

"Well, that *is* about the size of it," he admitted.

"Tricked me into coming with you! Said you wanted to take me out!"

Kenneth flushed slightly.

"It was absolutely true, sir. I did want you. I s'pose it was a trick; but, somehow, I didn't think you'd come if told you what I was going to do with you."

"And you think this is a proper way to treat me?"

"It's not a very usual way," Kenneth answered. "You must see that it's your own fault."

"My fault! How dare you! I suppose that bohemian put you up to it?"

"Which bohemian?" asked Kenneth sweetly.

"That damned girl! That Fenton girl!"

"Oh, Ursula! No, she doesn't know anything about it. I don't know that she'd altogether approve," he added reflectively.

The general took him by the arm.

"Listen! You can do what you damn well like, but I won't give my consent. Understand me?"

"I don't think *you* quite understand, sir," said Kenneth. "I shall have to keep you here till you do consent. I don't mind much myself, because I rather like this place, but I should think you'd find it a bit dull."

His father smiled grimly.

"My good youth, how long do you suppose it will be before Lorton discovers my absence?"

Lorton was his valet. Kenneth smiled, too.

"Well sir, I told Lorton that you and I were running down into the country for a few days. So I don't think he'll make any trouble."

"You told L——" Words failed the general. He grew purple in his rage, and he strutted round the room shaking his fists and spluttering. When his fury had spent itself, he turned to Kenneth. "You'll be sorry for this. I'd stay here for months rather than give in to you!"

"There—there isn't anything to drink, 'cept water," said Kenneth apologetically. "And there aren't any cigars."

The flood of invective with which the general greeted this piece of information left him weak and trembling. It had no visible effect on his son.

III.

THE general opened his eyes to a new day. He had not slept well. It seemed to him that the mattress on which he lay had been stuffed with potatoes. He gazed malevolently at the sun and thought over his unenviable plight. For some time his mind dwelt on a diet similar to last night's supper. He shuddered. There had been a packet of soup, diluted in water and boiled over a smoky fire. Kenneth had done the cooking, while he had sat apart in frozen silence. Following that unspeakable soup, had come tinned salmon and bully-beef, washed down by water. The general was not the man to deny that water had its uses; but he refused to countenance it as a drink. Kenneth had offered to brew some cocoa with the aid of tinned milk, but the general had refused the offer curtly. He had no opinion of his son's culinary skill. And he was a notorious *bon-vivant*, particular to the point of faddiness over his meals. To make matters worse, his cigar-case was empty. He had gone early to bed, ignoring all Kenneth's attempts at conversation.

Presently Kenneth tapped on the door.

"I say, sir, I've got your shaving water here, and I've got every kettle and saucepan on for your bath. 'Twon't be long. Can I come in?" He awaited no permission but entered, bearing a jug. This he set down on the rickety wash-stand. "Topping day, pater!" He dragged a tin bath from under the bed, and eyed it dubiously. "'Fraid it isn't frightfully large, sir. I'll bring the water up."

He disappeared, and the general crawled out of bed. He was in the middle of shaving when Kenneth came back, bearing a long-handled sauce-pan, which he emptied into the bath.

"Have to pump up every drop of water," he informed his father. "Awful fag!"

He went out again, returning almost at once with two large kettles. He then departed, leaving the general to his ablutions.

Breakfast consisted of porridge, slightly burnt, and bacon. The coffee was a little muddy; but, then, as Kenneth remarked, he wasn't used to cook-ing. Not until the meal was over did the general vouchsafe a word, then he frowned majestically at his son and growled:

"Well? Have you come to your senses?"

Kenneth took a large bite out of a slice of bread and marmalade. He said nothing.

"You will take me back to town today?"

"Yes, sir. On one condition."

The general's lips tightened.

"No!"

"Then I'm awfully sorry, sir, but—"

The general stumped out into the "garden". What he saw appalled him. A tall fence ran round the house, and inside it, some five feet wide, was a veritable maze of barbed-wire entanglement. The gate was stout and tall and on the top Kenneth had arranged more barbed wire and some broken glass.

During the day the general made two abortive attempts to escape. On both occasions he tore his trousers and became so hopelessly mixed up in wire which scratched him if he moved a finger that he had to roar for his son to come and rescue him. Kenneth came, begging his father not to do it again as he would certainly hurt himself badly. The general wasted half an hour in swearing at him, then he subsided and went to lie down. No word passed his lips during the rest of the day.

The next day found the general in a mood of black depression. As far as he could see, Kenneth was thoroughly enjoying the simple life. He showed no signs of boredom, he was unfailingly thoughtful and polite towards his father. He did all the work of the cottage, and sang as he worked. With a little encouragement he would have conversed cheerfully with the general, but he did not receive any encouragement. He drove out to buy milk and eggs in the morning, punctiliously locking the gate behind him. It was during his absence that the general tried to escape. After lunch the general descended to coaxing, and found it useless. He snarled at his son for twenty minutes, and then went to pace up and down the clay-field outside. He returned to the attack at dinner, and smashed two cups and a plate. As they had only two cups, they had to drink out of glasses at breakfast on the following day. Tea in a glass broke the general. He made one more attempt to reduce his son to a sense of law and order, and failing, gave in—blasphemously.

Kenneth was overjoyed. He tried to wring his father's hand and the general danced with rage. So Kenneth, realising that his father was hardly in the mood to forgive and forget, restrained himself.

"You'll come *at once* to Ursula's flat and tell her yourself?" he asked anxiously.

The general swallowed hard.

"Yes!" he swallowed again. "And I wish her joy of you!"

"We'll be off in half-a-shake!" cried Kenneth. "It's most awfully good of you, sir! But when you see her—"

The general made an indescribable noise, and Kenneth thought it wise to withdraw. He drove his car down to the village and sent an urgent telegram.

IV.

URSULA received the telegram just before one o'clock. She read it calmly, twice. She was a little surprised, but not much so. The telegram was evidently written in great excitement. It might even be termed puzzling.

"For the love of Mike get in whisky and Corona cigars for tea!—KENNETH."

Ursula wasted no time searching for a hidden meaning. She knew Kenneth. She put on her hat and coat and sallied forth in search of whisky. Luckily, it was opening hour, and she had no difficulty in buying it. She then bought the requested cigars, and went home. She supposed that Kenneth would explain when he arrived. Obviously he was coming to tea. So she changed her frock, made the studio look very cosy, and put another log of wood on the fire.

At four o'clock her front-door bell rang violently. She went to open the door.

"Hallo, Ken! Where've you been all—"

She broke off, staring at the general. "Who—who—?"

"My father, Miss Fenton," announced Kenneth proudly.

"W–won't you—come in?" asked the astonished Ursula.

Her eyes wandered to a jagged rent in the general's trousers, and widened.

Kenneth let his father into the studio. The general glared at Ursula.

"Are you Ursula Fenton?" he demanded.

Ursula nodded.

"Then you can marry my son!" snapped the general. "And I wish you joy of him!"

It seemed to Ursula that all was not as it should be between the general and his son. She looked from one to the other inquiringly.

"Bumptious puppy! Insufferable scoundrel!"

Ursula decided that she must take a hand. She pushed Kenneth before her into the kitchen.

"Wait there till I call you," she told him. "And keep quiet. What on earth have you been doing?"

"Kidnapped him," whispered Kenneth. "Got the cigars and the whisky?"

"Yes—no—go in!"

"I'm not going to leave you to tackle—"

"You'll do what you're told," said Ursula severely, and shut the door on him.

She went back to the general, who was fuming before the fire, and laid a gentle hand on his arm.

"I don't know what Kenneth's done," she said, "but I'm sure it's something abominable. Please take off your coat and sit down."

The general allowed her to extricate him from his overcoat. He sat down with a sigh of something approaching content.

"Abominable? I should say so! Scandalous! Iniquitous!"

"How dreadful!" Ursula was all sympathy. "Won't you smoke?"

The general bounced up, and saw the extended box of cigars. He snatched one unceremoniously, and inspected it. Some of the blackness went out of his look. Ursula went in search of a glass and some soda-water. When she returned, she found the general smoking blissfully. By the time she had supplied him with a whisky-and-soda he was able to tell her the whole story.

To her everlasting credit, Ursula did not laugh. She was properly shocked and indignant. And the more indignant she became, the more lenient became the general. The cigar was taking effect. When he had embarked on his second drink, he began to look on the humorous side of the affair.

"Young devil!" he said. "Carrying me off like that! Brazen impudence!" He chuckled a little.

"I think it was perfectly *disgraceful!*" said Ursula.

"So it was," he agreed. "But he's mad, you know. Barbed-wire entanglements—young Bolshevik!"

"Well, it's awfully decent of you to be so nice about it," said Ursula.

"Made me come here to tell you myself, damn him!"

"But I am so glad you did come," said Ursula. "I've so wanted to meet you."

"Where is he?" he growled presently.

"In the kitchen," answered Ursula. "I told him to stay there."

A gleam came into the general's eye.

"Told him, eh? And he obeyed you?"

"Of course," said Ursula. "He's nothing but a huge, mad baby!"

"Think you can manage him?"

Ursula dimpled.

"Yes, and you too, general."

"Minx!" But he looked at her with admiration. "Well, you can marry him, but I won't let you take him away. Understand that!"

Ursula patted his hand.

"I don't want to take him away. I want to come and take care of you as well. It seems to me that you both want a woman in charge of you. Of all the mad people—*well!*"

The general chuckled again. Ursula smiled at him.

"May he come in and apologise, general?"

The general shrugged his shoulders.

"If he wants to."

Ursula went to release her captive. When she got into the kitchen she was seized and hugged.

"You idiot!" she murmured, laughing. "Come along in and apologise."

The general accepted his son's apology in haughty silence, but over tea he unbent. But it was not until he finally took his leave that he showed Kenneth that he was forgiven. He kissed Ursula good-bye and turned to look at Kenneth.

"If you hadn't got your mother's eyes," he said, "I'd— Well, you have got 'em. Don't be late for dinner."

With that he stumped out, and Kenneth conducted him to the lift. When Kenneth came back, Ursula looked him over from head to foot. He stood meekly before her.

"Well?" said Ursula, with would-be sternness.

"It was just a sudden impulse," Kenneth excused himself. "And—and it *did* do the trick, darling, didn't it?"

"Do you always act on impulse?" inquired Ursula.

"N—yes. Usually."

"I *shall* have a busy time," she said. "Two mad, wild—"

"I say, Ursula, I want to kiss you!" he interrupted, and swept her into his arms.

"Is this a sudden impulse?" asked Ursula from his shoulder.

"No, by Jove!" cried Kenneth. "It's a never-ending impulse!"

THE END

READING "ACTING ON IMPULSE"

It never ceases to amaze me, the passivity of the Heyerian women in these contemporary tales of hers. Because, sure, our Ursula is presented to us here as an "independent" woman, who makes a living on her own and is account-able to no one, but ask her to marry an acquaintance of hers who will – apparently – take her away from all this artistic toil and make a lady who lunches of her, and she's apparently ready to agree almost immediately, with no intimation of any particular fondness for the gentleman on her part, before or since the proposal.

To me, that makes sense in the Georgians and the Regencies. But in the 1920s? Really? With all the flappers and the women wearing trousers and the suffragettes?

Really?

Now, don't get me wrong, I love this story. It is funny, it is charming, and both the competent Ursula and her impulsive fiancé, the dashing and charismatic Kenneth (oh, these names!), are likeable and attractive souls for whom shared happiness is all but certain. But for the two of them to go from "pals" to "let's get married!" in the space of a paragraph, without ever going on so much as a date or discussing things like whether they want kids, or where they're going to live, or even just making out, is wholly bizarre – even in the 1920s, surely. I mean, I've read Elinor Glyn; those people were totally doing it.

But not before marriage, in Heyer Land. As far as we're aware, Kenneth barely holds Ursula's hand before deciding she's the one for him… forever. What? No. That does not make sense.

It's adorable as hell, though.

And, oh, the poor pater. Obviously, his snobbishness regarding Ursula is not to be borne, but how dreadful, to find oneself shut up in a ramshackle house – purchased outright by Kenneth, if you please, just as a bolthole for a couple of days, because of course one could buy a house on a whim, once upon a time; galling, isn't it? – and deprived of the comforts of one's declining years, all so your son can get married to his chance-met acquaintance. It's disgraceful.

'Pater,' by the way, has to be one of the most time-specific endearments for a parent of all time. If you read a book in which the characters refer to anyone as "mater" and 'pater,' you are for sure reading a book that is set among the English upper echelons sometime around the World Wars. Giving the words an indefinite article – *the* mater and *the* pater – just solidifies the speaker's place in society, and also in time.

In the decades since, "mater" and "pater" have rightfully fallen by the wayside, and while I actively decry the loss of some words from our shared vocabulary – one day I *will* see "zounds!" brought back into vogue – those frightfully twee appellations can stay gone for good.

So, poor "pater" is starved into (whiskeyed and cigared into?) submission, and then Kenneth takes him to see Ursula to deliver the good news of the tortured man's forced approval of their ill-considered union, and then you really see the genius of Heyer at work—as well as the genius of Ursula. Earlier in the story, when Kenneth reports on his father's adamance against their marriage, she suggests she might go see the elder gentleman, and perhaps smooth the way. Kenneth advises against it, and Ursula accedes to his counsel, but it is evident that she is pretty sure she can turn the old boy around, if only she gets the chance to work her magic. Now, obviously the liberal doses of alcohol and tobacco help her cause, but one gets the impression that Ursula could have wrapped him around her little finger even without those inducements, because of course she can – she is pretty, she is smart, she is sympathetic and she knows how to manage him. General Mount is essentially Matthew Penicuik being turned up sweet by Miss Fishguard in *Cotillion*, or a dozen other cantankerous older gentleman who want nothing but an appearance of obedience and a kindly ear to make them believe they are in control. But Ursula emphatically has the upper hand over him, and Kenneth besides.

And we know all of this, from mere scraps of dialogue and inner-monologue.

Georgette Heyer really was astonishingly good at this.

And with "Acting on Impulse" she found her contemporary short story groove.

– *Rachel Hyland*

"WHOSE FAULT WAS IT?"

INTRODUCTION

Appearing in *The Happy Mag* in August 1923, Heyer's last for that publication, "Whose Fault Was It?" is Heyer's first domestic romance – a tale of conflict and love between a husband and wife. It is a sprightly story with some excellent and at times realistic dialogue, as George and Diana argue back and forth over the teacups. Heyer was still living at home in 1923, but since her own parents had been married for over twenty years, it seems likely that she would have witnessed or overheard marital disputes from time to time. While her father, George, was often described as charming and charismatic, her mother, Sylvia, was known to suffer from mood swings—and every marriage has its trials.

George and Diana, however, are only a year married, and though not long out of their honeymoon phase, are already becoming increasingly frustrated with each other. Heyer opens her story with a fiery interchange, in which Diana is surprisingly outspoken. There is no sign of the downtrodden wife or little woman here, even though her husband is self-absorbed and autocratic. Diana has been brought to live in "a beautiful Tudor house about twenty miles from London" where she has "her car and her horses and a large allowance." There seems little to complain of but Heyer understood relationships and she finds the weakness and uses it to powerful effect.

Although she had no direct experience of living in a grand house – Heyer had grown up in pleasant but mostly rented homes – at the time of this story's writing she was friends with Dorothea Arbuthnot. Dorothea was the great-niece of the Duchess of Atholl and had grown up in the Manor House in Hollingbourne with a retinue of servants; she was also the "Doreen" to whom Heyer would dedicate two of her novels. From girlhood, Heyer had enjoyed entrée to some of the "best" houses in Wimbledon where she had absorbed many details of how the wealthy and well-connected lived. Although the life she describes in "Whose Fault Was It?" had become less common after the Great War, it was still the dream of many. Having given her protagonists every reason to enjoy their marriage, Heyer teases out their one problem: Diana "had every intention of enjoying life. George, too, meant to enjoy life; unhappily their ideas of enjoyment did not blend." This is the crux of Heyer's story.

George is obsessed with Chinese porcelain and finds it "inconceivable that anyone could be bored when looking at a K'ang hi [sic] vase." He is outraged when Diana describes a recently-purchased vase as "ugly": "Ugly?

Ugly? My dear girl, this is a Ming vase!" (in fact, the Kangxi period belongs to the early part of the Qing dynasty). Heyer must have had a penchant for this sort of china, for years later she would write a superb scene in *A Civil Contract* (1961) in which the magnificent vulgarian Jonathan Chawleigh presents his aristocratic son-in-law with a Kangxi vase. Chinese porcelain forms a vital part of "Whose Fault Was It?" and Heyer uses it in several subtle ways to reveal character, to progress the plot and as a metaphor for how a broken marriage maybe mended.

The theme of compatibility in marriage was something she had been thinking about a lot, and she had recently completed a novel on the subject: *Instead of the Thorn*, which would be published just three months after "Whose Fault Was It?". Like the short, the book is about marriage and about the things that can go wrong between two people who don't really understand one another. Though the novel is far more serious in tone, both demonstrate the unmarried Heyer's interest and insight into marriage.

She had been observant from a young age and even her earliest writing shows how perceptive she could be about relationships and love. In this period Heyer was close to Joanna Cannan, who was married to Harold Pullein-Thompson. It was with Joanna that Heyer had often talked about the realities of wedded life and *Instead of the Thorn* is dedicated to her for having "discussed the fortunes of Elizabeth Arden not once but many times," and for "good counsel" and "sympathy in moments of depression." It is likely that the short story grew out of the novel, though it is considerably more humorous and much more lightly drawn than the longer work.

— Jennifer Kloester

WHOSE FAULT WAS IT?

THE eggs were hard-boiled, and there were no fewer than three printer's errors in George's article on Porcelain of the Yuan Dynasty. He looked up from the paper with a glowering brow and addressed his wife in a voice of icy politeness.

"I believe I asked you once before to speak to the cook about the boiling of eggs," he said.

Diana had slept badly and had awakened with a headache. She answered every mite as coolly, and without raising her eyes from her morning's correspondence.

"I daresay you did."

George's frown grew darker. One of the printer's errors destroyed the whole meaning of his paragraph.

"I should have thought that it was your business to keep an eye on the cook," he said with heavy sarcasm.

"I can't be forever nagging at her," Diana replied. "You complain about something or other every meal."

"That," said George, "is hardly my fault."

"It certainly isn't mine."

"Indeed! I suppose you'll say next that the management of the house is not your affair?"

"I'll say something more to the point," his wife answered, looking up at last. "I didn't marry you with the idea of being your housekeeper! I'm fed up with it!"

"I consider that a most unjust and uncalled-for speech!" said George sharply.

"Oh, do you? It's been perfectly evident to me ever since we came back from our honeymoon that you didn't want a wife at all, but a housekeeper. You don't care for anything except your beastly old china!"

"You're talking like a hysterical child. If you would take a little more interest in my china, and a little less in this everlasting dancing, and—"

"Thank you! I'm to sink my own tastes and inclinations, am I? It may interest you to know that if you were less absorbed in Chinese porcelain, or whatever it is, and thought more about what I like to do—"

"To hear you anyone would think that I neglect you!"

"So you do!"

"You know that's a lie."

"Oh, do I? You think of nothing but china from the moment you get up to the moment you go to bed. I believe you dream about it. I'm beginning to wish you had to work for your living. Then you wouldn't be able to gloat over your treasures all day long."

George rose with extreme deliberation, and picked up his coffee cup.
"I think it is a little too much if I'm to be subjected to senseless tirades at breakfast!" he said. "I shall finish my coffee in the library."

No sooner had the door closed with exaggerated softness behind him, than Diana began to cry into her half-eaten egg.

She had been married to George Doone for just a year, and this was by no means the first quarrel they had had. Diana had only been nineteen when she had married George, and she had sallied gaily forth into her new life with no idea of the pitfalls ahead. During her six months' engagement she had admired George's collection of china, and had tried her best to make intelligent remarks on it. George had been so attentive that she had not realised how big a place in his heart china occupied. Her mother had warned her, and had even suggested that Diana should study the subject, but she had only laughed, and shaken her pretty head.

The first months of marriage were months of bliss. Then they came home from their long honeymoon abroad, and settled down in a beautiful Tudor house about twenty miles from London. Diana had her car and her horses, and a large allowance. She had every intention of enjoying life. George, too, meant to enjoy life; unhappily their ideas of enjoyment did not blend. George was not a dancing-man, and he was not fond of theatre-going. Diana had known this, but she had not anticipated a stubborn refusal to learn to dance, or that George would grumble when she suggested a theatre-party.

George had known that Diana was ignorant on the subject of china, but he had never imagined that her interest in his collection during their engagement was mere politeness. To him it was inconceivable that anyone could be bored when looking at a K'ang Hi Vase.

He very soon discovered that Diana thought his hobby wearisome and dull. Even then they might have learned to adapt themselves to each other's tastes, if both had not been endowed with quick tempers. Neither had cultivated patience; any argument usually ended in a short but violent quarrel. It was not surprising that the quarrels grew more frequent. Diana began to think herself a neglected wife because George was often abstracted; George told himself that Diana was unreasonable and unjust.

HAVING rendered her egg wholly uneatable by her tears, Diana began to nibble at some toast, punctuating each bite with a watery sniff. To fortify herself for her coming interview with the cook-housekeeper she drank another cup of coffee. Then, being very young and inexperienced, she went in fear and trembling to the kitchen.

The interview with the cook made her headache worse, and she began to feel ill-used and worse-tempered than before. She went with lagging steps to the library, secretly hoping that George would not only make it up, but would comfort her and kiss away her unhappiness.

George was ripping open a small packing case. He had taken his coat off, and the frown had gone from his face. He was all excitement, and he hardly noticed his wife's entrance. Diana went to the window, trying to swallow her pride enough to make the first advances. Over her shoulder she saw George pull away the straw from the box, and insinuate reverent hands into it. Very carefully he drew forth what was to her only a dingy-looking vase. Over George's face had stolen an expression of worship. He set the vase on a table, and stroked it lovingly. Diana realised that he had not been aware of her entrance. She was conscious of a rising rage, but she managed to choke it down."

"George!"

"You—beautiful thing," said George softly.

She turned to run straight into his arms, but stopped short when she saw that he had not spoken to her, but to the vase.

"Put that piece of ugly china down!" she cried

He looked at her in amazement.

"Ugly? *Ugly!* My dear girl, this is a Ming vase!"

"I don't care if it is! It's ugly and dingy and *dead!* I'd like to smash all your horrible china! 1 would, I would!"

His face grew stern.

"I don't advise you to try," he said. "What you are pleased to call 'dingy' is a Ming vase with the aubergine glaze. What is it you want?" He spoke as to a refractory child, and Diana's passion got the better of her. She sprang forward, and in a flash had knocked the vase out of his caressing hands. It fell on to the parquet floor and was shivered into atoms.

Diana was pulled up short by her impetuous action. A wave of ashamed repentance swept over her; she put a trembling hand on George's arm.

"Oh, I'm sorry! I didn't—mean to! I'm very, very sorry!"

George shook her hand away. He was white with anger, but he spoke quietly.

"It's easy enough to say you're sorry, when you've broken the most precious thing I possess."

Diana quivered, and flung up her head. Through the tears her eyes flamed into his.

"Oh, indeed! *indeed!* The most precious thing you possess! Do you mean that?"

"Yes, I do!" said George angrily.

"Very well! If that's so you won't mind when I tell you that I'm going home to Mother! *She* doesn't rank a loathsome vase higher than me! *She* loves me! As for you—I wish I'd never set eyes on you!"

"It's come to that, has it?" he snapped back at her. "You break my vase out of wanton mischief and temper, and rail at me because I'm angry! Let me tell you that I've a good deal more cause for complaint than you have." With that, and forgetting the fragments of china on the floor, he turned on his heel and slammed out of the room.

Diana was left looking down at her handiwork.

Horrid, horrid vase!" she whispered, and bent to pick up one of the pieces. "Beastly, spiteful thing! I'm glad I broke you!"

MRS. GRAFTON exhibited no surprise when her daughter walked into the drawing room of her flat in Brook Street. She merely raised her eyebrows slightly, and even went on with her knitting.

"Hullo, Diana!" she said.

Diana pulled her hat off and threw it on to a chair.

"I've left George!" she said jerkily.

"Dear me," said Mrs. Grafton placidly.

"What's more, I won't ever go back to him!"

"What a brute!" remarked her mother, unrolling some more silk.

"He is! He's—" She broke off and looked suspiciously at her mother. "What do you mean? How do you know?"

"They always are," said Mrs. Grafton. "Do you propose to stay here?"

"Of course if y—you don't w-want me either—"

"Oh, I don't mind at all, my dear. Only I must have your bed aired. By the way, why have you left George, apart from his being a brute?"

Her daughter collapsed on to the sofa and began to hunt for her handkerchief. The day's calamities passed before her eyes.

"I slept badly and woke with a headache, Mumsy," she began.

Mrs. Grafton looked up, once more with raised brows.

"No doubt it's a sufficient reason," she remarked calmly.

"That's not all! The eggs were hard-boiled for breakfast, and George was hateful about it."

"So you left him? I see."

"N-no, that wasn't the reason," said Diana, doubtfully. "The—the eggs began it, but I've left him because he doesn't care for me."

"Doesn't he, really?" Mrs. Grafton was politely interested. "I wonder why he married you?"

"I'm sure I don't know! He only cares for his china. I—I smashed a Ming vase this morning—on purpose!"

"I hope he shook you!"

"You—Mother, don't you realise—"

"What?"

"I—I think you might be a little more sympathetic!"

"Oh, are you looking for sympathy?"

"No, I'm not!" said her daughter, rising. "I think I'll go and unpack my things."

"I should," said Mrs. Grafton.

Mr. Grafton was inclined to be worried over his daughter's return, but his wife assured him that there was no need for him either to "speak seriously to Diana," or to sally forth in search of George's blood.

"Well, but dear, hadn't I better go and see George?"

"Certainly not," said his wife. "George will come here when he has recovered. In the meantime a little uncertainty won't do either of them any harm. You leave it to me."

Mr. Grafton had never dreamed of disputing his wife's decisions; he was quite content to leave Diana's future in her hands. Mrs. Grafton started to devise a plan.

Secretly Diana was rather ashamed of having deserted her husband, and she would have been overjoyed had he appeared that evening to take her home. But he did not appear. Instead he sat humped over the library fire with his head in his hands and a pipe between his teeth.

As soon as his first anger had abated, he had gone up to Diana's bedroom, only to find that she had flown. Never for one instant had he imagined that she meant what she had said. The sight of her dismantled dressing-table was a shock to him. He sat limply down upon the bed, trying to realise that she had really gone.

At first he was indignant and thought himself badly used. This mood lasted until after lunch, when he was forced to excuse Diana's sudden departure to the maids. He went for a long walk that afternoon, fighting out the problem with himself. He came home to tea, tired and dispirited, and was conscious of a sickening gap in his life when he saw Diana's empty chair behind the tea-table. Except on rare occasions, the maids were not allowed to touch anything in the library, so that now the shattered Ming vase still lay upon the floor.

Gloomily George regarded it, reflecting on the loss of so wonderful a treasure. Then he thought of the greater loss of his wife and grew gloomier still. The sight of the smashed vase, lying lonely on the floor, induced a sentimental frame of mind. He reviewed the events of the day, and thought that, perhaps, Diana had not been altogether to blame.

As far as he remembered, he had been unusually irritable. He ought not to have snapped at her about the eggs. But that did not excuse her offence in breaking the Ming vase. Still, he should not have refused to accept her apology. It must have cost her something to beg his pardon so sweetly. He remembered her little clinging hand, and the repentant catch in her voice. Hang it all, he had been a bit of a brute!

Yet she had no right to say that he cared more for his china than for her.

She must have known that it was untrue. Even if he had been rather absorbed occasionally, she ought to have known that it did not mean that he loved his china best. Of course, she was very young. He had no right to make her feel herself neglected. Something would have to be done about that.

Gradually he came to a great resolution. He would try to be interested in the things that Diana liked. It was no good expecting her to feel as he did about china. He must try not to be so absorbed in it. In fact—he drew a deep, self-pitying sigh—he had better learn to dance.

GEORGE was summoned to lunch at Mrs. Grafton's club next morning. When that lady heard the worried note in his voice she chuckled, well pleased.

Over lunch she lectured him severely. He tried at first to justify himself, but collapsed at last. Mrs. Grafton told him that he would have to learn to adapt himself to Diana before she would return to him.

"But—won't she come back now?" he asked, miserably. "I thought if I told her I was sorry—"

"Don't dare to do any such thing!" said Mrs. Grafton. "You'll only have the same fuss all over again. You wait till Diana comes round."

"But will she? I mean—"

"I know quite well what you mean, George. You're wrong. Diana's a naughty child; she always was. It would be very bad for her if you started to eat humble pie. She'll come to her senses fast enough if you leave her alone."

"I can't leave her alone! I can't do without her!"

"George," said Mrs. Grafton, impressively, "am I or am I not a fool?"

"Of course not. But—"

"I've known Diana twenty years. You'll never understand her as I do. You're only her husband. Leave her to me. I don't want you both to run on to the rocks, which is what you would do if you made it up again in the same old way. You've got to learn to adapt yourselves; and because you're both peppery and impatient you'd better do the first part of the adapting apart. Now, are you going to take my advice?

George struggled with himself for a moment.

"All—right. I was thinking of learning to dance," he said.

"Excellent! " nodded Mrs. Grafton.

That evening she took her husband and daughter to dine with an old friend. Diana was unconvincingly gay, but she couldn't help liking Mr. Haskin.

He was a man of about fifty-five with a fascinating smile, and a collection of prints and china. Diana stiffened slightly when he mentioned his hobby, but she could not refuse to look at his collection. She listened carefully to all that he said, for she, too, had made a resolution, only half acknowledged.

"There's rather a curious history attached to this piece," said Haskin, picking up an old and rivetted plate. He told Diana the history, and as he was a good talker, she was interested. She became rather more enthusiastic, and ventured a guess that a certain vase on the shelf was very rare. Mr. Haskin showed her how to distinguish it from one of a later period, then proceeded to follow out Mrs. Grafton's commands. He would have done a great deal for Mrs. Grafton.

"You take an interest in china?"

She hesitated.

"N—yes," she acknowledged.

"I wonder if you're interested enough to help me with a catalogue I'm making? Or would it bore you?"

Diana thought that it was highly probable that it would, but she realised that this was a wonderful opportunity for acquiring knowledge on the subject of china.

"I'd love to," she said mendaciously. "But I know nothing about china. Should I be any use?"

Mr. Haskin thought privately that so far from being useful she would be a hindrance, but he did not say this. Mrs. Grafton was smiling at him.

"Mother," said Diana, when they were alone. "I'm going to help Mr. Haskin to catalogue his collection."

"Oh, are you?" said Mrs. Grafton ingenuously. "Won't it bore you?"

"Yes, I think it will, but I've made up my mind that I haven't been altogether fair to George. In fact, the row was a good deal my fault. And I'm not going back to him until I know something about his beastly—his china."

Mrs. Grafton put an arm about her waist and gave her a little squeeze.

"I PICKED up a genuine piece of old Sèvres yesterday," said Diana. "In a funny little shop in Soho. The man obviously didn't know its worth. His shop was full of the most awful oddments."

"Was it the same man who palmed off that faked—"

"No, it wasn't," said Diana haughtily. "And I wish you wouldn't keep ramming that down my throat. I know I was taken in, but it was over a month ago, when I didn't know anything about china."

"You don't know much now," said Haskin, twinkling.

"Anyway, I pointed the flaw out to you in that jug you wanted to buy."

"I should have discovered it—"

"The point *is*," said Diana triumphantly, "that I saw it first. By the way, I'm coming with you to Christie's this afternoon. My husband's very keen on Chinese stuff, and I'm hoping to find something really good."

"If it's really good, you'll have to pay a big price for it, young lady."

"What I'm looking for is—is a Ming vase," said Diana, bending studiously over her catalogue, and fingering the jagged piece of china that hung on gold chain about her neck.

"Lots of us are doing that," said Haskin pessimistically. "I suppose you're dancing, tonight, as usual?"

"I haven't danced more than twice since I came to town!" flamed Diana.

"Nor you have. Gone off it?"

"N—I'm not in the mood for it. As a matter of fact, I *am* going out tonight, with an old friend. To the Empress Rooms."

The old friend, one Stephen Markham, found Diana changed for the worse. He thought she seemed sad, and her newly-acquired habit of talking wisely, but not very learnedly, of Chinese porcelain, palled on him.

"Look here, Di, what's the matter with you?" he demanded at last. "I don't know anything about the what-you-may-call-it Ming stuff, and I don't want to. So chuck it!"

"Ah!" said Diana. "I used to think as you do. But I assure you, Stephen, it's a most *fascinating* subject. I don't know an awful lot about it, of course—"

"Quite enough," said Stephen, who had known her from her babyhood, and therefore never erred on the side of politeness.

"But my husband is a great authority on it."

"Oh, good lord!" groaned Stephen. He found that Diana had stiffened in every line of her body, and was staring fixedly across the hall. "What's up?"

"No—nothing," said Diana relapsing.

"Then shall we dance?"

"No—I mean—Stephen, can we sit in the outside room? It's so hot here."

"Certainly," he answered, rather mystified. "Do you feel ill?"

"No—thank you. Just too hot."

At the far end of the hall she had just seen George. George was fox-trotting with a girl she didn't know. Diana was quivering with indignation. That George—her husband—should dare to take a bare-backed *creature* out to dance! And what was George doing, circling round a dancing hall? He, who when she had asked him, had refused to learn to dance at all?"

"I want to go home!" said Diana suddenly. "This sort of thing has got to be stopped!"

"Look here. Di, what are you driving at?" demanded her aggrieved partner. "What sort of thing—and why?"

"Nothing. I spoke without thinking. I'm awfully sorry, Stephen, but I don't think I feel like dancing tonight. Anyway, not here."

"Why ever didn't you say so before?" said Stephen, relieved. "Of course, we'll go somewhere else."

Out of the corner of her eye she saw George laugh at something his partner had said. She rose quickly.

"I've changed my mind. We'll stay here. Come on, let's dance!"

"You're mad," Stephen told her, but he led her out on to the floor.

Then Diana began to flirt with him, much to his surprise. Her eyes and her cheeks were bright; to all outward appearances she was enjoying herself to the top of her bent.

George saw her, and observed her gaiety. He tried to catch her eye—and failed. He didn't know who her partner was, but he thought him an objectionable-looking fellow. He further thought that it would improve his appearance if someone were to hit him exceedingly hard between the eyes.

"I'm going to put a stop to this!" he said savagely.

The dancing instructress was bewildered. "Whatever do you mean?"

"Sorry. I wasn't speaking to you. Would you say that I could dance yet?"

"Oh, you're greatly improved!" she said. "Of course, you still want polish. Another six lessons ought to—"

"I'll let you know about it," he promised. "Er—I've just seen someone I know. Do you mind if I—?"

"Oh, not at all!" she shrugged. "As it happens, I'm engaged for the next dance."

But when George, having deposited her outside, returned to the hall, Di and her partner were nowhere to be seen. She had fled, dragging Stephen with her.

"This," said George, "is the limit."

HE was staying at his club, so it did not take him long next morning to reach Mrs. Grafton's flat. Mrs. Grafton received him with customary placidity.

"Ah, good morning, George! Dear me, how cross you look!"

"I want to see my wife," said George.

"You're just too late," answered Mrs. Grafton. "She's gone."

"Gone!" he almost shouted. "Where?"

"Don't roar, George!" she reproved him. "She has gone to Mr. Haskin's. She—er—does some work for him."

"Oh, does she?" said George. "Is he a loutish-looking ass with horrible black hair, and a nose that—"

"Good gracious me, no! He's as old as I am. Older."

"Oh!" said George, rather appeased. "Where does he live? I insist on seeing my wife at once!"

"My dear boy, you needn't keep on saying 'my wife' like that. I'm perfectly aware of your relationship. Mr. Haskin lives in Bolton Gardens. No. 6."

"Thanks," said George, and walked to the door.

Mrs. Grafton went back to her household accounts with a wise smile on her lips.

Haskin had left the library to fetch a magnifying glass when George entered the house.

"I want to see Mrs. Doone, please," said George of the man-servant.

"Yes, sir." James was accustomed to a constant stream of curio hunters. "She's in the library, sir."

"Thanks," said George.

Diana, in a large blue overall, was standing with her back to the door, carefully wiping the dust from a gracefully-shaped vase. She heard George's footstep, and spoke without turning her head.

"I don't care what you say about the ridiculous cheapness," she declared. "It is *not* a fake. Come here and look at these marks! If that isn't genuine Ming—! Besides, look at the colouring! It's the green, yellow, and aubergine of the Ming pottery. And you can just see here, on the bottom, a faint—"

"Diana!" gasped her husband. "Diana!"

Diana nearly dropped the vase. It almost slipped from her hands, but she managed to rescue it. For a moment, she forgot all else in her annoyance at nearly letting fall her treasure.

"Really, George, don't you know better than to startle anyone who's holding a priceless Ming vase? A nice thing it would have been if I'd dropped it. These pieces are unbelievably brittle!" She remembered the happenings of last night, and set the vase down. "George, who was that creature?" she demanded, paying no heed to his dazed expression.

George as suddenly remembered the reason of his visit.

"Who was that poisonous man?" he retorted, bringing his fist down on the table so that the china on it jumped.

"George!" shrieked his wife. "*Mind!* There's a *priceless* bowl on that table!"

"I don't care a curse for the beastly bowl!" he barked, forgetting his collector's instincts in husbandly indignation. "Who was that man?"

"Who was that girl?"

"Which girl? Don't evade the point."

"I'm not! The—the female you were dancing with! Look out, you'll knock that pedestal over if you're not careful!"

"Damn the pedestal! Are you taking about my dancing instructress?"

"Your—what?" cried Diana, stepping back a pace. "That fair, blue-eyed minx?"

"I don't know whether she's got blue eyes, but if you mean the girl I was dancing with last night, she's the girl who's teaching me to dance.

'*Who was your partner?*'

"Why, only old Stephen!"

"Only Stephen—!" George had often heard of him. "As far as I could see you were flirting with him."

"Well, that was only because—never mind. You needn't get excited, because Stephen didn't like it a bit. George, take *care!* That bowl will be—"

George had skirted the table, and taken her into his arms.

"What's a porcelain bowl to you, you darling?" he asked, hugging her.

"Why, George, don't you see? It's a M—"

"Yes, I do see. Oh, Diana, you adorable little witch, have you been studying china all this while?

Diana snuggled closer.

"Well, you learned to dance," she explained. "And, oh, George, it was all my fault, but I'm *awfully* sorry, and I've found another Ming vase—not *quite* as good as the other, I'm afraid—in the most unlikely spot! And, oh, George, were you at the sale where they had those beautiful—"

"Kiss me," he ordered.

"Diana, do you know that tricky new step where you take two chassée steps forward, then cross over, and chassée three steps sideways, and—"

"No, teach it me!" begged Diana, slipping out of his arms. "Two forward—I suppose it's backwards for me? Oh, bother! There's no room! George, do look at my vase! It's for you, but Uncle John's suspicious about it. But comparing it with this little piece—" She lifted the piece of china that hung on her long gold chain.

George took it in his hand.

"Diana, this isn't—?"

"Yes, it is. To—to remind me of what temper can do."

"Feel in my breast pocket," he said. She thrust her hand in. Her fingers encountered a broken piece of china.

"George! You didn't—?"

"Yes, I did. Same idea. A reminder. All that remains of the Ming Vase."

Diana flung her arms about his neck.

"Ahem!" coughed Haskin, from the doorway.

THE END

READING "WHOSE FAULT WAS IT?"

Am I the only one weirded out that the hero's name in this story is "George"? I'm not, right?

Because, as mentioned elsewhere, Georgette Heyer's father, too, was called George – she was named for him, of course – and if there is anything ickier than making your father the romantic hero of your narrative, I do not know what it is.

Unless, of course, your story is not so much a romance as it is an observation on the manifold unexpected trials of married life, and you have taken your parents as your subject. In which case, you'd think she might have tried to disguise it better. Sylvia and Diana are pretty obvious analogues, too: Sylvia's etymology leading directly from Silvanus, the Roman god of the forest, and Diana, of course, being the Roman goddess of the moon and, tellingly, the hunt. Coincidence? I doubt it.

It's interesting that for someone so notoriously private in her later life, Georgette Heyer was quite indiscreet as a young writer.

Her four contemporary novels – the much-aforementioned *Instead of the Thorn* (1923), *Helen* (1928), *Pastel* (1929) and *Barren Corn* (1930) – were vehemently withdrawn from publication by Heyer in the 1930s (alongside *The Great Roxhythe* and, oh the injustice! *Simon the Coldheart*), and while their relative quality has often been cited as the reason for this decision, it has been more convincingly speculated that it is those novels' revealingly autobiographical natures that may have given Heyer cause.

In *Instead of the Thorn*, heroine Elizabeth is a pretty conclusive case-study in asexuality (which it is indelicate to guess about, but is certainly not inconsistent with what we know about Heyer); in *Helen*, a would-be author of Great Novels deals with the sudden death of her beloved father and resulting writer's block (Heyer's own, very beloved, father died in 1926, which led to a two-years-long lull in her until-then prodigious output); in *Pastel*, heroine Frances loses the handsome love of her life to a fascinating rival and settles for the stolid Norman (again, not inconsistent with what we know about Heyer's early romantic life, and her husband Ronald); and in *Barren Corn* we see a husband emotionally abuse and gaslight his wife over her perceived imperfections, until eventually she becomes suicidal—along with a very real hatred of Communism. (However drawn-from-life the former might be, the latter unquestionably reflects Heyer's own political opinion.)

So what does "Whose Fault Was It?" say about Heyer, at age twenty-one, still living at home with dear old Mummy and Daddy? (She did not, surprisingly, go in for "mater" and "pater," no matter what her fiction might have suggested.) It could very well just be a fond dream, that her parents might have entered into each others' interests, and would thence have been content in their home life. It could be that Heyer had heard from young married friends – the like of Joanna Cannan – about the harsh realities of being treated like a "housekeeper" by one's husband, after the honeymoon was over. It could even be showcasing her deepest fears about marital compatibility, especially when either party is ruled by a particular passion. Like, for example, writing.

Or, it could just be that a cigar is a cigar, that the Chinese porcelain collecting household tyrant who learns to woo his wife through ballroom dance (consider that a lifehack, fellas!) was named George because it was a super-popular name, or as a tribute to Heyer's eldest brother, just four years her junior, whose name was also George – there were two Georges *and* a Georgette in that house; happily, the younger George was always known as "Boris," his middle name, thus rendering the dinner table much less confusing – or simply because she had by then befriended one George Ronald Rougier, who would become her husband only a few years later.

We'll probably never know, but it is fun to guess about it, isn't it? Especially since Georgette Heyer herself left us so comparatively little to go on.

One thing that is very obvious about her: she certainly understood the soul of a collector. Those of us who are captivated by anything esoteric or artistic or absurd, who search diligently for those objects of our devotion far and wide, and who proudly display our treasures while longing to share the experience, the enthusiasm, with others (especially those we love most), can only identify most strongly with George, grieve with him for his destroyed Ming – though *not* Ming, as it turns out – vase, and rejoice at the convert that Diana becomes when she begins to learn more about his special subject. The thrill of the chase, the joy of a bargain, it all sings in Diana's search for a replacement vase, and as the story comes to a close we can easily see ahead to their future Saturdays, haunting estate sales and flea markets and arguing agreeably over the provenance of assorted porcelain, before heading out to a dance hall to trip the light fantastic, united at last.

Is this what Heyer wished had happened between the real-life George and Diana (née Sylvia)? Is this story, entertaining and hysterical and ultimately charming as it is, her idealised vision of life at home?

I like to think so. And the knowing, wise woman of the world mother archetype she gives us here – who shows shades of Lady Malmerstoke in *Powder and Patch*, among many others – might likewise be her idealised vision of what her "difficult" mother (which *Pastel* also dwells upon) might have been.

– *Rachel Hyland*

"THE CHINESE SHAWL"

INTRODUCTION

Somewhat surprisingly, Heyer's seventh short story, "The Chinese Shawl" was first published in *The Quiver,* in October 1923. Founded in 1861 as a religious magazine, for its first forty years *The Quiver* originally concentrated on articles of "a highly moral and improving nature" and was "overwhelmingly pious." In 1909, however, a new editor was appointed. Herbert Dakin Williams reinvigorated the magazine, eschewing "goody-goodism" and "mere sentimentalism" while remaining committed to retaining the high moral ground. Through the War years, *The Quiver* published E.F. Benson's novel, *Michael* (1915-16) and H. Rider Haggard's *When the World Shook* (1918-19). In the post-War period it published Jerome K. Jerome's *Anthony Strong'nth'arm* (1922-23) and Warwick Deeping's series *The Green Caravan* (1926). By this time the magazine had "shifted its base from a religious to a woman's magazine, albeit with strong moral overtones." It was a crusading magazine, with an "Army of Helpers" who diligently raised funds for good works.

"The Chinese Shawl" was neither improving nor overtly moral, but rather a quiet story of struggle and luck with a little romance thrown in for good measure. It was Heyer's only short published in *The Quiver* and it is surprising that her agent, L.P. Moore, should have chosen to submit the story to such a "moral" magazine. In 1923, suicide was still illegal in England, yet in "The Chinese Shawl" the heroine's father has killed himself after losing all his money in the "smash." This was the same financial "smash" which had so adversely affected Bride's father in "The Little Lady" and Katharine Testram in "The Bulldog and the Beast."

The economic downturn of the early 1920s in Britain also affected Heyer's father. The year after his return from France where he had served as an over-age officer, George Heyer wrote a gently humorous but illuminating short story for *Punch.* It was entitled "Getting Fixed" and was about a man looking unsuccessfully for work after his war service. It was not until 1923 that George Heyer returned to his job as Appeals officer at the King's College Hospital and the financial strain on the family eased.

In "The Chinese Shawl" the heroine, Mary, has been left alone and penniless, and must work as a typist in a steel manufactory. Before her father's death she has enjoyed a life of wealth and ease: "a frivolous, expensive career" with "many friends, many love-stricken young men, delightful days at Lord's, or Hurlingham, or Henley; enchanted evenings in the murky vastness of Covent Garden; bright nights spent in dancing, with haunting music in the air, the buzz of laughing voices, and the scent of hot-house flowers."

How much of this was also Georgette Heyer's own experience is unknown, though she certainly attended dances and was a lifelong cricket fan who in later years attended matches at Lord's. When the story opens, most of Mary's friends have deserted her after the scandal of her father's death and she has cut herself off from them and from the life she knew before. She feels great bitterness and when a great-aunt sends her an exquisite shawl Mary is cynical enough to believe that "it was rather catty and patronizing of her to send it to me when she knows I'm no longer in a position to wear such things."

As always in Heyer, class beliefs are inherent. Her only friend at work is Malcolm, "who was of her class and wanted to be an artist." Her other friend is Janet, who is never fully explained but who appears to be Mary's flatmate, speaks the same well-bred language and is sufficiently attractive to become engaged to "an adoring, many-times-repulsed young man." It is Janet who shows Mary how to make the most of the Chinese shawl and it is this which pushes the story forward to its inevitable happy ending.

In the Heyer family albums, there is a striking black-and-white photograph of Georgette Heyer wearing an elegant embroidered Chinese shawl. The photo was taken sometime in 1923 – possibly to mark Heyer's twenty-first birthday – and it is likely that the shawl inspired the story. Certainly there are elements of "The Chinese Shawl" that would later appear in Heyer's final contemporary novel, *Barren Corn*.

"The Chinese Shawl" is rare, or even unique, among Heyer short stories in that it was translated into Danish. On 13 March 1924 it appeared in translation in the Danish (now defunct) magazine *Tidens Kvinder* under the title, "Det kinesiske Sjal." There is some suggestion that the story may have been published in Swedish prior to its Danish translation, but to date no such translation has been found. This would be the last Heyer contemporary short story of this kind, for her final short in the genre would feature a much older, quite independent, heroine.

– *Jennifer Kloester*

THE CHINESE SHAWL

I.

MARY drew it out of its tissue-paper wrappings and allowed the heavy silken masses to unfold themselves, hanging from her fingers in soft-hued radiance.

"How lovely!" Janet gasped. "How wonderful!"

Mary shook it out so that it trailed upon the floor.

"Lovely? Oh, yes, and useless! If my aunt wanted to make me a present—heaven knows why she has elected to do so; it's an unexpected event—she might have sent me something that I could use. What on earth's the good of this?"

"But, Mary, it's so beautiful! It must have cost pounds and pounds."

"I'd rather have the money, then. This reminds me of a cartoon I once saw. The presents rich people send to their penniless relatives."

"I don't know how you can talk like that! It's so perfectly lovely!"

Mary laid it over the back of a chair.

"I wish you wouldn't harp on its loveliness. It's beautiful, I know. If I were in the habit of going to the opera, and if I had the sort of frock that would suit it, I should think it a topping present. As I'm a miserable little shorthand-typist living in rooms and possessing one ancient evening dress, I don't quite see the point of it. No doubt I'm ungrateful."

Janet picked up the shawl and examined the sprawling pattern with admiring eyes and caressing fingers.

"I suppose it is rather a silly present," she sighed. "Still—can't you do anything with it?"

"We might use it as a bedspread or a tablecloth," shrugged Mary. Janet shrieked at this suggestion.

"Mary, you Goth!"

"Or I might sell it."

"You wouldn't!"

Mary looked at the shawl. It gave a bizarre air of affluence to the shabby room. It was indeed beautiful.

" I don't know. If I'm hard up I shall sell it at once. Now, I suppose, I must sit down and write an enthusiastic 'thank you letter' to Aunt Felicia. Come to think of it, it was rather catty and patronizing of her to send it to me when she knows I'm no longer in a position to wear such things."

Janet felt that this was an uncomfortable topic.

"She must he awfully rich," she remarked vaguely.

Mary had seated herself at the table and had drawn the inkstand towards her.

"She is; disgustingly so. She rather disgraced the family by marrying a jam-maker. Not that I blame her for that, if she liked him. She got such a surfeit of jam that it made her sour. That's a paradox. Do laugh."

"I don't see that it's particularly funny. I wonder she doesn't do something for you if she knows how badly off you are."

"She does," said Mary, beginning to write. "She sends me an embroidered shawl. As a matter of fact, she—very kindly—offered to give me a home when my father died."

"You don't mean to say you refused?" cried her friend.

"Of course I refused. I thought I'd see something of life on my own."

"Rich girls often think they'll like working for their living," said Janet, nodding. "They soon find out what it's really like."

"I never had any illusions about it," answered Mary. "This is a very difficult letter to write. Fold the shawl up, Janet, and shove it in a drawer."

Janet obeyed her, but sighed.

"It does seem a shame to put it away."

"It would be a greater shame to leave it lying about to collect the dust," said the more practical Mary.

There was silence for a time while Mary chewed her pen, and Janet laid the shawl to rest in the depths of a drawer.

"Mary," said Janet at last, "I don't want to be inquisitive, but why do you never see any friends? You must have had quite a lot."

"Um!' Mary started to write again. "Not so many as I thought."

"Why not? What do you mean?" asked Janet.

"Same old tale. Many so-called friends while there was money and position. Then comes the financial smash, the incidental disgrace, and my father's tragic death. It's the only grudge I have against father, that he didn't stay to face the music with me. Anyway, one of the greatest 'friends' cut me dead in the street. Others—just kept out of the way. So as soon as I could I turned and ran."

"They couldn't all have been so—so beastly!" said Janet.

"I daresay they weren't. I didn't wait to see. One or two called. I appreciated their kindness, but I'd realized that—I was no longer a desirable *connaissance*, so I didn't see them."

"Wasn't there—anyone special?" asked Janet shyly.

Mary looked up, smiling.

"Do you mean, was I engaged to be married? No."

"No, not quite that. Weren't you—wasn't anyone in love with you?"

"Evidently not." There was a note of bitterness in Mary's voice.

Janet wanted to know more, but Mary seemed to be absorbed all at once in her letter.

II.

JANET'S questioning had awakened memories that were not dead, but lulled by time to rest. Mary Nugent indulged in reminiscence that night as she lay in bed. She thought of the frivolous, expensive career that had been hers for years, not with disgust, but with an ineffable longing. There had been many friends, many love-stricken young men; delightful days at Lord's, or Hurlingham, or Henley; enchanted evenings in the murky vastness of Covent Garden; bright nights spent in dancing, with haunting music in the air, the buzz of laughing voices, and the scent of hot-house flowers. There had been the sweet companionship of Peter Devril, too, growing almost imperceptibly into something sweeter still. She thought, smiling cynically, of his fascination, of his wit, and of his good looks.

She remembered the hurt she had felt when he did not come to see her after the smash. Until lately she had kept the formal note he had written her locked in her writing-case. Six months ago she had discovered it there, and had burned it without one tear for the tragic past.

From Peter her thoughts flew to Bill Corkran, who had gone to America, a year before the smash, to get rich quick. He had been the dearest of all her friends; Mary wondered whether he would have held aloof after her father's suicide if he had been in England. He had been very fond of her; she knew that. Before he left for America he had said certain words to her that had implied that she was his reason for wanting to make money. She did not know where he was or what he was doing. He had probably returned to England, and certainly he must have heard of her changed circumstances.

Mary was a typist in a firm of steel manufacturers. She had but one friend in the place, Malcolm, who was of her class and who wanted to be an artist. He was twenty-six—a year older than Mary, but in every essential five years younger. He made no pretence of being in love with her, but occasionally they went out together, when he would pour his hopes and longings into her sympathetic ear.

III.

FOR months the Chinese shawl remained hidden in a drawer. Sometimes Mary would take it out (when Janet was absent) and wistfully finger the silken folds. It exercised a strange fascination over her; she liked to look at it and drape herself in it.

In January Malcolm came to her in jubilant excitement waving a pink and a yellow ticket in his hand. He explained that he had wangled them out of a chap he knew who knew the fellow who was running the ball at the Corinthian.

"Are those tickets for that ball?" asked Mary.

"Rather! One for you and one for me. You will come, won't you, Mary?" cried Malcolm.

"The annual ball at the Corinthian," repeated Mary stupidly. More memories of old times—times she had tried to forget—were conjured up. Her eyes lighted. "Oh, what fun!"

"Isn't it? On Thursday, Mary, and we'll dine at that nice little place I found last night. You will dine with me, won't you?"

"It's awfully kind of you, Malcolm." Her eyes had clouded again. "I'm— I'm afraid I can't, though. Get someone else."

His face fell.

"You can't? Oh, I say! Why can't you? Are you doing something else? Can't you possibly manage it?"

She smiled crookedly.

"I can't go with you because I haven't anything to wear," she said honestly.

Janet sprang suddenly out of her chair.

"Yes, you have, yes, you have!" she cried. "The shawl!"

Even Malcolm was dubious.

"I don't quite see how you can go to a dance in a shawl," he began.

"Nor I," said Mary.

Janet pushed Malcolm to the door.

"It isn't an ordinary shawl, idiot! Mary will go on Thursday, and you'll go now. Shut up, Mary, I've got a wonderful idea. Go away, Malcolm. I promise you that not only will Mary go to the Corinthian, but she'll be one of the best-dressed girls in the room. Go away!"

"You're mad," said Mary, when Malcolm had been hustled out of the house. "The shawl's all right, of course, but what about my dress?"

"The shawl *is* your dress!" proclaimed Janet, dragging it from its drawer. "The groundwork is black, so you can wear your old black satin shoes. And— and you'll clasp it on one shoulder with a crimson rose, and it'll be draped over the other. Oh, gorgeous!"

"Do you really think it could be managed?" asked Mary, taking off her skirt. "Let's try!"

IV.

MALCOLM gasped when he saw Mary on Thursday evening. Then he gave a long-drawn, admiring whistle, and said: "By *Jove!*"

"All Janet's doing, the dear thing," said Mary.

Janet had coaxed the shawl into Spanish lines. It was draped over one shoulder, but left the other bare. The heavy fringe fell about Mary's ankles; a dark crimson rose was in her black hair.

They dined at a little restaurant in Soho, where the waiters all wore white aprons and shouted unintelligible Italian orders down to the chef, and where one could have the most perfect French omelettes.

They drove to the Corinthian in a taxi, reckless all at once, and as she entered the brightly lighted ballroom it seemed to Mary that years had rolled back and she was once more "the beautiful Miss Nugent." The orchestra was playing a fox-trot; Mary's feet began to move. She slid into Malcolm's arms, and they danced.

"It's three years since I danced," Mary said. "I'm out of date."

"Rot!" said Malcolm. "Not a bit of it!"

For over an hour they danced, almost without a pause; then Malcolm remembered that he was thirsty, and that Mary must surely be thirsty too. He took her to an alcove and left her seated on a sofa while he went to collect refreshments.

Mary leaned back contentedly, watching the maze of dancers. Once she saw a face she knew, but in the vast hall it was well-nigh impossible to recognize anyone.

Suddenly she became aware of a man dodging in and out of the moving couples and making his way towards her.

"Mary!" cried this man. "Mary!"

She rose, trembling, wishing that she could escape, yet glad that it was impossible.

"Hallo, Bill!" she said jerkily.

Corkran seized her hands.

"My dearest girl, this *is* luck! I was coming along to see you tomorrow. I only got back the day before yesterday, and old Chalmer and his wife dragged me along here. I hoped I might see you. You're looking ripping! I say, let's sit down, shall we?"

"Have you been in America all this time?" Mary asked. She felt dazed, but curiously happy.

"Rather! I went to get rich quick, as I told you. I went gold-hunting in the Klondyke."

She laughed.

"You *didn't?* Bill, how—how mad, and how like you! Did you find gold?"

"Great Scott, no! That only happens in romance. I gained a whole lot of experience, though, one way and another. In a way it hasn't been a bad three years, but I'm glad to be back."

"And you didn't make a fortune out there, after all?"

"Nothing like it. Frightfully tragic thing happened. You know my cousin, Sir George Corkran?"

"N-no. I've heard you speak of him, that is."

"Well, the poor chap took a fall out hunting and was killed. Awfully sad, wasn't it? Net result is, I'm the giddy baronet."

"Oh, congratulations!" said Mary, but her heart had sunk.

"Thanks awfully. How's Mr. Nugent?"

She started. Then he didn't know? For her life she could not tell him the whole truth.

"He—he—died three years—ago," she said. The words stuck a little in her throat.

"I say, I am so sorry!" He was genuinely concerned; looking at him she recognized the worried crease between his brows, and loved it. "Dreadfully sorry," he repeated, and patted her hand. "Poor old thing! Where—where are you living now?"

Malcolm's voice cut into the conversation, to Mary's relief.

"Oh—er—how d'you do?"

"Bill," said Mary hurriedly. "This is Mr. Trent, a great friend of mine. Malcolm, Mr. Corkran."

Corkran rose.

"How d'you do? 'Fraid I've been monopolizing your partner. I haven't seen her for donkey's years, you see."

Mary started to sip the drink Malcolm had brought her. Desperately she hoped that Bill would forget to ask again where she lived. She felt that she could not tell him, not because she was afraid that he would draw away, but because she knew that he still wanted to marry her, and it was unthinkable.

Malcolm was talking to him now, making polite conversation. In a minute or two he turned to Mary.

"They're playing that topping tune again. We must dance it."

"Yes, we must," agreed Mary, getting up.

Bill put his hand on her arm.

"I say, you must dance with me soon, Mary. There's such a lot I want to talk to you about. We'll meet again after this dance."

HOW she managed to keep out of his sight she never afterwards knew. Somehow or other she did it, and when she and Malcolm at last left the hall Bill was nowhere to be seen.

"Jolly good show, wasn't it?" said Malcolm. "I do hope you enjoyed it!"

"Ever and ever so much!" she answered mendaciously.

V.

IT was the third time the advertisement had been in the newspaper. It headed the Agony Column, and was imperative:

> *"Mary N. Communicate your address at once, dear. Bill C."*

Mary N. was to write to Box No. 3175.

Mary's eyes were wet as she read the advertisement.

"Dear quixotic Bill," she murmured. "He'll—get over it—and be glad of his—escape."

"What did you say?" inquired Janet, looking up from her correspondence. She was wearing a sapphire ring on her third finger, which had been placed there three days ago by an adoring, many-times-repulsed young man. Mary felt unreasonably jealous of her happiness.

"I didn't say anything," she replied with dignity. "I've got a half-holiday tomorrow, and I'm going to take the Chinese shawl to a shop I know of and sell it."

Janet let fall her letters.

"You're not?"

"Yes, I am. I'm sick of it; and I want some money badly."

"I don't know how you can bear to part with it! I've got a sort of feeling about it—I don't know, almost as though it would bring you luck."

"Luck!" ejaculated Mary. "You're wrong. Anyway, I'm going to sell it."

Accordingly she set off next afternoon with the shawl tied up in a brown-paper parcel in search of a possible buyer.

It was a long time before she could make up her mind to enter a shop, and when at last she summoned up enough courage to do so, she was met with a chilly refusal to buy. Yes, the shawl was undoubtedly lovely, but Simpkins and Jones did not buy second-hand goods.

The same answer was waiting for her everywhere. Dispirited, Mary went home. The impossible crimson birds embroidered on the shawl seemed to regard her with derisive eyes.

"I shall advertise it," said Mary. "Horrid thing."

She spent her shillings in advertisements, and still the shawl remained unsold. The only people who answered her advertisements wanted to buy the shawl at half the price she asked for it. Mary threw their letters into the fire. It seemed as though fate were willing her to keep her aunt's gift.

But at last a belated offer to buy arrived, accompanied by a request that Mary would send the shawl first on approval.

"Aha!" said Mary. "It is going to be sold after all!"

Mary sent the shawl to the prospective buyer, and in due course received a wad of notes in return. Mrs. Mellowe was delighted with her purchase.

"Well—well—I've *sold* it," said Mary.

"You're sorry now, I reckon," Janet told her.

"I am not. Only—no, I'm not sorry. I'm glad."

VI.

MEANWHILE Corkran, in despair, had enlisted a detective on his side. After what Netta Chalmer had told him of Mary's misfortune, and realising that she had slipped through his fingers, he felt that, whatever happened, and no matter what the cost might be, Mary was to be run to earth.

Her father's old lawyers knew nothing of her whereabouts; they were rather averse to discussing the Nugent family with anyone. Mr. Nugent had not proved himself to be a distinguished client.

Corkran advertised in more papers, with the same discouraging result. He set his lips tighter, and vowed that Mary was the most obstinate, trying little wretch a man could possibly wish to marry. In the hope of meeting her again by chance he visited dance halls and theatres, naturally with no success.

On one of these hunts Netta Chalmer accompanied him. They went to a first night (Mary had made a hobby of first-nights in the old days), and sat in a box so that Corkran might rake the house with his opera glasses.

"I don't see how one could expect her to be here," complained Netta. "I have told you her father's death left her practically penniless. In fact, I don't understand how it was that she came to be at the Corinthian. Unless, of course, she was taken."

"My dear Netta," answered Bill irritably, "I tell you that Mary was in a most ex-pensive rig."

"I'd like to know what sort of a judge you are," said Netta superbly. "She was probably in a black three-year-old hack frock, but, of course, you'd think it a Paris model."

"It was nothing of the kind. It was a priceless-looking dress, sort of swathed about her, Spanish fashion, with a fringe and quaint-looking red birds over it, like that shawl thing that woman in the fourth row's wearing. See!"

"Oh, yes, I know the sort of thing you mean. It couldn't have been one of those, though."

"I tell you it *was!*" indignantly reiterated Corkran. "And—hallo!"

"What?" Netta followed the direction of his opera-glasses, straining to see what had caught his attention. "What is it? Tell me!"

"I thought it was Mary," explained Corkran disappointedly. "It isn't, but—I'll swear it's her dress! Here, you take a look! The woman getting into her seat in the sixth—no, the seventh row. Quick!"

Obediently Netta focused the glasses on to Mrs. Mellowe.

"No, it's not Mary, but what a beautiful shawl! I've never seen one quite like that before. Are you sure it's Mary's?"

"Dead sure! I remember the way those red birds were flying about all over it. Hang the curtain going up! I'll have to wait till the interval."

"You can't very well go and ask her where she got the shawl," whispered Netta, giggling.

"Can't I!" he retorted.

As soon as the interval came Corkran left the box. With a beating heart Netta watched him appear downstairs and make his way towards Mrs.

Mellowe. Netta saw him smile and bow to Mrs. Mellowe. Through the glasses she observed Mrs. Mellowe's startled and puzzled frown. The man who was with her seemed to be amused; he gave up his seat to Bill and went outside, presumably to smoke. Bill entered deep into conversation with Mrs. Mellowe. To her relief Netta saw that lady laugh and nod. Evidently the two were hatching some plot, for Bill did not return to his box until the curtain was rising on the second act.

"What happened? Who was it? Does she know?" demanded Netta.

"Sh! I'll tell you after this act," said Bill. He was smiling, and his eyes were shining.

VII.

"HOW very queer!" said Mary. "Whatever can she mean?"

"Who?" asked Janet.

"The lady I sold the Chinese shawl to. I have just received this letter from her. She says she has 'discovered something rather strange about the shawl, and should be so very grateful if you could make it convenient to call here one day, when I will explain to you what I mean.' Did you ever hear of anything so mysterious?"

"I always said it was no ordinary shawl!" exclaimed Janet. "What on earth's it been doing? Sounds rather uncanny. Are you going to do as she asks you?"

"I suppose I must. She writes very politely and nicely, and she asks me to choose my own day. It'll have to be Saturday. Hand me my writing-case, will you, Janet?"

On Saturday afternoon Mary dressed herself with unusual care. At three o'clock she let herself out of the house, intending to go to Mrs. Mellowe's house by omnibus. To her surprise a large saloon car was standing by the kerb, evidently awaiting someone. She descended the steps, staring, and as she did so the man in the driver's seat turned to look at her. Mary fell back a pace, wondering whether she could escape, and what Bill was doing here.

Corkran slid out of the car.

"Ah!" he said sternly. "At last! Get in, please."

Mary began to stammer. Corkran gave a great sigh.

"Get—in!" he repeated, and took her firmly by the arm.

"B-but I c-c-can't! I don't know how you f-found me, but I d-don't want to see you, and I won't go with you, and I wish you'd go away!" She found that she was being forced relentlessly into the front seat. "No, Bill, I can't possibly go with you. I—I've got an appointment!"

"I'll drive you there," said Corkran, shutting her in. He went round to the other side and got into the seat beside her, setting his foot on the starter. "Now, then, young lady! Did you or did you not see my advertisement in the

Personal Column of the paper?"

"Yes," murmured Mary, gazing straight ahead of her.

"Why didn't you answer it?"

"Because I—oh, because I—I didn't want to!"

"Am I supposed to believe that?"

"Yes, of course!"

"Oh!" he smiled. "You're an awful little silly, Mary dear. What possessed you to cut and run, as you seem to have done? I heard all about it from Netta. She was ever so upset when you disappeared. After we've seen Mrs. Mellowe I'm taking you to her."

"What!" Mary started. "What do you know about Mrs. Mellowe?"

He chuckled.

"That's how I found you. I saw her at the theatre in your shawl. Recognized it at once, and tackled her. Between us we hatched this plot to find your whereabouts. Now this, Mary, is Battersea Park. I'm going to stop the car and talk to you very seriously."

She uttered unintelligible protests. Bill took her hands in his.

"Mary, you know how much I love you. I always have loved you. Do you—could you care enough to marry me?"

She tried to pull her hands away.

"I can't! I can't! Please let me go!"

"You don't care for me that way?"

"It's not *that!*" she cried impulsively.

His grip on her hands strengthened. His voice lost its worried note.

"Then that's all right. You do care for me. Why won't you marry me?"

"Oh, Bill, don't you *see?*"

"No, I'm afraid I don't."

"How—how *c-could* I marry you? How could I let you marry a—a—suicide's daughter?"

"Why not?" he asked imperturbably.

She gasped.

"But—but—oh, don't be so silly, Bill! I couldn't *bear* to have all that old scandal raked up and—and attached to you! People would talk so!"

"Why should they?"

"Because—Bill, don't be dense! You *must* understand! For one thing I haven't a penny to call my own, and—and everybody would say I married you for your money."

"I was waiting for that platitude," he remarked. "Wondered whether you'd be foolish enough to bring it out. Do you seriously believe people would say that?"

"Yes—no—I don't know. Didn't the Chalmers tell you about—about father?"

"Yes, but I don't see what that's got to do with you and me."

"But it *has* got something to do with us! You've no idea what—what a dreadful scandal there was. You can't possibly marry me! It's—dear of you and—and quixotic, but—"

"Quixotic be hanged!" he said. "I'm getting my proposal in before anyone else has a chance to. You seem to think that because your father was—er—unlucky, the blame and the disgrace will rest on you. Ridiculous, child! If you'd only waited you'd have had ample support from your friends, and no one would have stared at you or whispered about you."

Mary seemed to shrink suddenly. She tried to pull her hands away, and, failing, bowed her head over them.

"People – cut – me!" she whispered brokenly. "I c-couldn't—face them—after that. And I won't, I couldn't possibly marry you!"

Bill took her in his arms, where, after a slight struggle, she remained, weeping softly into his shoulder. Man-like, he patted her shoulder by way of comfort.

"How soon can you be ready?" he asked gently when the muffled sobs had abated.

"I won't! I couldn't! I'm not going to."

"One thing," said Bill severely, "is very evident; you've got a lot too pig-headed through living on your own all this time. I'm not going to stand any more nonsense. Understand?"

"I won't—"

"You'll do as you're told. D'you suppose I'm a child that I don't know my own mind? You've told me you care for me—"

"I didn't!"

"You wouldn't be crying your eyes out on my shoulder if you didn't. No, lie still, Mary! There! As I was saying, you admit that you care for me, and yet you won't marry me, because you don't think you're the proper sort of wife for me. Are you listening? Very well, then, perhaps you'll explain what you mean by trying to interfere in my concerns? If I want to marry you that's my affair. I'm not going to be dictated to on the choice of a wife by you. Mary, you darling, you're laughing!"

"I c-can't help it! You're s-so idiotic!"

"Not a bit of it. I'm talking sound sense. There have been many too many 'I won'ts' from you. You're going to do as you're told—aren't you?"

"I can't—"

Bill bent his head to kiss her.

"Aren't you?"

"I—"

He kissed her again.

"Aren't you?"

"Yes, Bill," she said weakly.

VIII.

WHEN Mary returned to her lodgings it was late that night, and she, too, was wearing a ring on her third finger. Also she was carrying the Chinese shawl over her arm. Janet sat up in bed and stared.

"You've got it back? But—whatever's happened, Mary?"

Mary danced to the bed.

"Oh, Janet, it's a wonderful shawl, and it did bring me luck, after all, because I'm engaged to be married, and, oh, Janet, everything's too wonderful for words!"

"Engaged! The shawl! Sit down at once, Mary, and tell me what you've been doing!"

Thus adjured, Mary perched on the edge of the bed and told Janet the whole story.

"And then Bill insisted on buying the shawl back again, and Mrs. Mellowe was awfully good about it. And after that Bill made me go with him to the Chalmers, and it was so glorious to see them again! I'm to be married next month. Oh, and I've got to give notice at the office, because I'm to go and stay with the Chalmers until the wedding!"

"It's—it's like a fairy tale!" said Janet, hugging her. "I *am* so glad!"

Mary slid off the bed and began to undress.

"To think that I was sore with Aunt Felicia for sending me the shawl," she marvelled. "If she hadn't sent it I should never have gone to the Corinthian, and if I hadn't gone to the Corinthian I shouldn't have met Bill. And if I hadn't sold the shawl to Mrs. Mellowe Bill would never have found me. I'll never part with it again. I love it!"

One of the crimson birds smiled sagely in the candlelight.

THE END

READING "THE CHINESE SHAWL"

So, you're a hopeful gentleman in love with a much-admired young woman. She comes from money, and you don't feel you can support her in the style to which she has become accustomed. You hope you can strike it rich and be worthy of her, so you leave the country... and three years later, without a letter or a phone call or (considering the times) telegram, with merely a bare suggestion of your feelings before your departure, you return home and, fortuitously finding her still single, expect her to immediately wish to marry you.

What an odd time it was for romance, the 1920s.

Also a very odd time for selling things. Can you imagine sending your goods off to a complete stranger on spec nowadays? eBay doesn't even give that as an option—funnily enough. How trusting – or perhaps just how honourable – were the people of the past. It's like that story of how P. G. Wodehouse used to just throw his letters, stamped, out the window to save himself a trek to the local post box. He was so certain of his fellow man's noble nature that he believed not a one of them would hesitate to post his letters for him, should they find one on a London street. (Cheek, I call it.)

But back to Bill and Mary. Just like Kenneth and Ursula of "Acting on Impulse," every facet of their relationship, the fact that they even have one, is entirely at the man's discretion. Just as Ursula had never, apparently, even considered marrying madcap Kenneth before he abruptly decides she should, Mary actively denies any desire to marry Bill *more than once* but he insists and insists and because it is easier to give in (to the life of ease and comfort he is offering her as much as to his stern importunities) she just meekly goes along with it. Cicely, Katharine, Ursula, Mary – for all we know, Diana also married George because he told her to; at least Ruth had enough backbone to stand up to Peter, before "The Little Lady" sent him crawling back to her – these women are all almost entirely at the whim of the men who might choose to marry them, and by god, that is annoying. Way more so here than in any historical romance, even in those that employ the Forced to Marry trope, like *A Civil Contract* and *Friday's Child* and so very, very many penned by Barbara Cartland and her ilk.

Part of the problem, of course, is the brevity of these stories – we learn a lot about the players, major and minor (except for most of the people in "Linckes" and, sadly, Ruth) because of Heyer's gift for characterization in an economy of words, but the development of relationships must be necessarily truncated in an offering like this, so abrupt denouements are somewhat to be expected. But this dictatorial "you will marry me" nonsense, this whole "you need me to take care of you" rigamarole, this infuriating "you're nothing without me" rubbish, just makes me so mad.

Yet these stories are... pretty great. This one isn't close to my favourite in the collection, but it's still better than ninety percent of romantic shorts I've ever read—and which number in the thousands. Georgette Heyer is so good that even when she drives you crazy, you still love her.

Plus, hey! Good thing that Mary's friend Janet espouses the Maria from *Sound of Music* school of fashion design – pre-*Sound of Music*, of course – or else bullying, bizarrely-confident-after-three-years Bill would never have found his carefully selected bride.

And then what would she have done? Married someone she actually *chose*, when she was actually ready to do so after she'd properly processed her father's death and her changed circumstances and learned that she did not need a man to take care of or complete her?

Pshaw!

– *Rachel Hyland*

"THE OLD MAID"

INTRODUCTION

"Helen King-Eyre, who was thirty-six and looked forty, stood by the window with her back to her friend and said nothing at all." Such is the unusual beginning of Georgette Heyer's last known contemporary short story. Published in *Woman's Pictorial* in August 1925, it appeared under the name "Stella Martin," the same pseudonym which two years previously she had published *The Transformation of Philip Jettan*. "The Old Maid" is undeniably a Georgette Heyer story, and reading it, it is tempting to think that it has several autobiographical elements – which may be why she used a pseudonym.

It is interesting to note just how often Heyer used the name "Helen" in her fiction: Hélène de Courvonne in *Simon the Coldheart* (1925), Helen Marchant in *Helen* (1928), Helen North in *A Blunt Instrument* (1938), Helen "Nell" Stornoway in *The Toll-Gate* (1954), Helen "Nell" Merion, Lady Cardross, in *April Lady* (1957) and Helen Morland in "Hazard" (1936) (reprinted in *Pistols for Two,* 1960, and *Snowdrift,* 2016).

It is also worth noting that Heyer's friend Dorothea "Doreen" Arbuthnot's middle names were "Helen Mary." The two must have been very close, for Heyer dedicated *Simon the Coldheart* (1925 US edition) and *Barren Corn* (1930) to "Doreen." Of course, Doreen was not a name she could use in her historical fiction, so it is possible that her repeated use of "Helen," and even of "Mary" (Mary in "The Chinese Shawl" and Mary Challoner in *Devil's Cub*, to name but two), was a subtle tribute to her friend.

The Helen of "The Old Maid," however, resonates strongly with what we know, not of her friend, but of Georgette Heyer herself, for there are several parallels between the budding author and the fictional heroine. Helen is a famous author; Heyer's fame was growing. Helen is frank and yet shy, as was Heyer, and both women have "humorous grey eyes." But it is perhaps Helen's description of herself that seems so in tune with what we know of Heyer:

> *She had had her success; men called her "great"; she was the biggest satirist of her day; she had hosts of friends, but she was lonely, for none of the men who admired her genius considered her as a woman. She was a "good fellow", she was witty, and unusual, and an invigorating companion, but she was too downright to be attractive, too competent and independent.*

This is similar to what Heyer's first biographer, Jane Aiken Hodge, wrote of her in 1984:

Georgette was a self-confessed blue-stocking, that dangerous phenomenon, a female author... She had been shunned at Miss Head's School because of her sharp tongue, and probably still used unusual words, talked in sentences, and maybe even indulged in an occasional Latin tag... the fact that she was beautiful may well have been counterbalanced by the equally unconcealable fact that she was witty. Friends from every stage of her life remember her dry tongue, her elegant speech, the laughter they shared.

Like Helen, Heyer was frank and competent and independent; like Helen, she was not demonstrative. As an adult, she did not believe in overt displays of emotion or of speaking openly about her deeper feelings – her writing was her outlet for emotion. As an adolescent attending school she had struggled to make friends of her own age because she was mature beyond her years and related more easily to the teachers than the students. As a wife and mother she was kind and generous and proud of her husband and son, but she was not effusive in her affection. Heyer did not readily hug or kiss people beyond what was strictly necessary; she was reserved and shy with all but those inside her close inner circle. The Helen of this story is the same.

In manner and speech she is also very much like the eponymous heroine of the autobiographical novel, *Helen* (1928), yet to come. The short dialogue between Helen and her friend Anne could almost have been lifted from *Helen* had it not pre-dated that novel:

"Helen, you needn't pretend with me.
A hot flush rose.
"Never have."

Interestingly, the writing of this final short story coincided with the return from Nigeria, after eighteen months away, of Heyer's dear friend, Ronald Rougier. In 1923 he had qualified as a mining engineer and in October of that year had sailed to Nigeria to take up a position with the Niger Company. It is not known whether Ronald proposed before he left, but if he did, he was not accepted. It was only after his return in the spring of 1925 that Heyer agreed to marry him. Just as Helen is reunited with her old love, Maurice Parmeter, after a long absence in India, so Heyer was reunited with Ronald after his time in Africa. They were engaged in May 1925 and it's possible that Heyer wrote this story as an outlet for her feelings. For most of her writing life, her books and stories would be an outlet for her emotions.

"The Old Maid" is fascinating for what it appears to tell us of Heyer, but it is also a very entertaining story. The characters live, the dialogue is crisp and revealing, and there is a gruff humour of the type at which Heyer excelled. There is also an element of Jane Austen's novel *Persuasion*, with its story of lost love and second chances. Like Anne Elliot, Helen strives to hide her true feelings, and like Captain Wentworth, Maurice Parmeter learns that honesty is the best way forward.

This was to be Heyer's last contemporary short story. She would, however, write three more contemporary novels. They would sell well, earn good reviews and achieve multiple reprints. Not only would Heyer suppress them within ten years of their publication, she would also exclude from a comprehensive list of her novel and short story publications all but one of her nine short stories that were published in the 1920s. Only the Danish title of "The Chinese Shawl" would remain in her records – a tantalising clue for those keen to know more of a wonderful writer and her feelings about these early, youthful works.

– Jennifer Kloester

THE OLD MAID

HELEN KING-EYRE, who was thirty-six and looked forty, stood by the window with her back to her friend and said nothing at all. Mrs. Dering eyed her speculatively from her seat by the fire, and surreptitiously smiled.

"You do remember him, don't you, Helen?" she said softly.

Helen swallowed hard. Did she remember Maurice Parmeter! She'd tried to forget him all these weary years, and miserably failed. And now he was coming home from India for good, and, if Anne Dering was to be believed, he wanted to see her again.

"Yes. I remember him," she said curtly.

Anne spoke more softly still.

"Helen, you needn't pretend with me."

A hot flush arose.

"Never have."

"Yes, you have. You've never told me how you feel about it."

Helen answered with some difficulty.

"It's never easy to admit you were a fool."

"Ah!" Anne straightened in her chair. "I guessed it. You've always been sorry you didn't marry him?"

"Yes."

Anne went to her, and put her arm around her shoulders.

"It's not too late, old girl."

Helen laughed shortly.

"Much too late. I haven't even seen him—since—since I sent him away. And I was twenty-five then. Don't suppose he ever thinks of me."

"He isn't married, dear. And he says in his letter that he wants more than anything to see you. He wouldn't say that—being Maurice—unless he still cared."

"Bosh!" said Helen inelegantly. "Probably he's got a sentimental feeling about me. That won't last when he sees me."

"Helen, without any more nonsense, if Maurice still cared would you marry him now?"

"Yes!" said Helen fiercely.

"Very well," replied Anne, in a business-like manner. "It's up to you, then. And I'm determined you shan't let this last chance slip. You'll come to stay with me just as we'd arranged before I heard that Maurice was coming."

"I won't."

Anne opened wide her eyes.

"Dear me, why not? Are you afraid of the man? After all these years I really can't see that you need be shy of meeting him."

This had the desired effect. "Shy!" snorted Helen.

"That's settled, then. You'll come. And Helen, don't—don't frighten him! I know what you are. Men don't like a woman to be as brilliant you are. And, oh darling, do, *do* be more feminine! Don't shock him!"

"Anne, if you think I'm going to try and—and catch—Maurice—"

"You'll be a fool if you don't," said Anne serenely. "And considering your views—"

"Damn my views!" said Helen. She turned, and her whimsical, dancing smile dawned. "It's all rot, Anne. I'm getting old, and if he'd wanted me he'd have come before now."

"I don't see it," Anne replied. "You sent him away pretty decisively in the first place, and he wasn't the sort of man to hang on after that. And when he was on leave the first time you were lecturing in America. And the next time, my dear, you were engaged to Rupert Arden."

At that Helen winced.

"What did you do it for, darling?"

"I don't know. It was madness. I was lonely. I admired his genius. We— we had things in common. Heavens, what a fool I was!"

"And now," Anne said briskly, "you're sane and unattached, and we shall see what we shall see."

WHEN Anne Dering had gone, Helen went to the glass and carefully studied her reflection. She saw humorous grey eyes, a face that was lined a little, and innocent of powder, brown hair that was unwaved, screwed into a careless, untidy knot, with ends that escaped from it and straggled over her ears and brow. She saw, too, her neck grown thin and her tall body clothed in a shape-less green garment unworthy of the name frock. All about her, in this expen-sive flat, was beauty; only she was ugly there and incongruous.

She'd let herself go; she'd thought that her brains counted for more than her looks. When she had sent Maurice away she'd been on the threshold of success. Her first book had been published and the critics were enthusiastic. She had thought that her career must stand first; she couldn't make up her mind to go with Maurice to India. India belonged to Kipling, but London was hers.

She had had her success; men called her "great"; she was the biggest satirist of her day; she had hosts of friends but she was lonely, for none of the men who admired her genius considered her as a woman. She was a "good fellow"; she was witty, and unusual, and an invigorating companion, but she was too downright to be attractive, too competent and independent.

"One thing is certain," she told her mirrored self. "You can't meet him like this. You're a perfect sight."

THE long, low touring car, the pride of Helen's heart, was nearing its desti-
nation. Helen sat in the back of it, consumed with unaccustomed
nervousness. She was a transformed being. She wore a marvellous little hat
over carefully waved hair; her face had been massaged and very skilfully and
delicately rouged; her feet were in high-heeled shoes, and a sable coat hid a
frock that spelled Paquin quite unmistakably.

"I shall never keep it up," she thought. "Damn these shoes! Yes, and
that's one of the things I must not say. This man will be the death of my poor
car!"

She leaned forward to say a few well-chosen words to her chauffeur but
remembered in time her new rôle of helpless femininity. But it was hard to
see her car driven by anyone but herself.

They swept into the drive of the Dering's house; Helen saw Anne on the
porch, and Don, her husband, and a tall, square-shouldered figure, the sight
of whom made her heart do strange things

"Don'll give it away, sure as eggs is eggs," she thought desperately. "I
was a fool to come!"

The car drew up; Helen pulled herself together and gazed limpidly into
Anne's astonished eyes.

"Dear Anne!" she murmured, and sweetly smiled.

Anne recovered herself with an effort, and stepped forward.

"Dear Helen!" she cooed.

Maurice was waiting to hand Helen out of the car; as she stepped down
she looked at him from under her darkened lashes, and her pulses beat fast.
He was the same, save for a few grey hairs at his temples. His eyes held the
grave, honest look she remembered so well, and—yes, they were full of
admiration.

Don, who had been standing as though rooted to the spot, opened his
mouth.

"Good lord, Helen, what in thunder—"

"How delightful to see you, Don!" Helen said and held out her hand. As
he took it, struggling for words, she trod heavily on his toe, and whispered:
"Shut up, you fool!"

Don looked rather relieved: this was the Helen he knew, and liked. What
she was doing in these extraordinary clothes, and why she talked in a soft,
society manner he could not imagine. However, he understood that he was
to say nothing, so he grinned cheerfully and wrung her hand.

"You remember Maurice, of course," Anne was saying.

HELEN found herself looking up into those dear grey eyes.

"Of course," she answered. "What ages it is, Maurice! You are home for
good now?"

"Yes, for good," he said, smiling at her. "This is a very great pleasure, Helen."

Then Anne bore Helen upstairs, agog with excitement, and almost pushed her into the spare room.

"Helen!" she gasped. "You—you *marvel*. I never saw anything to equal it! My dear, you look lovely! I nearly had a fit!"

"Don's probably having one now," said Helen. "Did you see his face? Oh, Anne, he's just the same as ever!"

Anne gathered that her friend was not referring to Don. She smiled.

"And did you see *his* face? Helen, it's the most wonderful thing I've ever known. You're perfect! That hat! Your hair! Manicured nails! I can't get over it."

"I feel a stupid fool," said Helen, and tossed her hat on to the bed. "And a beastly, low-down cheat!"

"You've even brought a maid!" went on Anne, unheeding. "Where did you get that dream of a frock? I hardly knew you! Helen, you're made up!"

"Too much?" asked Helen anxiously.

"No, not a bit; but you couldn't take me in. Oh, come downstairs again, my dear! This is the most thrilling thing that has happened for ages!"

There was a twinkle in Helen's eyes.

"I'll come as soon as I've changed, dearest," she said in a mincing voice.

The maid came in. Anne met her friend's wide blank stare, and fled.

TEA was brought to the low, panelled hall, where a fire burned in a barless grate. Slowly, and a little late, Helen came down the stairs, dressed in a tea-gown of filmy mist-blue, her hair elaborately arranged, her feet in tight shoes of silver brocade. Not her usual cheery grin curled her mouth, but a faint, controlled smile.

"Am I late?" she said. "How dreadful of me! Give me a comfy chair by the fire, Don, please. That will be delightful."

Don swallowed hard, but his lips trembled despite himself. Maurice came to give Helen tea, and he left his own seat to sit beside her. Helen hid her shyness—and she was very shy—and turned towards him.

"Are you glad to leave India?" she inquired. "It seems to get such a hold over people."

"It has its fascination," he answered, his admiring eyes on her face, "but on the whole I'm glad to be home again. I'm going to try and find a house to settle down in. You've become very famous, Helen."

Ordinarily she would have nodded, and laughed. Instead she made a little deprecating gesture with her hand.

"Oh! That's very kind of you."

"I've read all your books, of course. I think that *Miriam* is my favourite."

She sat up at that, and for one instant the real Helen showed.

"Why do you say that? I regard the book as—" she broke off, on the very brink of hot argument. "I am so glad you liked it," she said.

When tea was over Anne, in some miraculously unobtrusive way, took Don away and left her guests together. Maurice drew his chair nearer, and offered Helen a cigarette. She thought it more in keeping with the part not to smoke, so she shook her head.

"Do tell me all your news!" she said prettily.

"There is nothing to tell. You have done far more than I have. But then, you always had the divine spark in you."

Helen started to say "Rot!" and changed it to:

"You mustn't flatter me, Maurice."

"Impossible," he said. "You are quite wonderful."

"You find me changed?"

He frowned.

"Y—es. And yet I don't know." His eyes smiled. "You're more elegant than the Helen I remember. And just as lovely."

Helen flushed, and began to talk rather hurriedly about India. The time flew. Helen made Maurice talk; she abstained from contradiction, and said very little, but sat smiling and interested. The dressing gong for dinner interrupted them.

"I must fly!" said Helen. "I mustn't be late again!"

Maurice looked at the clock.

"In the old days," he remarked, "you used to tear upstairs three minutes before dinner and, I verily believe, dive into the first garment that met your eye!"

"Oh, but I'm older now!" she answered.

"You don't look it."

ANNE came into Helen's room on her way downstairs. At a nod from her mistress the maid departed.

"Heavenly frock," said Anne. "My dear, he's struck!"

"Struck what?" said Helen disagreeably.

"Struck nothing. Struck with you."

"Don't be vulgar! If—if I could—I'd chuck this horrid sham!"

"Yes, but you can't, my dear. And it's just perfect. This room reeks of smoke."

"Rather stinks of it," Helen agreed. "I must smoke somewhere, though. Oh, that's the gong! I wish I'd never come!"

There was no doubt about it—Maurice was attracted. During the days that followed he looked on her with mingled awe and admiration; and sometimes Helen thought that she could see a puzzled gleam in his eyes. He treated her as though she were made of sugar, which irked her exceedingly. They went for sedate little walks on tarred roads, and if a spot of rain fell, Maurice, absurdly anxious, hurried Helen homewards. He seemed always to expect her to be tired, and several times she almost let her mask fall, because she wanted so much to tell him not to be a fool. He drove her out in her car sometimes, and that was not all joy for Helen. She yearned to say: "Look here, old thing, I love you, you're the dearest person in the world, but you don't know a thing about cars." But it was quite impossible to say anything of the sort, especially as she was not at all sure that Maurice still loved her. Her love for him choked her; for once, in her independent life, she hungered to feel his arms about her, and his kisses on her mouth. It did not happen. Maurice was tender, and solicitous, and admiring, but he seemed to hold himself aloof, watching her. Once he said:

"I don't expect the sort of house I'm after would be much in your line. You're a town bird, aren't you?"

She wasn't. She only lived in London because of her loneliness. She wanted "his sort of house," with dogs, and horses, and a garden to tend.

He went to look at Airedale pups, and took her with him. He was not familiar with the breed and Helen, in impotent wrath, watched him select a hopeless specimen and listen guilelessly to the breeder's eulogies. Helen held herself in check, but her impulse was to say a few illuminating words. Instead, she murmured:

"It seems rather a lot to give. Perhaps you'll find one less expensive."

She couldn't bear to see Maurice be swindled. Luckily he decided to think the matter over before purchasing the pup.

She had been with the Derings for three weeks when Maurice heard of a house for sale. It seemed to be just what he desired, and as it was possible to motor there and back in a day, they arranged to go over to look at it, lunching on the way, and arriving home in time for dinner. Everything was planned when Anne, worried over the slow progress of the matchmaking, developed an intangible ailment, and declared that she did not feel "up to it." Don, blindly obeying orders, refused to go without her, and it seemed as though the expedition must fall through. But Anne insisted that Maurice and Helen should go, and after a great deal of argument Helen agreed.

MAURICE took Helen in her own car, wrapped her in many rugs, although the day was very mild. They lunched at a little inn on the way, and arrived at the house about four in the afternoon. It was all that was most beautiful, a long, low Tudor building set in big grounds, with a rose garden, a pleasaunce, a small farm, and tennis courts. They wandered all over it, enchanted, and could hardly bear to tear themselves away. But it was growing late and they had had no tea. They reluctantly went in search of a confectioner, and wasted fully an hour there discussing the house. Then Maurice saw that it was already six o'clock, and sprang up.

"Oh, Helen, this is too bad of me! I'm afraid we shan't get back till nine, and Anne said eight o'clock dinner. I'm so sorry!"

"It doesn't matter a bit," she replied. "I've so enjoyed it. We'd better be going now, though."

"I'm afraid you'll be very tired," he said worriedly. "Do you mind having dinner on the way?"

"Not a bit; I should love it," she said truthfully.

They drove back through the fast gathering dusk, and presently the darkness came, and Maurice, looking at the clock before him, under its little light, said: "It's nearly eight. I think we'll stop at the first decent inn we see. Are you quite warm?"

The words were hardly out of his mouth when there were sundry strange sounds from the car's interior, and they stopped in the middle of the deserted road. After a moment Maurice got out.

"Something's rather wrong," he said "I didn't think she was running very well this morning. I say, I am sorry, Helen!"

"What is it?" she asked. A note of anxiety had crept into her voice, for this car was the pride of her heart.

"I don't know," said Maurice, and groped in the engine. "Can't see. Have you a torch?"

"Left hand—er—I expect there is one in one of the pockets," Helen said, clinging to her role of helpless female. Maurice came and looked for it, and drew it forth triumphantly.

"Good! Now we shall see!"

He clicked the switch of the torch, and it was evident that they were not going to see at all. A frown was gathering in Helen's eyes.

"Of all the rotten luck!" said Maurice disgustedly. "The battery has run down."

And then something seemed to snap in Helen. She forgot all about her pose, and cast the rugs from her, and stepped out into the road.

"That," she said crisply, "is what comes of letting that fool of a chauffeur mess about with the car. I might have known it."

Maurice stood transfixed with amazement, staring at this suddenly trans-formed woman. Helen did not see his surprise. She flung off her coat and hat and demanded a match.

"Just come and hold it for me," she said. "In all the years I've driven a car never once have I come out without a spare battery. Hold the match there, will you?"

Meekly he obeyed. He hid his astonishment, for fear of chasing this old, dear Helen away. A wild elation filled him; he wanted to hug her as he had never wanted to hug the immaculate woman who had taken her place.

She dived into the car, and her capable hands groped here and there. Out she came, and strode to the switchboard. Then she came back again, and once more disappeared into the bonnet. When she again emerged her hair was awry, and a large smudge of grease adorned one cheek.

"No good, I can't see!" she said curtly. "Give me a cigarette!"

MAURICE began to shake with inward merriment; he handed Helen his cigarette-case, and watched her sit down on the step of the car. Helen smoked rather violently for a minute.

"This is the most putrid luck," she presently announced. "Any ideas?"

"One only. Push the car to the side of the road."

"Righto!" said Helen, and got up.

They pushed the car as he suggested, and all the time Maurice thought: "Helen has come back!"

"Now," he said, "I think you'd better tuck yourself up inside while I go to the nearest village and get some sort of a convenience."

Helen stared at him in the light of the car lamps.

"What did you say I'd better do?"

"Get inside, and keep warm. You'll be quite—"

"Now, I ask you, Maurice, does that elegant little scheme sound like me?" she demanded.

Maurice spoke deliberately.

"It sounds remarkably like the you I've known for the past three weeks," he said.

There was a sudden, frozen silence. Helen gulped, reddened, and turned away, horribly uncomfortable.

"Explanations, please," said Maurice sternly, but she saw his eyes were dancing.

"I shall not explain anything," she said with dignity.

"Oh, won't you? Shove on your coat and come along!"

"I believe I'll wait for you as — as you suggested," she said.

"I don't. Do buck up!"

Helen put on her coat, jammed the luckless hat on her head, and set out beside Maurice. They strode down the road for some way in silence.

"What I want to know first," said Maurice, "is this: what was the meaning of Rupert Arden?"

A low chuckle came from beside him.

"Oh, he hasn't much meaning," Helen answered.

"Why did you get engaged to him?"

"Well he had his points. Not at all a bad sort of creature. Only I got bored with him. Didn't know one end of a dog from the other. Which reminds me. That Airedale pup. No good at all. Bad quarters, no bone, too full in the eye."

Maurice laughed.

"All right, we won't have him. But we were talking of Rupert Arden."

"He gassed about his Art," said Helen pensively. "Capital A."

"I see. But why were you engaged to him?"

"Look here, what's that to do with you?"

Maurice stopped and faced her.

"I'll tell you what it's got to do with me."

"I was engaged to him because—because I thought I liked him," said Helen in a hurry.

"We'll let that pass. You will now tell me why you've been behaving like an animated doll for the past three weeks."

"I shan't!"

"Don't be so bad tempered. Out with it!"

"Oh, shut up, Maurice! Don't bully!"

His hands were on her shoulders.

"You, darling! And don't you deserve to be bullied? Helen, have you ever regretted that you sent me away?"

SHE looked up into his face, and what she saw there made her heart bloom again.

"Yes."

The grip on her shoulders tightened.

"And you got yourself up to look like a dress-maker's model to vamp me?"

"Here, that'll do!" said Helen. "I'm blowed if I looked like a—"

"*Did* you?"

"Yes!"

"I hope you're ashamed of yourself."

"Maurice, I'm —I'm sick of this! Let me go!"

" I'm not going to let you go—ever. You beast, Helen, I've been miserable because you seemed so different. I've wanted you, and wanted you. I came back to try and make you love me, and instead of the old, haphazard Helen, I found a dressed-up—"

"That'll do," said Helen. "I don't want to hear any more."

"—a dressed up minx. And it may interest you to know, my sweetheart—"

"No, not at all! I'm not your sweetheart! I—"

"Drop it. It may interest you to know that it was not a fashion-plate that I wanted, but the adorable, mad creature who shoved her head into the bonnet of the car, cursed the chauffeur, and came out with a smudge of grease on one cheek. Got that?"

"Yes, thank you. Do you mind letting me go now?"

"I do," he said. Then the laughter left his voice, and he drew her nearer. "Helen, all these years I've longed for you. Will you marry me now?"

"No, no, no! If I hadn't thrown myself at your head—"

"Well?"

"You —wouldn't have—thought of—marrying me!"

"If you call this throwing yourself at my head—"

"But I did! Anyway, I won't marry you!"

"Dear idiot, if you'd kept up that elegancy you certainly wouldn't have married me. I wasn't having any. Didn't you notice that?"

"Oh Maurice, you brute!"

Then she could not say anything more for quite some time, because the breath was literally crushed out of her. And presently, holding her tightly against his shoulder, Maurice asked:

"Helen, will you, or will you not marry me?"

Helen's voice quivered irrepressibly.

"May as well," she said.

IT was close on midnight when Anne and her husband heard a car scrunching over the gravel drive. They went out at once, in time to see Helen jump out of an aged Ford. Her hat was over one eye, her face and hands were smeared with car-grease, and she had lost her gloves. Behind her came Maurice, with a broad grin.

"Hullo!" said Helen. "We broke down. Towed the car to Littleharbour, and left it."

"Helen, your face!" wailed Anne.

"My face," said Helen cheerfully. "The game's up."

Anne looked quickly from one to the other, then held out her hands.

"You dears!" she said. "When's it going to be?"

"As soon as possible," Maurice answered. "We're buying the house, and we shall probably breed Airedales."

"And I am not going to be beautiful anymore," said Helen blissfully.

THE END

READING "THE OLD MAID"

None of Heyer's contemporary works is quite as indicative of her state of mind at this particular time of her life as is "The Old Maid." At the ripe old age of twenty-three she was clearly terrified of living alone, of being over-looked and left on "the shelf"; this story shows us Heyer looking deep into the abyss of singledom and finding it unacceptable. She fast-forwards her writerly life, Ghost of Christmas Future-style, and sees what shifts she will be driven to if she continues on as she is, striving for literary greatness while turning down a perfectly eligible proposal from a man who has long carried a torch for her, in all her introverted eccentricity.

Heyer gazes ahead and sees that years later, having become a spinster, she'll have to get a makeover and put on airs and let a chauffeur drive her car, and all because she was the "toast" of literary London and didn't want to go to Africa to follow her man.

As it happens, Heyer eventually did end up going to Africa to follow her man, of which we are most brutally assured by her frankly upsetting non-fiction article "The Horned Beast of Africa," which was published in London newspaper *The Sphere* in June 1929. She and her husband Ronald – whom she met in 1920 and married in 1925 – had been living in Tanganyika (now Tanzania), and mining engineer Ronald had also become something of a big game hunter, taking down black rhinoceros by the seeming dozen. Heyer describes his expertise with a nonchalant glee which was very much of its time – though we've all seen *Beatrice at the Dinner* and those shots of various plutocrats; people still do such things, after all – and one can't help but think of Helen King-Eyre, and what she had to endure in her *Sliding Doors* version of the future, in order to not be an old maid until she was so positively ancient at thirty-six.

But looking forty. Whatever that means.

I really like this story. I especially like how bluff, sharp-tongued Helen, alone of all Heyer contemporary heroines, has very real agency: she has decided she wants to marry Maurice, and she single-mindedly sets about win-ning him in a very determined fashion. Of course, she gets terrible advice from her well-meaning friend on how to accomplish this, because there are always those who will not understand how Different and Special the "not like other girls" heroine is, and will inadvisably try to make her just like everyone else.

It's practically the law.

But of course Maurice refuses to fall for these tricks, because we couldn't respect a man who did, nor could we support one who didn't steadfastly adore our heroine Just the Way She Is.™

Again: law.

I also like how, in the fear-fuelled future fantasy that is her life, Heyer has recast herself as a darling of the literati, an acclaimed and best-selling "satirist," not a romance novelist of any kind. It was always evident that Heyer had aspirations beyond the scope of her most popular genre playground – she wanted to be Thackeray, or Dickens, or at the very least Scott. But in "The Old Maid" she gave herself the legitimacy she craved, and even in that flight of fancy, the respect of the kinds of critics who would plague her in real life still wasn't enough to fill a life she would consider empty without a husband to call her own.

Whatever travails occurred after her marriage to Ronald – up to and including the wholesale slaughter of magnificent, now critically-endangered, creatures – I really hope that she continued to feel that way for as long as they both did live. Helen is brought to life so vividly here that I almost believe she is an alternate history version of Georgette, and I want her to never have felt the need to be "beautiful" in order to be happy.

Actually, I want that for everyone. And I think Georgette would have, too.

– *Rachel Hyland*

"LOVE"

INTRODUCTION

First published in 1919, *The Sovereign Magazine* was initially aimed at women readers. During its short life (it folded in 1927) it published mainly adventure and romance stories. In its earliest years it serialised swashbucklers such as Rafael Sabatini's career-making novel, *Scaramouche*, Achmed Abdullah's desert romance, *Shackled*, and Sapper's *The Black Gang*, featuring Bulldog Drummond. From 1922 there was a marked increase in the number of "weird mysteries and ghost stories," but there were also shorts from soon-to-be famous writers including Agatha Christie, Leslie Charteris and Margery Allingham.

The magazine favoured dramatic covers and the edition in which "Love" appeared had a particularly lurid example. It featured a wild-eyed young man about to bring an axe down on the head of a bearded assailant who has in his grasp a terrified and nearly-topless woman. Though the sketches inside the magazine were well drawn and Heyer's historical short story had an illustration of people in Georgian dress in a sumptuous drawing-room, the magazine's cover cannot have endeared itself to the author. It is hard to imagine Heyer being impressed with this sort of image and it is perhaps unsurprising that she never had a story in *The Sovereign Magazine* again.

Published in November 1923 – the same month as *Instead of the Thorn* – "Love" would prove to be the only tragedy among Heyer's short stories. It would also be the only one of her historical shorts published in the 1920s; she would go on to write several historical shorts in the 1930s and 1940s, most of which would be included in her 1960 anthology, *Pistols for Two* and in the 2016 reissue, *Snowdrift and Other Stories*.

"Love" was the culmination of an intense writing period for the young Heyer. Between September 1922 and October 1923 she had written and successfully published three novels, seven contemporary short stories and this historical short. She had also written the bulk of the novel that she described as "a sequel" to *The Black Moth*. This draft manuscript, which she had nearly finished in January 1923, would eventually become her perennial bestseller, *These Old Shades* (1926). At the age of just twenty, Heyer was already demonstrating her remarkable ability to slip easily from one genre to another; from historical to contemporary and back again.

Though set in the same era as Heyer's novels *The Black Moth* and *The Transformation of Philip Jettan*, "Love" is very different from those light-hearted romances. It is the story of Henry, a married man trapped in a loveless marriage; his wife is capricious, demanding and given to fits of uncontrollable hysteria. He loves another woman, Mary, and she loves him, but Mary's brother is smitten with Henry's wife, Sophia. When the story opens, Mary is desperate to see her brother freed from Sophia's clutches before he is ruined.

This is a story about love – true love and fickle love, love of things, love of power, and love's sacrifice. It is not a happy story but it is very well-written and, like the ending of *These Old Shades*, the reader believes in these people and in the melodrama that is their lives. It is, however, a departure from Heyer's usual type of story and it is possible that a recent stay in hospital had turned her mind to tragedy rather than comedy.

She'd had serious surgery in the first week of September, just two months before "Love" was published. She'd written a story on the eve of her operation and it is likely that the story was "Love." The surgery kept her in hospital for three weeks and had left her with "a very hot line in tubes sticking out of my neck. When I eat I can feel it move inside! Perfectly filthy!" She'd sent the story to her agent after the operation and later wrote to him to say:

> *I don't know in the slightest what the story is about! In fact, I never even read it through! When my surgeon heard how I spent the eve of my operation he was filled with awe and wonder! But it reads like that, doesn't it? The operation was entirely successful and you'll be relieved to hear that I behaved like a perfect lady throughout. I also managed to shake off that chewed banana feeling quite quickly, and am now quite well and cheery, if a trifle exhausted.*

She ended the letter with a characteristic postscript, 'Have just read this through. If the construction and phraseology of my story is anything like this it must be choice.' Of course, being Heyer, the prose was polished, the dialogue elegant and evocative, and the plot well-executed. But, though it is a Heyer story, "Love" has a very different message for her readers. In her long career, out of twenty short stories and fifty-five novels, only "Love" (1923), *Barren Corn* (1930), *Penhallow* (1942) and *Cousin Kate* (1968) would deal in tragedy.

– Jennifer Kloester

LOVE

I.

THE woman in the high-backed chair sat very still, her hands clasped tightly in her lap, her eyes upon the man by the window. He was standing with his back to the room, looking out into the fog. A flame, springing to life in the open hearth, cast a shimmer over the sleeve of his peach-satin coat where it caught the light. His thin hand lay on the window-sill, listless.

The woman spoke, low and evenly.

"It is common talk now, my lord—they laugh about it at White's—how Lord Farquhar's wife has a lover in Mathew Hatton, and Mathew's sister in Lord Farquhar."

My lord turned his head; his eyes were very weary, set in a face of extraordinary beauty; young still, but marred by lines telling of late nights and dissipation. His mouth was finely curved, with pale lips and very white teeth.

"I know," he said. There was a note of sadness in his voice, and of disillusionment, never absent. It was very sweet and level.

The woman moved her hands restlessly.

"I cannot go on, Henry. She is ruining Mathew. He is changing under mine eyes."

My lord was silent, looking out once more into the fog.

"I am his sister, Henry. Can't you—understand what it means to me? To see him swayed by—your wife's—influence?"

My lord flung out his hand in an appealing gesture.

"Mary, I know all this. We have spoken of it so many, many times! To what avail? It is to talk to you that I have come, and of our lives. Of what concern are these others?"

"He is my brother," she answered quietly.

"He is no longer a child."

"And she—is your wife, Henry."

He came back into the room, to the fire-place. A bitter smile hovered about his mouth.

"Ay, my wife… Why rake all this up again, Mary? God knows I tried to act rightly by her, but she made everything impossible. It is over now, and we tread different paths."

Tears came to the woman's eyes.

"It is not right," she said. "You could win her again."

"You counsel that, Mary? You?"

"I must," she whispered. "It is—Mathew, you see. He is—all I have."

My lord winced imperceptibly.

"I am nothing, Mary?"

"You—should be, my lord."

"You'll make me so?" Still more bitter became the smile.

"God help me!" she said, and covered her face with her hands.

He went to her, his silks rustling, and the jewels on his fingers glittering in the firelight.

"My dear..." he said, and knelt beside her chair, drawing her into his arms. "You're over-wrought, love. You cannot mean what you say! It's our lives, dear one, yours and mine. Can't you forget Mathew? Can't you trust yourself to me?"

She was weeping now, quietly, her cheek against his.

"You are fighting still, Mary? Nothing matters save that we love."

"Ah, no, no!" she sobbed.

"Listen, Mary! I want to take you home—to my home in Italy. I will be so good to you, dear—I swear it! I want to take you to find happiness. There is so little in the world, child, one should seize what comes gratefully. I want to take you to Venice. Do you know it, my dear? There is a house there, an old, old house, deserted now, where I was born.

"I have not seen it since my boyhood—oh, a long time ago, Mary! But it is there still, as it was left, awaiting my return. Do you think I have not dreamed of you there? I see you as its mistress, dear—its wonderful mistress. I see you in every room, in every corner of its gardens. And I want to go back there—with you. Ah, Mary, don't turn away! It would be the fulfilment of my dreams!"

She loosened the clasp about her with trembling fingers.

"Do not, oh, do not, my lord! I—I am not that kind of woman! I cannot... I cannot...!"

He carried her hands to his lips.

"Afraid, dear heart? Afraid, and with me?"

She looked sadly down into the tired, wistful eyes.

And you, Henry? What would you do there?" She touched his cheeks lingeringly. "You think to cast this fashionable life behind you, but I know it is impossible."

"Ah no, by God!" he cried. "Do you think it cures me? I hate every minute I spend in London when not at your side! I am sick unto death of the life we all lead. I want to start afresh, with you at my side!"

"I cannot! Don't ask me, Henry! Please, please be merciful! I want you to help me—you've always been—so kind! Don't fail me now!"

He still held her hands.

"What is it you want of me?" he asked. His voice had sunk back into its level sweetness.

"Separate them. Hurry, for my sake! It—it is the last thing I shall ask of you." She pressed his fingers, leaning forward. "You could win her from him,

Henry! You could!"

He seemed to shrug.

"For how long? A month? A day? An hour?"

"Long enough, my dearest. Just to give me back my brother! You could do it!"

"Ay, I could do it. Do you know what it means? It means feigning a love I do not feel. I must hold her in my arms as I hold you now, and I must kiss her painted lips. Have you thought what that means, Mary?"

Her head was bowed.

"She is your wife," she whispered.

"And you are my love."

"You would make me—your mistress."

He did not answer, and for a long while nothing broke the stillness save the crackle of the wood in the hearth. It was my lord who spoke first.

"So this is the end," he said wistfully. "We might have been so happy, dear."

She shook her head dumbly. He sighed.

"Well… what now, Mary?"

"My lord—if you would but—send him back to me!"

"'Tis only Sophia can do that, love."

"You could—induce her. Henry—for my sake!"

"For your sake…" He touched her hair caressingly. "Very well, child. He shall be sent back to you, but 'twill be the end. There can then be nothing more between us. You know that."

"It—is best," she answered dully. Suddenly she caught at his shoulders. "You won't—think hardly of me? I love you so, my lord! I love you so!"

For a minute she lay against his heart, clinging to him. Then she drew herself away resolutely.

"Please—go now, my lord. You will find them together—as always. Please go!"

He rose, she also. She gave him her hands, and for a long moment he held them, looking down into her brave eyes. Then he bent and kissed the quivering fingers very tenderly.

"God keep you, child—and give you—happiness."

"And you," she whispered, broken-hearted.

II.

HE walked home through the clearing fog, his hand clenched on his snuffbox, his cloak swinging open from his shoulders. Someone hailed him from across the street, but he neither saw nor heard. He was thinking drearily of what lay before him.

His wife for six years… He remembered her as she had been when first they were married. He thought of her sensual desire for emotion, her hysterics, the luxury of her repentances. He had gone through all that. A hundred times she had transgressed, a hundred times returned to his arms, lapped in yet another sensation.

He had tried to hold her, God knew! but she would not have it so. Then, at last, sick to death of the constant quarrels, of the unrestrained reconciliations, worn out with the anxiety of trying to hold a wife whose heart was too shallow for constancy, he had given up the never-ending struggle.

For three years now they had met as chance acquaintances, although she lived still in his house, spending his money. He allowed her to tread her own path so that he might have peace… Then Mary, with her sweet mouth and her steadfast eyes. That was over too. He must take back Sophia for Mary's sake, bear with her moods, submit to her caresses.

Mr. Hatton was in the boudoir with my lady. Lord Farquhar was indifferent to the curious glance the footman bestowed on him. He threw down his hat and cloak and walked to the great carven-oak staircase. He mounted it slowly, one waxen hand on the baluster, dreading the scene that awaited him. Every fibre of his body was shrinking from it, but his face was impassive as ever, the eyes quietly cynical, deadly tired.

He opened the door and went in, shutting it behind him. He stood looking at his wife, and at Mathew, bending over her.

The air was heavy with some sickly perfume, the room over-furnished and almost voluptuous. Sophia sat on a cushioned couch by the fire, richly dressed in bright-hued silks, cut low across her thin chest. She was not yet thirty, but only traces of the beauty that had been hers remained.

Her cheeks were raddled by the paint she laid on them, her eyes were haggard and restless, tired as his own were from endless gaieties and uncontrolled emotions. She saw him, and cried out, paling beneath her rouge.

"La! You startled me, I vow! Indeed, and what brings you to my room thus unexpectedly? I should be honoured, I suppose!" Her voice was nervous, high-pitched and jangling.

Young Hatton sprang up, defiant.

"My lord, I—"

Farquhar held up one hand, silencing him. Emeralds glittered on it, and diamonds. He walked forward, pressing his handkerchief to his lips. His hand was very steady. He began to speak in his sweet, deliberate voice. My lady was conscious once again of his wonderful fascination. She caught her breath, listening.

"There was once a man, Mr. Hatton, who desired always to act well in the eyes of the world. Alack, he was but a frail creature, and it seems at every turn he failed. He married a lady"—his eyes flickered to Sophia's face—"very beautiful, very charming. He loved her, Mr. Hatton, but in some way or other things went awry between them. There was another man—a boy—too young for such pastimes."

"My lord—"

"Ah, hush!... The husband came home one day, and found this man—with his wife." Again, Farquhar touched his lips with the handkerchief. Sophia was watching him closely, leaning forward, eyes gleaming, a red spot on either cheekbone. "I have said, Mr. Hatton, that he desired always to do that which was best."

Sophia spoke, her unmusical voice contrasting strangely with his.

"And the end of the story, my lord? The end?"

"Was between the husband, my dear, and his wife."

She flushed deeper, glancing from one to the other of the two men.

"I don't understand the meaning of this rigmarole," cried Hatton. "What part does the other man play—in the end?"

My lord withdrew his gaze from my lady's face. His eyes rested on the younger man's face almost compassionately.

"None, Mr. Hatton. Between that husband and his wife that other man was, you see, nothing."

"That, my lord, is for Sophia to say! Not you!"

"A man and his wife are one," replied Farquhar gently. "But let her speak, if you wish it."

Mathew flung round to my lady's side. She put up her hand, warding him off, she was looking at her husband, uncertain yet, but suppressedly eager.

"You have me at a disadvantage, Henry. This new attitude sits strangely on your shoulders, after these years of neglect."

"It is as I said, my dear. I have desired to act well by you. But somehow things have gone awry. You know best how far I am to blame. I desire now to set things right between us."

She sprang up jerkily, her thin bosom panting.

"I don't understand you! You wish everything to be—as once it was? You?"

He took her hand.

"Is it not possible, Sophia?"

Mathew brushed forward.

"By heaven, Sophia—"

She waved him aside. Beside my lord he was as nothing.

"Oh, you weary me! Be silent, pray!"

The boy fell back.

"You—you tell me—to go?"

She stamped petulantly.

"It was but a game! I am tired of it! Leave me! Leave me!"

Again Farquhar glanced at Mathew with that same compassion. Mathew turned to him.

"My friends will wait on you, my lord!"

My lord smiled faintly.

"My dear lad, that is for me to say. And I do not say it. Go now."

Mathew flushed angrily.

"You think me a blackguard, sir—"

"No."

"—but what of yourself? This magnanimity becomes you not at all. Do you think I am ignorant and—" He stopped, and under my lord's steady gaze his eyes sank. He grew redder, and muttered beneath his breath.

"You are very young," said Farquhar. "One day perhaps you will understand a little. Go now."

Hatton strode to the door. With his hand on the knob he turned.

"One thing, Lord Farquhar, I wish to make clear to you! As your doors are closed to me, so are mine to you!" There was triumph in his look, but my lord only nodded:

"Ay."

He waited for Hatton to go out, then he sighed and released his wife's hand.

III.

MY lady's eyes brimmed slowly with easy tears. Her hands fidgeted with her kerchief; her mouth was twisted.

"Henry...!" There was a sob in her voice. Suddenly she sank down on the floor beside the couch, her face buried in the cushions, luxuriant in grief. Her shoulders shook with a tempest of sobs, noisy, unrestrained.

My lord watched her for a moment, his lips firmly together. Seeing her thus and listening to her weeping brought back so many past scenes akin to this. An hour on and he would have forgotten her tears, even the cause of them. A feeling of nausea stole over him; he wanted to fling open the windows, to let the heavy sickly perfume escape. His thoughts carried him to the quiet room from which he had come with only the fresh scent of flowers in the air, and only a still, great-hearted woman seated there by the fire...

He raised his hand to his eyes as if to shut out the sight of this picture, but let it fall again. He bent and touched his wife's powdered hair. Her hands clasped together, convulsively.

"Oh, God! Oh, God!"

"My dear..." he said, even pitifully. "Calm yourself, Sophia, I beg of you."

"It is you who have brought me to this! It is you, you, you!"

"Hush, Sophia! The servants will hear you. Has there not been scandal enough?"

"It is your coldness!" she sobbed passionately. "You do not love me! You have never loved me!"

"Never, my dear? Have you forgotten?"

She seemed to sink deeper and deeper into her sea of misery.

"You'll say 'twas my fault! You never understood me! Never knew me!"

"I tried, Sophia. I did my best—only it was never good enough. Can we not—start again?"

"You don't mean it! You don't really love me!"

He was silent.

"God help me! Oh, God help me! I am so unhappy! You never made me happy! You never tried! You never understood! You are cruel!"

He knew that it was hopeless to soothe her. He drew away to the fire and stood with his hand on the mantel-shelf, staring down into the blaze. On the floor by the couch Sophia wept on, alternately pouring forth recriminations and broken appeals for forgiveness.

But presently her sobs abated, and she crouched listless on the thick carpet. Then he went to her, and raised her. It was the old routine; the three past years might not have been. He brought her her salts, and sat beside her, holding her hand. At last she opened her eyes.

"You want to take me back?" she asked, husky from crying.

"Yes, Sophia. Have we drifted too far?"

"Oh, no, no, no! I am a wicked woman, but I *will* be better! Oh, Henry, take me away! It is London that gives me these megrims, and the worry—the dreadful worry! The dice—the cards—I cannot help it—forgive me! oh, forgive me!"

"It is forgiven, Sophia. Don't speak of it again."

"How good you are! I worship you! Oh, you will take me away, before I ruin you with my play! God knows we have come near it!"

"Hush, dear! Yes, I will take you away."

She flicked her hand across her eyes.

"Yes, oh yes! These joys are killing me—I never go abroad, you have never taken me; you would never! It was unkind, Henry! Unkind!"

"Yes, Sophia, it was unkind. But I will take you now."

She sat up, already smiling.

"I want to go to Italy! Lady Pamela Palmer went, and my dearest Kitty, last year. Oh, how I *longed* to go!" She caught his hands. "And you—why, you are half Italian! Farquhar, you've a title—an Italian title! And an estate! That is where I will go! Oh, say you will take me!"

He pulled his hands away.

"No, not there!" For the first time since he had entered the room his voice lost its even tone. It sounded harsh even to his ears. "Anywhere but there!" He got up and went back to the fire.

The jealous, peevish light sprang to her eyes again. She sank back on to the cushions with a long wail of discontent.

"Oh, you do not love me! You refuse me the one thing I ask!"

He winced.

"For God's sake, Sophia, no more hysterics!" he said sharply.

She quivered and burst into tears.

"Go away, go away! You don't care, it's nothing to you! Oh, I am miserable!"

"Sophia, anywhere but there! Paris, Vienna—where you will, but leave me that one—" He broke off, pressing his handkerchief to his lips.

"No, no, no! I want to go to Venice! Oh, is it so much to ask?"

My lord straightened himself. Once again he was quiet and collected.

"No, my dear, it is not much. I will take you."

She sprang up, her silks crumpled and her hair in disorder.

"Ah—!" She came to him, and he saw that the tears had made ugly marks on her painted cheeks. "Now I know that you love me!" She swayed towards him, and mechanically he took her in his arms. She heaved a great sigh, full of triumph. "You do care, don't you, Henry?" she murmured, and stole her hands up to his shoulders. Her face was upturned, expectant.

He hesitated a moment, fighting his sudden repulsion. Then he bent his head and brushed his lips against hers. She closed her eyes, leaning on him.

"Ah!" she sighed again. "Now I know! This—is Love!"

He looked down at her, but for a fleeting instant it seemed to him that it was Mary's face he saw, grave and steadfast, bravely smiling. He drew a deep breath.

"Ay," he said slowly. He still looked down at her, but now he only saw a painted, sharpened face that filled him with something akin to hatred. He raised his head, looking over hers into space. His voice grew softer. "This—is indeed—Love."

THE END

READING "LOVE"

Angst. That single word could well be this story's title – and blurb. It's all Scarlett O'Hara selfish histrionics and Sydney Carton "It is a far, far better thing I do" self-sacrifice and while I very much admire the skill with which Heyer somehow manages to evoke my sympathies for the cheating Lord Farquhar, I am much more interested in how she managed to make both the women in this story utterly unlikeable.

First, we have Mary. (Ha! Another Mary!) Mary is having an – at least – emotional affair with Lord Farquhar, and is on intimate enough terms with him that she calls him "Henry," but Lord Farquhar's troubled, coquettish wife has ensnared Mary's impressionable brother in her toils and the only way that she can be persuaded to release him is if Henry woos her back to his side and, presumably, bed. So Mary, knowing how much Henry loves her and hates his wife, throws him to the wolves – or, she-wolf, at least – in order to save her brother from a fate that he could very easily avoid if he just didn't hit on married women. Which you wouldn't think would be too hard.

So Lord Farquhar (I really, really want to type Lord Farquaad every time his name comes up), after some grousing and an unsubtle suggestion of elopement and lifelong adultery, goes home and finds brother Mathew in his wife's bedchamber, which is totally normal and everything's fine, which we know because we've read about cicisbeos in a dozen Heyer novels. But our Henry makes a big deal about it and pretends he cares, tricking his long-neglected wife into thinking maybe he might care for her, and sure, she's immature and manipulative and clearly unstable, but if you had a husband who was palpably bored and/or disgusted by you and who won't take you to his childhood home and who also has spent at least several months demonstrably in love with another woman, might not you also be kind of a wreck? Might that not be a good reason for some sympathy?

Not according to Heyer. According to this story, Lady Farquhar (interestingly, the story mostly refers to her as Sophia, as though disassociating her from even her husband's name) is greatly at fault for even such declarations as "I am so unhappy! You never made me happy! You never tried! You never understood! You are cruel!" even though we can tell that she's probably right, he never really did try, for all that he claims to have loved her once, that she was "inconstant," that he was "never good enough." There are two sides to every story, of course, but what we see very clearly from Henry is that he has indeed been so "cruel" to his wife as to actively seek out the company of a woman to whom he was attracted, enough that he grew to fall in love with this woman and offer to throw away everything, including his wife and her reputation, all for the illicit thrill of it.

It's all very well to be all noble and "I will give you up to save your brother" about it, except *you have a wife and it's the eighteenth century and all these broken hearts are entirely your fault, Farquhar!*

I am feeling very emotional about this story.

It's all made worse, of course, because Henry is so very articulate and cutting and clever. He's another Andover/Avon effort, a specialty of Heyer's – *The Talisman Ring*'s Ludovic Lavenham, *Cotillion*'s Lord Legerwood, *Frederica*'s Lord Alverstoke, among so many others, have the gift – except not when he's with Mary, there he's all ardent schoolboy, as callow as brother Mathew defiantly declaring himself attached to Sophia. But have him contemplate his fate as a husband, newly invested in his marriage at his true love's behest and confront the youngster who is the reason for his predicament, and he's all icy looks and cool remarks and of course Sophia went looking for love in all the wrong places, you're a passive aggressive asshole!

Wait, I'm supposed to feel sorry for him, right?

I don't.

As far as I'm concerned, he deserves his fate.

Everyone here does.

– *Rachel Hyland*

THE SEARCH FOR "ON SUCH A NIGHT"

Here's what I knew.

In 1935, Georgette Heyer sold a short story entitled "On Such a Night" to an Australian magazine.

And that's pretty much it.

That's all I knew.

That's all anyone knew.

What the story was about, even what era it was set in, no one had any idea. The first I heard of it was a brief mention in my dear Jennifer Kloester's seminal 2011 work, *Georgette Heyer: Biography of a Bestseller*, and I had been intrigued enough then to have checked out multiple microfilm recordings of some of the bigger women's magazines of my nation from that time – the *Australian Women's Weekly*, the *Australian Woman's Mirror, Australian Woman's World* – spending hours and hours and *hours* at the State Library of Victoria to see if I might stumble upon this lost gem, like Indiana Jones seeking the Holy Grail, but marginally less dusty.

My hunt went unrewarded, unsurprisingly, and it was years later that I again got involved in the search, when I began to plumb the depths of digitized back catalogues around the world for all things Heyer-related that might be of interest to readers of *Heyer Society*, both the book and website. In the course of this investigation I stumbled across "The Chinese Shawl" printed in *The Quiver* – previously, the only known version was a Danish-language translation – and, riding high on that discovery, went further and came upon a listing in the radio program guide printed in the *Sydney Morning Herald* for Monday, December 6, 1937 that read:

11.45 - Story: "On Such a Night" by Georgette Heyer

Woah. Really?

This was new information.

If nothing else, we now knew that "On Such a Night" was short enough that it could be read aloud in fifteen minutes.

The station it was broadcast on was Sydney's 2GB, and armed with this knowledge, a new avenue of research opened up. The game was afoot! I was filled with a new zeal—could I actually be the one to crack this mystery, all these years after my first attempt? After Jen, and so many learned others, had already attempted it? And could it be that it would go beyond ceaselessly sifting through microfilm and delicate copies of long-ago publications, but I'd be able to chat to radio buffs about the history of the medium, as well?

My first stop, of course, was 2GB, to inquire if perhaps they had archives going back that far. When my initial e-mail went unanswered for a month, I called into their offices, only to be told by a disinterested operator that they did not have either physical copies nor transcripts of their programs from further back than the 1970s. Fair enough.

I then reached out to Ian O'Toole, curator of the Sydney-based Kurrajong Radio Museum, with whom I had a most instructive chat about how radio stations used to record their programs – on pressed vinyl discs similar to LP records, but much larger – and how they would then dispose of them indiscriminately when their storage capacity was reached. The hitch in his voice was obvious when he told the anecdote of how a Brisbane station manager would take his employees down to the banks of the river on Friday afternoons and they would frisbee years-old broadcasts into the water. I'm a collector of the old and rare myself, so that tale of thoughtless, wanton destruction similarly affected me.

Ian's collection, sadly, did not boast the needful, but he sent me to the National Film and Sound Archive of Australia, in the hope that there might be something there. Within hours I heard back from Zsuzsi Szucs (which has got to be one of the greatest names ever, not to mention a phenomenal Scrabble score), the institute's collection coordinator, who regretfully told me that they only had four 2GB recordings from the period, and none were what I was seeking – and, of course, the odds of that being the case would have been pretty astronomical. Then she sent me links to the short story collection *Snowdrift* and Georgette Heyer's Wikipedia page, which I am sure was very kindly meant.

It was quite heartening to learn that that of the four 2GB radio recordings still in existence, however, all were radio dramas, and I found the listings for them on Trove, the National Library of Australia's digital collection, in radio magazine *Wireless Weekly*, which began publication in 1922 and – astonishingly – only came to an end in 2001, then under the title *Electronics Australia*. I dove into the *Wireless Weekly* edition for the day of the "On Such a Night" broadcast, and discovered yet more information I didn't have before: the story was read over the airwaves by one Dorothea Vautier. To wit:

11.45: Dorothea Vautier—On Such a Night, by Georgette Heyer (Story)

Oooh! Now we had a name!

But who the hell was Dorothea Vautier?

It turned out that she was something of a radio glamour girl of 1930s Sydney radio. She became host of the *Australian Women's Weekly* radio sessions in 1935, first on 2UW and then 2GB, and was hailed by *Wireless Weekly* as "one of Sydney's most attractive broadcasters" in 1938. Now, given that the *Australian Women's Weekly* had a positive addiction to serializing Georgette Heyer's novels, as well as publishing several of her short stories over the years, and that Dorothea Vautier read the story, one might have thought that the "Australian magazine" mentioned in Jen's biography, and to which the story was initially sold was, in fact, the *Women's Weekly* all along. Maybe they just forgot to publish it, and only aired it on the radio? Because I had personally checked every edition of the magazine from the entirety of 1935 – 1940, as had Jen, as had others, and it simply wasn't there.

So *where* was this story published? And if it wasn't in the *Women's Weekly*, why was their radio-based poster girl the one to read it on air?

Next, it was time to look into Dorothea Vautier. Was there the slightest chance she was still alive? And, total long shot time, would it be possible that she, or her heirs, could have archives of her radio career that included the story, or even that she might perhaps remember what the story – that she read aloud, once, eighty-two years ago – was about?

I could only ask, right? But first, I had to find her.

Was she the Dorothea Vautier who produced a slim volume of stories and poems, circa. 1931, entitled *The Story of Teddy Koala*, with illustrations by Noel Burnet of Koala Park? Sadly, no dedication page or identifying information is present in that book, but it seemed likely.

I thought I was on her track, when I found a listing on familytreecircles.com, tantalizingly detailing the marriage of one Dorothea May Vautier. But when I dug further, that Miss Vautier married a Charles Roger Darvall in Victoria in 1931, and further reading in the *Wireless Weekly* archive led to the news that our Dorothea Vautier was married to one Bill Power, and moreover that in 1939 she had moved to the US to try her hand at radio announcing over there.

For a while I thought she might be the Dorothea Vautier I found on a listing at Ancestry.com, but that one was born in 1908 in Charlton, in country Victoria and died in 1977 in Richmond, a suburb of Melbourne, her father Alfred Clark Vautier, and mother Willamena Sarah Klug. A profile of Vautier from *Wireless Weekly*, however, cited her as the daughter of C. A. Vautier, a well-known New Zealand architect, so she was clearly not the Victorian Dorothea. And I still did not know when (or if?) she had died.

But wait! A *Wireless Weekly* "Portrait Gallery" from December 1933 – captioned "The first portrait of a woman announcer to be published in our series" – included the news that back then Vautier was married to Mr. F. W. L. Esch, a somewhat radical Sydney journalist. And, among other outlets, Esch wrote for *The Australian Women's Weekly*! He covered New Books, as well as writing some feature articles. (My favourite: "Eating of Sugar Once Was Terribly Wicked!" – an article written in 1934, and of which echoes can be found in paleo blogs and the like across the internet to this day.)

For all his works, however, not much is now known of Mr. Esch's life and times. I know he was still alive in 1976, because a founding member of the D. H. Lawrence Society of Australia spoke to him regarding Lawrence's visit to our shores, something Esch had researched as early as the mid-1950s, and which is very intriguing in its own right.

And I know he is now dead, because artworks from his estate were sold in 2014.

But, this is interesting! Turns out the Bill Power to whom Dorothea was married in 1939 is William Power, a playwright and "brilliant radio dramatist" (cf. *Wireless Weekly*) who also worked at 2GB. Wonder if they moved to America to avoid the scandal, when she left the journalist for the dramatist? Was divorce still scandalous in 1939?

Then, in 1940, Vautier was working for CBS radio. And then: nothing. I can't even find an obituary for a Dorothea Power anywhere, let alone a Vautier or an Esch.

So, she's vanished from the record, best I can tell.

But yes, she did write the book about the koala.

IT seemed like the radio angle, at first so tantalising, was going to be a dead end. (Or, in Dorothea Vautier's case, a presumed dead end.) So next I returned to the microfilm that had typified my long-ago forays into "On Such a Night" research, spending many, many more hours at the State Library immersing myself in the magazines of yesteryear.

Magazines that were full of the "ex-King," Edward VIII-turned-Duke of Windsor who abdicated the throne for love, long-forgotten matinee idols and the "Quins" – the Dionne Quintuplets, born in Canada in 1934 – while the newspapers carried news of Japanese war efforts and the rise of Adolf Hitler in Germany (while many book review sections give a disconcerting number of column inches to thoughts on *Mein Kampf*, which I never thought of as having been translated and sold under the English title *My Struggle*, but yeah, it was), and advertisements exhorted the joys of "damp setting" one's hair and the miracle food that was the "rindless" and "completely digestible" Kraft Cheese. There were short stories by H. G. Wells, and book reviews of the newly-released *Gone with the Wind*, and reference to a host of long-forgotten and out-of-print authors who were once so prolific and popular – just another reminder of how rare it is that Georgette Heyer's works have so long outlasted her, when so many of her contemporaries have fallen by the wayside. She's certainly up there with Wells and Margaret Mitchell, at any rate.

The problem with all this was, once I had rechecked the *Women's Weekly* and its well-known competitors – many of which were now digitized on Trove – I was at something of a loss of where to look next. What I needed was some kind of listing of all the likely publications that would have been in print at the time. A concordance of women's and literary magazines, that would have done nicely. In vain did I search, until I at last had the happy notion of asking a librarian for help.

I know. I'm a genius.

"Excuse me," I said to one of the experts at the help desk. "I'm not sure how to find this, but I'm looking for a listing of all the women's... and I guess also literary," I remembered *The Quiver*, "magazines that might have been published in Australia in the mid- to late-1930s."

She got a deer in the headlights expression. "I... you know, I think we used to have a list like that." She turned to her colleague. "Martin, do you remember that list of literary magazines we had? I think it'll be in the Australian literary magazines file."

Martin went off to dig it out, and Kirsty – for such was her name – began an extensive catalogue search for what I was after. "We have so many directories of so many magazines, but I just don't know if we have..." Her eyes opened wide, as she had a sudden realization. "You know, we have a... there's a kind of book for advertisers... I can't recall the title, but it was something like the *Newspaper and Magazine Guide*..." Feverishly, she began a new search, while Martin proudly handed me a grimy manila folder, slim and dispirited looking with a hand-written label that read "Literary Magazines – Australia." Not terribly hopeful, I looked inside to find several tissue paper-thin requests that dated back to the 1970s, from the National Library of Australia to assorted institutions asking to know their holdings in the genre, most of which did not seem to have received a reply. A list starkly labelled INCOMPLETE also stared back at me, as did a note about *If Revived*, a magazine that was issued fourteen times from 1949 – 1959, and the first editor of which was Rupert Murdoch.

This research was turning up all kinds of fascinating ephemera.

"*The Press Directory!*" a triumphant whisper-shout came from Kirsty at her desk, and I ran over to find her requesting the volumes from 1935 and 1938 for me, to be viewed the following day. "It's a pretty complete listing of the magazines and newspapers in print back then," she said sunnily. "Good luck!"

RETURNING the next day, I collected my *Press Directory* booty and painstakingly copied down the titles of each viable journal that I thought might conceivably play host to a lost Georgette Heyer story. I still couldn't quite understand why she might have sold the story to a magazine other than the *Women's Weekly*, her usual haunt on this side of the world, but she manifestly had not, so it had to be elsewhere.

My list of likely candidates wasn't as long as I had feared, but was also not as long as I had hoped. If there weren't many magazines in which it could have been printed – and surely many of them would be digitized already? – then the chances of finding "On Such a Night" grew exponentially smaller.

I identified about fifteen publications that might be potential hunting grounds, from *Adam and Eve* to *Woman*, and I began eliminating them by the simple expedient of first checking if they had already been digitized, and if they had not, combing through them issue by issue with painstaking and careful precision, one, two, even three rolls of microfilm, each covering at least six months of a publication, per session, ten days in a row. By the end of it, I'd searched nine publications in their entirety (for the most probable period), but some were unavailable at my location, and I'd variously need to travel to the State Library of New South Wales in Sydney, the State Library of Queensland in Brisbane and the National Library of Australia in Canberra in order to check those final possibilities off my list.

In the meantime, I had greatly enjoyed the search, and my immersion in that previous time. I'd loved seeing the articles on the changing roles of women, discovering new writers, seeing the gorgeous outfits on sale for ludicrous prices, and skimming over remarkably familiar-sounding advertorials on "slimming" and make up and "how to keep your man." (Often all three at once.)

But with my interstate trips now booked for a couple of weeks away, I decided to return to my radio-based search, figuring it wouldn't hurt to peruse the *Wireless Weekly*, in which Dorothea Vautier had so often and prominently been featured. It occurred to me then that I hadn't actually thought to look further into the magazine the week that "On Such a Night" was broadcast – maybe there'd been some kind of advertisement of the story in its pages? After all, Georgette Heyer was an ever-rising star in women's fiction at the time – and was already a best-seller in anyone's language – and so it seemed impossible to me that any story of hers would be given short shrift by any right-thinking editor and consigned either to the back of a magazine, or completely ignored by some lucky radio station's advertising department.

It was only as I began to sift through that edition of the *Wireless Weekly* did I notice an oddity. "On Such a Night" wasn't only broadcast on Monday, December 6, 1937; it was broadcast *every day* that week. Not on Saturday and Sunday, but every weekday, from Friday, December 3 through to Thursday, December 7. Now, it would make sense to maybe broadcast a short story multiple times, to give those who missed it a chance to tune in, the kind of thing TV networks used to invariably do before streaming and binge-watching came along and foiled their repeated episode model. But to repeat the story *every day* across two different weeks? That seemed… odd.

But then, fifteen minutes isn't very long. Perhaps "On Such a Night" was one of Heyer's longer short stories, and it required five days to complete the thing. Or… maybe even more days?

I called Jen. "So… this is weird," I said. "You know how I found 'On Such a Night' in the radio listing for that one day in 1937? I've now realized it was broadcast every day for that whole week."

"What?"

"So I'm wondering... could it be a short story we already know? Like, one of the longer ones – maybe even 'Lady, Your Pardon', which was published in the *Women's Weekly* in 1936? You did say that Heyer mentioned in her notes that she didn't remember a short of that title, and I know you've said that 'Pharaoh's Daughter' was the original title of that one, but could it be that 'On Such a Night' was her first stab at it—"

"No," Jen said definitively. "Because we have correspondence about her deciding what to call it: whether to say 'Faro' or 'Pharaoh'. And we know she was furious with *Woman's Journal* editor Dorothy Sutherland for renaming it, although I've never found it published there and have always thought that she must have made a mistake, and it must have been the *Women's Weekly* editor she should have been angry with. Wait, let me check..." After a moment, she is back, clearly with her primary source material at her fingertips. "Here we are, Georgette's list of her novel and story sales, typewritten by her, and with notes in her own hand."

"Wow."

"Yes, it's quite remarkable. And 'On Such a Night'... here it is, under short stories. Oh, that's interesting."

"What?"

"It says here it was sold to the *Australian Women's Weekly*."

"What?!"

"'Serial rights' to the *Australian Women's Weekly*." A pause. "She—she must have made a mistake... She *must* have. I've been through the whole of it—"

"Me too!"

"And so it *must* have been a different magazine. But why she would have—"

She trailed off, and there was a helpless silence as we both digested the implications of this.

"Let me take another look at the *Wireless Weekly*," I said, trying to remain positive, "and see what else I can find out about these broadcasts. I'll call you back."

Subsequently, I started digging into the following edition of the *Wireless Weekly*, and discovered that, actually, "On Such a Night" didn't just run for five days. It didn't even run for ten days. I kept going further and further forward in time, until at last I found that the last broadcast of "On Such a Night" on Radio 2GB took place on Friday, January 14, at 11:45 a.m.

Then I went backward, and found a *Wireless Weekly* listing for it on Friday, December 24, though no earlier. So not only had it been broadcast over more than one week, it had been broadcast in two separate *years*. I turned away from *Wireless Weekly*, and went back to the *Telegraph* radio programme listings. According to that source, "On Such a Night" by Georgette Heyer was first broadcast on Wednesday, November 17, 1937. And assuming it did indeed run every weekday until January 14, 1938, as the schedules seemed to indicate, then this "short story" was apparently read aloud on no fewer than forty-three days over the course of ten weeks. That was over ten hours of airtime dedicated to it—call it at least seven or eight hours, factoring in station ID and a jingle and probably commercials either side.

So either Dorothea Vautier *really* liked reading the same short story over and over again for a cumulative eight hours across more than two months.

Or this was no short story.

This was a novel.

I TOOK a look at the *Wireless Weekly* listing for Monday, January 17, the week after "On Such a Night" would have come to an end. In the same time slot the schedule simply read "Dorothea Vautier – Serial," but contemporary newspaper listings, and subsequent *Wireless Weekly* editions, have the title of it as *She Went to Paris* by Fanny Heaslip Lea, which was read until Thursday, February 24, 1938.

That slot was not for a short story read over and over. It was for a "Serial." Hell, after *She Went to Paris* came to an end, Vautier started reading out *Pride and Prejudice* for the next couple of months.

This *had* to be a book.

I called Jen, and explained what I had discovered.

"Then *why* does she have it listed under her short stories?" she cried, exasperated. The whereabouts of this "lost" Heyer short story had been puzzling her for more than a decade.

I sighed.

"I don't know…" I thought some more. "Wait. Let me go and check all the Heyer stories and novels that the *Women's Weekly* published. Then I'll also check to see if there are any ads for Dorothea Vautier's radio sessions in the *Weekly* itself."

A minute's searching in Trove and I came across and an ad in the for the first episode of *She Went to Paris* that simply read:

WEDNESDAY, January 19 – 11.45 a.m.: Serial (a modern romance).

I was exultant. Perhaps, I thought with mounting excitement, the *Weekly* will have a similar listing for "On Such a Night." Perhaps we can, if nothing else, at last learn the genre of this long-lost story!

Less than fifteen minutes of paging through back issues later, searching for the unobtrusive text boxes tucked away toward the back of the magazine in which were listed the programming for the *Women's Weekly* Radio Sessions on 2GB each week, and I had my answer. The listing read:

WEDNESDAY, November 17 – 11.45 a.m.: Serial (romantic thriller).

Oh my.

So, not only was it now confirmed that this – which the *Wireless Weekly* and Sydney newspapers of the time gave under the title "On Such a Night," and persisted in calling a "story" – was in fact a *serial*, but also that its genre was "romantic thriller."

I started flipping back through the *Wireless Weekly*, and soon found this confirmatory nugget, in the "Broadcasting Gossip" section of the November 26 issue that I had foolishly overlooked:

> *Dorothea Vautier is the latest to join the ranks of serial readers. Each week day at 11.45 a.m. she is reading "On Such a Night" from the pen of the ever-popular Georgette Heyer.*

Had I found that earlier, I would have known we were dealing with a serial and *not* a short story, despite what Georgette's notes might erroneously claim. It must be one of the detective novels, I thought in resignation. Or perhaps *The Talisman Ring?*

Seriously? Has "On Such a Night" really just been *The Talisman Ring* this whole time?

Maddening.

I applied myself to some simple deduction, in order to figure out which of the novels it could possibly be, going back through the *Women's Weekly*'s enormous Heyer-based output.

Death in the Stocks was printed, in an abridged form, as a "book-length novel" in the *Women's Weekly* in June of 1935, and *The Unfinished Clue* received the same treatment in August of that same year. Those would both tally with the 1935 sale date of this so-called *On Such a Night* – but Heyer's notes, according to Jen, had said "serial rights," and neither of those were serialized.

Behold, Here's Poison! was, however, printed in instalments from November 23, 1940 – February 1, 1941, having been published in book-form in 1936, which would kind of fit in with all the available dates – might Heyer might have pre-sold the rights to that novel to the *Weekly* in 1935, and then changed the title before the book's publication? ("No," said Jen. "The Shakespearean allusion of the title was always very important to that book.")

And the question must be asked: does "On Such a Night" even work with that novel, as a title? And can the novel we know as *Behold, Here's Poison!* really be classed as a "romantic thriller"?

Looking at what the *Women's Weekly* had to say about the serials when they published them, they stigmatized *Behold, Here's Poison* as merely a "mystery serial", while *The Talisman Ring*, which was serialized in the magazine from December 5, 1936 – February 13, 1937, is variously called "our thrilling new serial", "our brilliant serial of romance and adventure in an old-world setting" (catchy!), "our romantic serial of love and adventure" and "our splendid adventure-romance serial."

Although, *An Infamous Army*, also advertised as "thrilling", was likewise serialised in the *Weekly*, beginning January 22, 1938, just a week after this alleged *On Such a Night* concluded, but since it was not published until 1937, it seems a stretch that even so clever a rights-seller as Heyer could have meant that when she referred to the 1935 sale.

Unless she made a mistake with the sale date, as well.

What is so frustrating about this is that, announcing the change to their programming that came about on Wednesday, November 17, the day "On Such a Night" began to air, the *Weekly* makes a big deal about the new 2:45pm "Homemaker" segment, hosted by one Mrs. Eve Gye, but annoyingly off-handedly mentions "another new feature will be a serial" and mentions the time, but nothing about the title chosen for this first-time honour.

Months later, *Pride and Prejudice* gets namechecked. But Heyer, who at this point had had no fewer than four short stories – "Runaway Match," "Lady, Your Pardon" (aka "Pharaoh's Daughter"), "Love is a Hazard" (aka "Hazard") and "Pursuit" – published in the *Weekly*, had had three of her novels serialized and two others published in full (if abridged) form, barely rates a mention.

It's like they were actively *trying* to confuse us.

I CALLED Jen with my working theory. I told her that I thought that when Heyer sold the serial rights to *Death in the Stocks* – which is both thrilling and quite romantic, given all the pairing off that goes on – to the *Australian Women's Weekly*, she'd decided to use the title *On Such a Night*. Then either she or her publishers went with *Death in the Stocks* instead – retitled *Merely Murder*, in the US – but in her accounting she continued to refer to it by its original name. The *Weekly*, meanwhile, had decided not to serialize the book, after all, but to print it as an abridged full-length novel, so they had to purchase the rights again, this time to print it in its entirety, and therefore under its new title. But they still had the serial rights to it as *On Such a Night*, so when they broadcast it on the radio, they used the original title instead of the updated version—perhaps for legal reasons; perhaps because radio standards and practice wouldn't allow the word "death" to be bandied about in an 11:45 am timeslot; or perhaps it was even a ploy to trick people into listening to it, thinking it was a new Heyer story they had yet to read – like when *Envious Casca* was recently reissued under the title *A Christmas Party* for no discernible reason.*

At that point, Jen was flabbergasted, but also resigned. It seemed an elegant enough theory that fit all the facts, except for the title change, which

Jen couldn't quite buy. "I don't think Georgette would have allowed a title change," she said.

"She did in the American version," I contended. "Not to mention how *The Corinthian* became *Beau Wyndham* over there, as well."

"True."

A DAY later, Jen called me. She'd gone into full literary detective mode, and trawled back through the Heyer Archive – both the cache of letters held by the University of Tulsa and the papers given over to her by Heyer's son Richard – to see if she could help confirm my hypothesis.

Instead, she blew it out of the water.

"I think it's *They Found Him Dead*," she said excitedly.

"Really? But, the *Women's Weekly* never published it as a serial. Why would they have broadcast it on the radio?"

A faint buzz grew at the back of my brain, about that particular book and the UK's *Woman's Journal*, which I remembered from Jen's Heyer biography. As I recalled, it had not been serialized there, but was supposed to be, and there had been some hard feelings as a result.

"Well, listen to this letter Heyer wrote to her agent's assistant in January of 1937," said Jen.

Here is that letter – which is partially quoted in Jen's Heyer biography – printed in full:

> *Dear Norah*
>
> *I'll sign the contract & send it back to you as soon as Ronald has seen it. It looks to me a very fair sort of an agreement, & I suspect your hand has been at work on some of the clauses. I will also send you back the proofs so that you will get them on Monday.*
>
> *I have been thinking over the situation with regard to the serial rights, & I think Miss Sutherland might well be jolted. She really is not treating me at all fairly. When you consider that I rushed the book on so that she might receive it early in December, & further made alterations in the story at her request, & handed them in three days before Christmas, her dilatoriness is not only inconsiderate but extremely rude into the bargain. I do not wish to hear from her that the altered succession is to blame. I don't doubt that it has given her a lot of work to do, but I can hardly believe that her papers are to be allowed to lapse because of it. Presumably they are all appearing just as usual. Saving your presence, she is treating me to a startling example of the folly of Woman at the Helm. A bigger example of incompetence than this going into a flat spin would be hard to come by. All she has to do is to read through the first 4 chapters, as corrected by me (or to delegate this task to a subordinate) which will occupy perhaps half an hour of her valuable time.*
>
> *I should like to make a point quite clear to the lady. If she reads an M.S. of mine &, disliking it, turns it down, I have no cause for complaint. But when*

she holds my M.S. from the beginning of December to the middle of January without giving me any definite reply, & in the knowledge that by so doing she is ruining all chance of finding another market for it I have a great deal of cause for complaint.

It would be as well if she were to ask herself whether I am very likely to offer her any further stories. And I will take the opportunity to repeat in writing what I think I said to you the other day: If Miss Sutherland refuses the M.S., or postpones its publication in serial form to the prejudice of H. &S's publication of it in book form no further MSs of mine are to be offered to her. I am now working on the Waterloo** book, which, though not precisely a sequel, follows on to Regency Buck. If she wants this she'd better get a move on with They Found Him Dead. If she doesn't – well, she knows what to do about it.

If she finds it incredible that I should be prepared to sever relations with her you can, if you choose, tell her that her handling of my work has from start to finish been an annoyance to me; her criticisms always seem to me illiterate, & her alterations even more so. Accompany these compliments by any rude gesture that suggests itself to you.

If she pulls herself together, & sends you a cheque, I think she might as well have the Waterloo book.

But as she doesn't seem to me to like my mysteries I should much prefer to tackle a different market for the next. I shall do my best to let you have it in good time, so that you will have plenty of opportunity to find another opening.

** This is *An Infamous Army*, of course. And *Woman's Journal* never did end up serializing it.

Wow. Leaving aside the "folly of Woman at the Helm" crack, which had been quoted in the biography – oh, Georgette! – this letter helped make a few things more abundantly clear. One, *They Found Him Dead* was under option as a serial to *Woman's Journal* as early as December 1936, months before its publication in May of 1937. (This makes sense, since the purpose of these serials was to drum up interest in, and sales of, the novels when they were released, so they would necessarily have to be organized far in advance of each book's launch). Two, *Woman's Journal* editor Dorothy Sutherland did not think it was good enough as-is, and asked Heyer to make some considerable changes before it could be published in her august pages. Three, we already know that Sutherland had a propensity for altering Heyer's titles – hence *Gay Adventure* instead of *Regency Buck* – and so could very well have changed the title of *They Found Him Dead*, especially as she wanted Heyer to "stress on the love interest" (*Georgette Heyer: Biography of a Bestseller*, pg. 163), perhaps making it into more of the "romantic thriller" that the 2GB radio sessions claimed: *They Found Him Dead* does have some romance, as do most Heyer works, but that designation does seem something of a stretch for it as it exists to us, quite honestly. And then there is this, also from Jen's biography:

> *In December, King Edward VIII abdicated to marry Mrs. Wallis Simpson. The change in the Succession meant a change in Woman's Journal editorial policy. Dorothy Sutherland felt that a murder mystery was not wanted in an edition about the abdication and the Royal family and consequently had decided not to serialize They Found Him Dead.*

It was in response to this move that the above-printed letter was so furious – and, as the biography points out, it would be ten years before *Woman's Journal* got to serialize another Heyer work.

But none of that really explained how the *Australian Women's Weekly* ended up serializing *on the radio* a book that was probably *They Found Him Dead* under an alternate title most likely bestowed by Dorothy Sutherland.

Jen and I discussed this at length, over a number of days, eventually referring once more to the original sales list on which the discovery of "On Such a Night" as a "short story" hung. The list, in part, read:

TITLE	SOLD TO	RIGHTS	LANGUAGE
HAZARD			
1936	Australian Women's Weekly	One Serial Use	Australian
1938	Ullstrated Familie Journal	"	Scandinavian
ON SUCH A NIGHT			
1935	Australian Women's Weekly	Serial rights	Australian
GAY ADVENTURE			
1935	Australian Women's Weekly	Serial rights	Australian

So, *Gay Adventure* was included in that list, and we know that was not a short story. And while the definite short story that is "Hazard" was sold to both the *Women's Weekly* and "Ullstrated" [sic] *Familie Journal* (most likely Danish publication *Illustreret Familie Journal*, aka *Familie Journalen*, also published in Sweden and Norway) for "One Serial Use," both the ersatz *On Such a Night* and *Gay Adventure* were sold as proper serials. (Let us also take note that "Scandinavian" and "Australian" are both, apparently, languages.)

Another piece of the puzzle. This was all coming together. Except…

"Hey! Why did the *Women's Weekly* title *Regency Buck* as *Gay Adventure* when they serialized it, when we know that it was *Woman's Journal*'s Dorothy Sutherland who changed the title? Why would that have happened? Are they related publications?"

"No, I don't think so."

"Hmm. So… what? Maybe the *Women's Weekly* used the same abridged version of the novel that *Woman's Journal* did? Maybe they even bought it from them, to save doing it themselves?"

"That's very possible."

"*And* since Dorothy Sutherland apparently liked retitling Heyer's works, maybe she also retitled *They Found Him Dead* as *On Such a Night*, and that is how the *Women's Weekly* bought it. But then Sutherland never published it, ostensibly because of the abdication—and perhaps the *Women's Weekly* never did either, for the same reason. But, unlike Sutherland, they never revoked their serial rights, because they really valued their relationship with Heyer, and so still paid for them. So when, a couple of years later, they were looking for a story to read aloud during their revamped radio sessions with Dorothea Vautier – and remember, the Heyer serial was the first one they broadcast in that timeslot, before that it was dedicated to sections from the magazine; it also seems to have been a pretty hasty decision on their part, given that they didn't have time to alert the *Wireless Weekly* to the change in programming in enough time for them to amend the listings – they dug it up out of their archives."

Silence. "That makes sense," Jen said.

AND with that, I am considering this case closed.

Because the upshot of all of this, after hours upon hours, across months and years, of exhaustive, exhausting research and obsessive cross-correlation, is that I am now one hundred percent convinced that "On Such a Night" never was. Most likely, Georgette (or her assistant, agent, or accountant – that portion of her records is type-written and could have been done by anyone) simply made a mistake when she listed the title under her "Short Story" sales, as she did with *Gay Adventure*, and neglected to note that it was an alternate title to an existing work. After all, what is more probable – that there is a whole other Georgette Heyer novel-length story out there, that she inexplicably sold only to an Australian magazine, and never had published in book form anywhere, at all; *or* that mistakes were made and titles were changed and incorrect listings were published and muddled records were kept, and *On Such a Night* is merely the title of a book we already know and (probably) love?

I vote the latter.

So is "On Such a Night" indeed *They Found Him Dead?* Or is it *Death in the Stocks?* Is it *The Talisman Ring?* Is this reasoning even more faulty, and it is indeed *An Infamous Army*, or *The Unfinished Clue?* Does it even matter?

Honestly, not a whit. In the final analysis, all that matters is that "On Such a Night" does not, in fact, exist.

But oh, how I wish it did.

– *Rachel Hyland*

* Turns out the reason was that Georgette Heyer's working title for *Envious Casca* was "Christmas Party" – and when the publishers at Random House found out that little tidbit from Jen, they decided it would make an excellent Christmas release.

GEORGETTE HEYER'S BIBLIOGRAPHY

Georgian Novels

The Black Moth (Constable, 1921)
The Transformation of Philip Jettan, aka *Powder and Patch* (Mills & Boon, 1923)
These Old Shades (William Heinemann, 1926)
The Masqueraders (William Heinemann, 1928)
Devil's Cub (William Heinemann, 1932)
The Convenient Marriage (William Heinemann, 1934)
The Talisman Ring (William Heinemann, 1936)
Faro's Daughter (William Heinemann, 1941)

Regency Novels

Regency Buck (William Heinemann, 1935)
An Infamous Army (William Heinemann, 1937)
The Spanish Bride (William Heinemann, 1940)
The Corinthian (William Heinemann, 1940)
Friday's Child (William Heinemann, 1944)
The Reluctant Widow (William Heinemann, 1946)
The Foundling (William Heinemann, 1948)
Arabella (William Heinemann, 1949)
The Grand Sophy (William Heinemann, 1950)
The Quiet Gentleman (William Heinemann, 1951)
Cotillion (William Heinemann, 1953)
The Toll-Gate (William Heinemann, 1954)
Bath Tangle (William Heinemann, 1955)
Sprig Muslin (William Heinemann, 1956)
April Lady (William Heinemann, 1957)
Sylvester, or the Wicked Uncle (William Heinemann, 1957)
Venetia (William Heinemann, 1958)
The Unknown Ajax (William Heinemann, 1959)
A Civil Contract (William Heinemann, 1961)
The Nonesuch (William Heinemann, 1962)
False Colours (The Bodley Head, 1963)
Frederica (The Bodley Head, 1965)
Black Sheep (The Bodley Head, 1966)
Cousin Kate (The Bodley Head, 1968)
Charity Girl (The Bodley Head, 1970)
Lady of Quality (The Bodley Head, 1972)

Historical Novels

The Great Roxhythe (Hutchinson, 1922)
Simon the Coldheart (William Heinemann, 1925)
Beauvallet (William Heinemann, 1929)
The Conqueror (William Heinemann, 1931)
Royal Escape (William Heinemann, 1938)
My Lord John (The Bodley Head, 1975)

Contemporary Novels

Instead of the Thorn (Hutchinson, 1923)
Helen (Longmans and Co., 1928)
Pastel (Longmans and Co., 1929)
Barren Corn (Longmans and Co., 1930)

Detective Novels

Footsteps in the Dark (Longmans and Co., 1932)
Why Shoot a Butler? (Longmans and Co., 1933)
The Unfinished Clue (Longmans and Co., 1934)
Death in the Stocks (Longmans and Co., 1935)
Behold, Here's Poison (Hodder & Stoughton, 1936)
They Found Him Dead (Hodder & Stoughton, 1937)
A Blunt Instrument (Hodder & Stoughton, 1938)
No Wind of Blame (Hodder & Stoughton, 1939)
Envious Casca (Hodder & Stoughton, 1941)
Penhallow (William Heinemann, 1942)
Duplicate Death (William Heinemann, 1951)
Detection Unlimited (William Heinemann, 1953)

Short Story Collections

Pistols for Two (William Heinemann, 1960)
Snowdrift and Other Stories (William Heinemann, 2016)

Short Stories

1.	A Proposal for Cicely	1922 Sep	*The Happy Mag*
2.	The Little Lady	1922 Dec	*The Red Magazine*
3.	Bulldog and the Beast	1923 Mar	*The Happy Mag*
4.	Linckes' Great Case	1923 Mar	*The Detective Magazine*
5.	Acting on Impulse	1923 Jun	*The Red Magazine*
6.	Whose Fault Was It?	1923 Aug	*The Happy Mag*
7.	Chinese Shawl	1923 Oct	*The Quiver*
8.	Love	1923 Nov	*Sovereign Magazine*
9.	The Old Maid	1925 Aug	*Woman's Pictorial*
10.	**Runaway Match	1936 Apr	*Woman's Journal*
11.	**Incident on the Bath Road	1936 May	*Woman's Journal*
12.	*Hazard	1936 Jun	*Woman's Journal*
13.	Lady, Your Pardon	1936 Apr	*Australian Women's Weekly*
14.	**Pursuit	1939 Nov	*Queen's Book of the Red Cross*
15.	*Snowdrift	1948 Nov	*The Illustrated London News*
16.	*Full Moon	1948 Nov	*Woman's Journal*
17.	*Pistols at Dawn	1949 Dec	*Woman's Journal*
18.	*Night at the Inn	1950 Mar	*John Bull*
19.	*A Husband for Fanny	1951 Nov	*The Illustrated London News*
20.	*Bath Miss	1952 Sep	*Good Housekeeping*
21.	*The Pursuit of Hetty	1953 Jun	*Good Housekeeping*
22.	*The Duel	1953 Feb	*Good Housekeeping*

23.	The Quarrel	1953 Dec	*Everywoman*
24.	*Pink Domino	1953 Dec	*Woman's Journal*
25.	*A Clandestine Affair	1960	Unknown

*Indicates those stories included in the Georgette Heyer anthology *Pistols for Two* (1960) in which the 1953 short story "The Pursuit of Hetty" was renamed "To Have the Honour".
** Indicates those additional stories added to the anthology when it was reissued as *Snowdrift and Other Stories* (2016).

FURTHER READING

Georgette Heyer: Biography of a Bestseller, Jennifer Kloester, William Heinemann, 2011
Georgette Heyer: A Critical Retrospective, Mary Fahnestock-Thomas, Prinny World Press, 2001
Georgette Heyer's Regency England, Teresa Chris, Sidgwick & Jackson, 1989
Georgette Heyer's Regency World, Jennifer Kloester, William Heinemann, 2005
Heyer Society – Essays on the Literary Genius of Georgette Heyer, Overlord Publishing, 2018
The Private World of Georgette Heyer, Jane Aiken Hodge, The Bodley Head, 1984
Reading Heyer: The Black Moth, Rachel Hyland, Overlord Publishing, 2018
Reading Heyer: Powder and Patch, Rachel Hyland, Overlord Publishing, 2019

Overlord Publishing
overlordpublishing.com